Dark Goes the Stage

Lance S. Barron

Lance S. Barron

Paperback ISBN: 978-1-64719-522-9
Epub ISBN: 978-1-64719-523-6
Mobi ISBN: 978-1-64719-524-3

Published by BookLocker.com, Inc., St. Petersburg, Florida.

The characters and events in this book are fictitious. Any similarity to real persons, living or dead, is coincidental and not intended by the author.

Printed on acid-free paper.

BookLocker.com, Inc.
2021

Also by Lance S. Barron:

Dark Are the Steps of Time

DEDICATION

For Barbara, my wife

ACKNOWLEDGEMENTS

This is a work of fiction. The modern events and characters are fictional. Events and personalities from the past are mostly real. Mammoth Cave is real, although I have made fictional adjustments. Some readers may recognize some of the more modern character names, but I applied these names, with permission, to fictional characters who have only a passing resemblance to any persons living or dead. Several friends have graciously permitted me to use their names in this work. For those considerations, I am grateful. Emory University Professor John Ammerman, who brought Edwin Booth to life on stage in his one-man play "Booth, Brother Booth," generously allowed me to use his name in this book. And to Kathleen McManus, who won our hearts in many performances, thank you for allowing me to use your name.

Over the last forty-five years, I have experienced some of my best times in Mammoth Cave. Among the best of those were times spent with Bob Cetera, trailing, and later guiding with him on the ten-thirty Scenic and the five fifteen Frozen Niagara. Bob was kind and patient enough to let me tag along on after-hours photography trips, which included Zona, his wife now for over 60 years. Through the years, Bob and Zona have included Barbara and me in their photography trips in Mammoth Cave and out on the surface. Through Bob and Zona, I have maintained my connection to and interest in The Mammoth Cave. For that, I am eternally grateful. They, and Mary Bowers, Zona's sister, have been patient and understanding readers of the manuscript.

Keven Neff had guided cave tours at Mammoth Cave National Park for seven years when I reported for my first summer. He was on an earlier shift than I, but his sense of humor and enthusiasm for Mammoth Cave were very apparent in the guide lounge, on the information desk, at pot-luck dinners at seasonal housing, and after-hours photography trips in the cave. Keven is appreciated not just by me, but by thousands of visitors to Mammoth Cave and by his many co-workers. Thank you, Keven and Myrna, for kindly reading several versions of this manuscript.

Daran Neff, John and Pam Yakel, and Charles Burton were kind enough to read versions of the manuscript and offer helpful suggestions.

Many thanks to Angela Hoy and her team at Booklocker.com.

My loving, wonderful wife, partner, and editor-extraordinaire, Barbara, has labored as a full-fledged co-author, editor, and first reader. In addition, she has put up with me during less than pleasant times. She has supported me in every way imaginable. Without her, there would be no story. Of the remaining mistakes and errors, I claim full responsibility.

TABLE OF CONTENTS

Prologue

"Holy Moly!" said Barbara. "This elaborate nightmare has spooked you to the point where we have to drop everything and rush up to Mammoth Cave this weekend?"

"That's about it. Except, it feels bigger than a dream, or even a nightmare. You know, I seldom remember my dreams," I said.

One
What about Walt?

"I don't want to go into the cave with a crazy man!" said Bob.

"Walt isn't crazy. He's eccentric. Maybe," said Zona.

"Walt and Barbara haven't been up here in years. Then, out of the blue, he calls up and asks if they came up this weekend. He said something about a dream he had. About the *Spirit of Mammoth Cave!* A dream that made him need to see the cave. What's that about? He's at least unstable."

"I don't know. Did he sound agitated or irrational?"

"You know how he can get overexcited about the cave. Not irrational, other than the cave spirit called to him in a dream, and that he needed to come see. I like my spirits in a bottle, my spooks undercover, and my ghosts toasted."

"What are you talking about?"

"I enjoy reading about ghosts and horror, not living it. I'm not sure I feel like a ramble through the cave with eccentric, if not unbalanced, Walt. On top of that, I'm burned out on the Historic tour. It's two hours of walking with twenty minutes of talking. Push, push, push."

"Well, now. You have to go. You've teased him all along about those horrible changes they've made to Mammoth Cave. You can't back out. He'll be so disappointed. You can see that."

"He can buy a ticket and take a tour. Why does he need me?" said Bob. "When did they say they would be here?"

"They said they would call when they crossed the Kentucky line. It should be any minute," said Zona.

Bob and Zona Cetera sat at the kitchen table in their large, comfortable home outside Cave City, Kentucky. Bob sipped from a cup of strong coffee. The table by the French doors lay in late afternoon shadow.

"I don't know anything about Walt's dream," said Zona. "You understand how busy they've been. They try to schedule a trip, and then something comes up."

"Maybe. I'm not sure. I hope he doesn't want to go on a photography trip. I'll disappoint him for sure on that."

"He's never been pushy before. He didn't mention photography, did he?"

"No, but his dream about the cave could involve anything. He could have a breakdown. I don't want to be on my own with a crazy man in the cave. No."

"He's not having a breakdown. It's been a long time since we've seen them, let's relax and enjoy their visit. Maybe you can talk to Walt about retiring. It could be excellent therapy," said Zona.

"Maybe. I'm having a Scotch. Do you want some wine?" He grunted as he got up from the chair.

"Not yet. I'll wait for Barbara. It pleased you they're coming. I'm looking forward to seeing them."

"I was pleased. Still. I'm too old. I'm in horrible shape. He's getting more eccentric." Bob opened the drinks cabinet, and from the back, pulled out an unopened bottle of single-malt Scotch.

"Walt will understand my going first." Bob broke the seal, unstoppered the bottle, and poured a finger into an expensive crystal whisky glass.

"You're walking four to six miles some days with all those steps and hills. You won't keep up that pace if you retire."

"Zona, you are right about the walking," Bob said and chuckled. "And it will feel good to not wake up to a four-mile hike."

"Only for the first week, then you will miss it like crazy. You will, you know."

The house phone on the wall on the far side of the kitchen chirped twice. Zona rose from her chair, crossed the floor, and grabbed the receiver.

"Hello," she said in her low voice. A pause. "Well,   hello there, Walt," she said, changing to an upbeat trill. "Where are you?"

Another pause. Bob looked out the French doors at the back deck.

"No, I don't think so, but let me check. Bob, Walt says they're south of Bowling Green, and he asks if we need anything from there."

"No, don't stop," he said, facing Zona. "Tell him to come on."

"Walt, Bob says to come on to our house." Bob sipped his Scotch and walked around the kitchen island.

"I'm going to put the lasagna in the oven. I should take it out as you walk in the door. It's from the home delivery truck," said Zona.

A long pause.

"Very good. See you soon. Drive careful."

"Bye."

"How did he sound?"

"Just as he always does. He's not crazy. Relax."

"Did they say why they're running late?"

"They got mixed up in traffic in Nashville. They're south of the first Bowling Green exit."

"I'll be glad when they get here," said Bob.

"What? Now you're anxious they should come on?"

"I am reluctant to go on a cave trip with Walt. I want to. Cave guiding seems boring now. I never thought I would grow bored with Mammoth Cave."

"I never thought I'd hear you say it. Their visit should revive your interest, don't you think?"

"It might. If he gets deranged in the cave, that could make up my mind, too."

"He won't get deranged. Don't be silly. Go do something to take your mind off that line of thought."

"I'm taking the dog for a walk. Jessie, let's go. Let's go, Dog. Ready for a walk?" The big, black, shaggy dog—part

Newfoundland and part Lab—lumbered into the kitchen where Bob snapped the leash on her collar.

"I'll keep an eye out for them," said Bob.

"Good idea. You do that. I'll set the table."

Two
Back on the Sinkhole Plain

Barbara steers our red, station wagon around curves and over hills along the narrow road leading out of Cave City. The Cetera's house sits on fifteen acres of the Sinkhole Plain. I spot sinkhole after sinkhole in the pastures.

"Is this the house?" she asks.

"There's Bob and Jessie out in the hayfield." Barbara blows the horn. Bob waves. Jessie sits at Bob's side.

As we pull up at the garage door, Bob and Jessie join us.

"Hey, Walt. Hey, Barbara," says Bob. He hugs Barbara. He shakes my hand and grabs my shoulder. He gives it a shake, like he's taking the feel of me. He looks at my eyes and stands back.

"Hello, Bob, it's good to see you," says Barbara.

"Hello, Walt and Barbara," says Zona who joins us outside the garage. Greetings continue, and we move into the house through the garage. I carry a few bags when we go. Jessie barks and stops. Bob feeds Jessie a dog biscuit before entering the kitchen.

"Jessie gets a biscuit after her walk," says Zona.

Jessie barks.

I carry our bags to the guest room in the rear corner. When I go back for the big stuff, Bob follows.

"How was your trip up from Georgia?"

"Except for Nashville, no problem. How are you?" I say.

"Fine. Well, I'm getting older and lazier. How are you feeling?"

"I feel great. Tired from the trip, but glad to be back in cave country."

"Good. That's great," says Bob. He's not smiling. He's not quite frowning either. What's going on here? I wonder.

"Are you taking any pictures?" Bob and I bonded over taking cave pictures when I worked a summer seasonal position at Mammoth Cave National Park in 1976 and 1977.

"I'm focusing mostly on portraits. You've seen the studio, haven't you?"

"No. The building back there?" I point to a building further in the woods on the left.

"That's it. We'll take you on a tour. Tomorrow, maybe."

"Sounds great." I lift two large suitcases from the back of the car.

"Here, let me take one."

* * *

Barbara and I settle our luggage, and we freshen up from our five-and-a-half-hour trip from the northwest suburbs of Atlanta. As I come into the den, Barbara and Zona talk across the kitchen island. Bob stands at the drinks cabinet.

"Are you able to have a Scotch?"

"Yes, I'm able," I say. What kind of question is that?

"Sounds great. Are you having one?"

"Already in progress. Hope you don't mind if I started early."

"No, certainly not. What label? Not that I'm particular. Peculiar, yes. Particular, no."

"Someone gave me this a couple of years ago. I've been saving it. It's from an island off Scotland. Some spirit haunts the distillery."

"Can you taste the spirit in the Scotch?"

"I think you're punning me there," says Bob.

After taking a sip, "Nice. It must be way too expensive for everyday use. Thanks for sharing."

"Let's go out on the deck. Don't worry. Tomorrow night, you're grilling. Zona put a lasagna in the oven for tonight."

"OK. It smells great." Bob always makes his guests grill. Cuts down on complaints. Complaints to Bob, that is.

* * *

Over dinner, Bob's guiding career leads the conversation.

"Are you still guiding regularly?" I ask. "This lasagna tastes great, Zona. And the garlic bread. The wine is wonderful."

"Zona and I were talking about my career as a cave guide before you arrived. Guides reach a time when they're too old and too out of shape to make the trips. I'm feeling like that now."

"But he's getting some great exercise he wouldn't get at all if he quits guiding," says Zona. She's up refilling wine glasses.

"I know little about wine. The guy in the liquor store recommended it because it goes well with lasagna. Not too pricey either. Glad you like it," says Bob.

"The white zinfandel is nice," says Barbara. Zona nods.

"And guiding bores me. Especially the Historic. I'm not sure I even like that tour anymore."

"Wow. I didn't expect you'd get bored with it. But then, I only worked for two brief summers. After a while, I guess it could wear on you," I say. "While we haven't been here in ten years, it's difficult to think about you not being at the park."

"Nice of you, Walt. He would miss it terribly," says Zona. "And, we have missed you guys."

"Here we come—and on short notice—making you go into the cave on your day off. My taking away your relaxation time can't be good. I can see if I can get a ticket for the Lantern tour," I say. "But, we're glad to be here with you folks. I like it back here on the limestone. Limestone with great enormous holes in it."

"No, don't worry about the time. There's no pressure. If you're feeling up to it, we'll ramble. Take it easy. You'll be astounded. I have to confess, I'm worried that the changes may overwhelm you."

Bob has the idea that I've been having mental problems. "It will help to have you with me rather being stuck at the back of a tour with a trailer I don't know."

"Well, if you're sure. Anyway, you can see Keven in action. He gives a great tour. As you know. I am more than curious about the dream that motivated you to come up."

"It was strange. You took me through the cave to show me the changes made by the sponsor. Very intense. I needed to see for myself."

"Right. Who's ready for dessert?" asks Zona. Bob eyes Zona when I ask for decaf. With our blueberry pie and vanilla ice cream, we sip coffee and relax.

"Can you tell us about your dream?" says Bob. "Do you remember it at all well?"

"Let's clear something up first. You two have not bought a small commercial cave called Mystic Onyx on Egdon Knob, have you?"

"What? No!" Bob and Zona say together.

"No, we haven't," says Zona. "Bob, have you heard of either place? Certainly not the cave, right?"

"No. Neither one is familiar," says Bob. "Are you saying, in your dream, we owned a commercial cave? And it was called *Mystic Onyx*?"

"A commercial cave and fifty acres on Egdon Knob southwest of Cave City."

"Isn't Egdon a name from Thomas Hardy?" says Barbara. "The name of the heath in *Return of the Native*?"

"Yes, it is."

"Zona, have you heard of Egdon Knob? I haven't."

"Not familiar. Do you remember all of your dream?" says Zona, going to refill Bob's cup of strong, black coffee.

"It's like a movie running in my head. It's weird."

Zona says, "You haven't hit your head, have you?" She stands by my side and runs her hand over my balding pate. "No unusual bumps?" I shake my head. Where have they got this idea I'm ill—or unbalanced? It seems like they all pause and ponder whether I've gone off the deep end.

I glance up from the pie. "What?"

"Would you tell us your dream? I've often wondered about owning a commercial cave," says Bob.

I peer at Barbara.

She says, "Tell us about it."

I lean back in my chair and place both hands on the table. "I know this sounds like I'm crazy, but I feel like the cave has reached out to me. In a distress call."

"Fascinating and a little scary," says Bob. "I'm eager to hear it."

I nod, "Let me finish my pie."

Three
Dreaming of Mammoth Cave

"Walt, this cave dream sounds intriguing!" says Zona, back in the kitchen.

"I can't tell you where it came from. You owned a nice little, vertical cave. Lots of steps. Great formations. Once you got the movie sets cleared out, it would be classic."

"Movie sets?" asks Bob. He perks up and rises from his chair.

"Down in your cave, there are sets from Keven's favorite movie franchise. Spaceships, little green men, the entire lot."

"Spaceships sound worse than gnomes," says Zona.

"And harder getting them out of the cave," says Barbara, "By the way you say *sets*."

"The previous owner of Mystic Onyx sold cave water, calling it a crystal elixir. He sold the elixir in six-ounce bottles with a little calcite crystal in each. Same bottles used for pepper vinegar. He made enough money from the elixir and from the sale of the cave to retire to Costa Rica."

"We didn't keep selling that elixir, I hope," says Zona.

"No, you stopped selling and poured most of the elixir back in the cave."

"I'm glad to know we were more responsible owners than to sell cave water."

"How much were they selling it for?" asks Bob.

"Twenty bucks for the bottle and a little booklet with suggestions for use."

"Twenty bucks for six ounces? Incredible," says Bob.

"He left two cases of twelve bottles in the gift shop. You saved one bottle for your collection."

"My word," says Zona.

"Is there more about Mystic Onyx in your dream?" asks Zona.

"There is more, but if you don't mind, I'll save Mystic Onyx for later and jump to the part about Mammoth Cave. In the dream, Bob took a picture of me at the entrance sign—with its garish pink and blue plaid logo for PharmARAMA. It looked awful."

"Horrible. In real life, the sign is even worse," says Bob.

"But did they install an industrial entrance on the left this side of Frozen Niagara?"

"Oh, yes. They did, but I didn't tell you about the Industrial Entrance. At least, I don't think I did. How could you know about that? I had planned to let you find it on your own."

"You let it surprise me in the dream. When we drove by the top of the Snowball elevator, you told me the sponsor replaced it."

"Your dream is tracking actual changes. They installed a for-real, mine-shaft elevator with an open cage. More like the original one. Shortly after they installed the new one, resource protection closed the Snowball Dining Room." says Bob.

"With the dream being more predictive than I suspected, I'm more frightened now than the other night."

Bob, ever the theater director, says, "Well, you've done my work, setting the mood."

"The entertainment value of this dream has decreased substantially. I can tell you think I'm crazy," I say.

"It may be too early to rule anything out." He chuckles. Barbara and Zona laugh. But no one smiles.

"Now, about a couple of more things. The oxen and other stuff can wait."

"Oxen?"

"Has the sponsor put surveillance monitors throughout the cave?"

"Not monitoring of visitors. I'm not aware of any. Do you mean the traffic counters used in museums?" asks Bob.

"Could be. I didn't understand it completely," I say. "Have they built a hotel in Wright's Rotunda, like Doctor Croghan envisioned?"

"A hotel?" says Zona. "I don't think so, have they, Bob?"

The mere fact Zona would ask sends a frisson down my spine.

"I forgot about Doctor Croghan's plan. Holy cow! No, no hotel at Wright's Rotunda or anywhere else. And say nothing else about this dream outside our house. If you do, we may have worse changes for your next visit."

Dr. Croghan, the owner of Mammoth Cave, from 1839 until he passed away from tuberculosis in 1859, developed plans for constructing a hotel far back in the cave with horse-drawn carriages delivering guests from the surface. Mammoth Cave lucked out he did not realize his plans.

"What a dream," says Zona. "Did you eat strange food before you dreamed all this?"

"No. No curry or anything like that. Let's leave it for now. I'm reassured not all of what I dreamed comes true. Scary still."

"How about new medications?" says Bob. They really are trying to track down what's wrong with me. Oh well.

"I understand that I've been coming across as a little off kilter, but I want to assure you. I'm not any crazier than before. Right, Barbara?"

"Only usual," she says and smiles at me. I feel reassured like only she can.

"I have to admit, Walt. You did have us wondering. I feel better about your dream now. Thanks," says Bob.

"The crime of selling cave water as a—what was it?" says Zona.

"A crystal elixir. Have you ever heard of such a thing?" I ask.

"That part scares me the most," says Zona.

"No, I haven't heard of it. But keep the elixir under your hat, too. Otherwise, the rock shops around here will be selling it. It could give them a side-line—or a blind for moonshine." Bob laughs.

"Cave elixir would be funny." I continue with the dream's other elements, including the oxen and the War of 1812 re-enactment. The explanation takes longer than I expected. Barbara and Zona have cleaned up the kitchen, and we stand around the kitchen island.

"Why don't we go to bed and see if the cave issues more warnings?" says Barbara.

Four
Cave City

"We're on schedule," says Bob. We gather on the driveway outside the garage.

"Well, we don't have a schedule," says Zona. "You guys go ahead to the park. We're picking up Mary and heading to Bowling Green."

I give Barbara a hug and a kiss.

"Be careful down there in the big city," I say.

"You're the one who should take care," says Barbara. "Don't let Bob get you into anything dangerous."

"Let's go out to the studio," says Bob, ignoring Barbara. "I'll give you the nickel tour and grab my camera bag." When the Ceteras built their house here in Kentucky, they included a state-of-the-art darkroom in the basement. Years later, they added the stand-alone portrait studio.

Bob's photographs of Mammoth Cave have appeared in commercial posters, playing cards, the *Mammoth Cave Official National Park Handbook*, *Mammoth Cave: The Story Behind the Scenery*, a stamp for the National Park Service Passports, and hundreds of slide shows and evening programs.

"Are we taking pictures today?"

"I'm not planning any in the cave. If you're asking if we're lugging a bunch of gear underground, sorry, no." Bob says. "However, Bill Soonscen told me about a baby owl he's seen in a dead oak tree on the Green River Bluff trail. You probably wouldn't know Bill. He's worked here about two years."

"No," I say. "His name's not familiar. This cool morning air refreshes me. Energizes me," I lift my arms over my head and say, "Great." During my first summer working at the park, the cool nights surprised me. During the day, the temperature climbed into the nineties. Afternoon thundershowers, sometimes severe thunderstorms, would roll through Cave Country, driving the relative humidity to match the temperature. Overnight, the temperature dropped into the sixties. Glorious weather.

"Well," says Bob, "Today, we could get a thunderstorm. Do you have all you need? Any medication or anything?" He's still got that I'm ill in the forefront of his mind.

"I'm good. Let's go."

* * *

We load the gear into Bob's SUV, and he turns out of the driveway toward our destination, the visitor center at Mammoth Cave National Park. Along the narrow, winding road, we pass farmhouses and tobacco barns. Some set right beside the road, others farther back on hillsides. Sink holes, some marked by rings of oak and hickory trees, dot the fields and pastures. Rough, circles where the bedrock collapsed into underlying cave passages. Cave Country.

Farmers will soon make their first cut of hay for the year. Tobacco plants stand several feet high already requiring hard manual labor. Tightly packed rows of corn form those thick green walls common throughout central and western Kentucky. Corn and tobacco grow on rich, red soil developed over the residual clay left by hundreds of thousands of years of erosion of the limestone bedrock.

"Bob, I don't see as much tobacco out here."

"You have a trained eye. The state encourages alternative agriculture, and they're buying up the farmers' tobacco allotments."

"Are there alternatives to tobacco in Kentucky?"

"It might surprise you what some farmers grow now. After all the years of dry counties and local liquor options, some farmers have put in grapes—vineyards," says Bob.

"Vineyards?"

"Exactly."

"An enormous change. But then, they're still planting corn."

"Yes, and they're still distilling Bourbon. It seems making wine commits a sin, but distilling Bourbon follows God's natural order," says Bob. "Or moonshine."

"The natural order."

Bob and I talk about current and former park employees. Some new ones I never met, one-summer, seasonal cave guides he doesn't remember, and more we both recall. Most of the time our dates and remembrances coincide. We will play this game the whole time of our visit. The two principal topics of conversation between us will be Mammoth Cave and theater.

Bob steers the SUV along the curves and hills of the narrow, paved road to the intersection with U.S. Highway 31W and turns right toward Cave City. We cross the Sinkhole Plain, formed on the bedrock of the St. Louis Limestone, and I muse on the rock. For many years, everyone understood the big caves lay under the ridges. Mammoth Cave Ridge and Flint Ridge in the park held the known big caves. Then Jim Quinlan, a National Park Service geologist, fielded teams of professional cavers who found and mapped huge trunk passages out beneath the Sinkhole Plain. Miles and miles of cave. Huge cave. Wet cave.

A fellow graduate student at the University of Kentucky, Duke Hopper, once one of Jim Quinlan's professional cavers, took me into some of those wet-suit passages. However big they were, they flooded. Duke tells a scary story based on the control of the water level in Green River, and therefore in that cave. He had to beat a retreat through rising water, his head turned sideways, one ear in the water, and his hard hat scraping the roof.

Bob turns us on to Kentucky Highway 90 at an intersection with a landscaping shop and a farm supply store. Highway 90 connects with Kentucky 70 at the edge of downtown Cave City and takes us toward the park. Across the interstate, we enter a gauntlet of tourist attractions and souvenir stands.

At the interstate, I say "Man, that PharmARAMA sign must be the ugliest billboard I have ever seen."

With the topic right in front of us, Bob says. "It began about three years ago. Believe it or not, Homeland Security takes part in this—studying the microbes of the cave."

The bacteria *Nitrobacter* species forms calcium nitrate which builds up in the cave dirt over the millennia. During the War of 1812, enslaved Black men hauled cave dirt from the farthest known reaches of the cave to two sets of big vats nearer the entrance where they leached calcium nitrate from the soil found in the dry, upper-level passages of Mammoth Cave.

On the surface, other enslaved workers converted the calcium nitrate or false saltpeter, into potassium nitrate, which is real saltpeter, and a key ingredient in black powder. They shipped the crystallized saltpeter over wagon roads to the facilities of a black-powder manufacturer on the eastern seaboard, an essential component of the war effort. I wonder if our focus on terrorism is dragging the cave into another war.

I put my nightmares, both waking and sleeping, aside and enjoy the countryside on the way to Mammoth Cave. I love to read travel books. Any trip, but most often trips to the cave area, cause my version of a travelogue to play in my mind, and, to Barbara's consternation, sometimes out loud. My travelogue stays in my head for this journey. Bob knows it all better than I do. And today, it seems, I need to be careful of prattling on.

* * *

As we leave the tourist development behind, the SUV climbs the easy, winding road along the Dripping Springs Escarpment. This line of cliffs leads from the sinkhole plain up onto Mammoth Cave Plateau. The plateau comprises a series of narrow, limestone ridges capped with sandstone. Karst valleys incise the ridges on either side. The term Karst describes landforms, or topographic features, resulting from the dissolution of limestone bedrock. The better-known Karst features include caves and sinkholes.

The rich green forest of oak, hickory, and tulip poplar interrupt broad views of these Karst valleys, ones with no streams in their bottoms. Most of the water flows underground in this part of Kentucky. Helen Fitz Randolph, in her book *Mammoth Cave and the Cave Region of Kentucky*, describes the journey to Mammoth Cave across these streamless valleys. She refers to Edgar Poe's "Hollow Vale." Poe used part of a Bishop King poem which referenced the metaphorical "vale" on the other side—the heavenly vale.

Perhaps a more fitting reference would be Wordsworth, in his poem, "Near Dover, September 1802," where he wrote, "Inland, within a hollow vale, I stood." In the non-metaphorical world of Kentucky, water has sculpted the vales out of limestone. Here in Cave Country, the valley walls and floors are hollow with cave passages.

Juniper and green spikes of woolly mullein adorn ledges in the road cuts through the limestone. The highway runs through the limestone of the escarpment onto the sandstone cap of Toohey Ridge, our first ridge of the Mammoth Cave Plateau.

Extensive cave passages extend beneath this first ridge. Over the years, cavers found connections between the Toohey Ridge caves and the passages spreading out from the Frozen Niagara section of Mammoth Cave, which lie northwest of this ridge, the general direction of our travel.

With the recent connections, these new and extensive parts of the Mammoth Cave System lie beyond the boundaries of the National Park. Because of the nature of speleo-politics, some cavers resisted having *their cave* being included under the growing dominion of the more famous Mammoth Cave. Now, it's one big integrated system, but with separate, albeit cooperative, cave organizations.

As we approach the park, we pass a few specialized souvenir stands called rock shops. They advertise cave rocks, but offer few, real speleothems, stalactites, and stalagmites.

They sell limestone and sandstone rocks, geodes, and mineral specimens purchased wholesale from out West.

In the seventies, glass factories in the Midwest produced glass slag, a by-product of glass manufacturing, in colors across the spectrum from red to violet. The rock shops bought multi-colored glass slag at bulk prices. Thus, few cave guides escaped the question, once they led their tours into the depths of the cave, surrounded by gray and brown limestone.

"Where can we see all the brightly colored cave rocks?"

The guide explained what the rock shops were selling. In the following silence, facial expressions told the guide which visitors already owned a chunk of glass slag. The shop owners did not identify the glass as cave rock, but if the customer didn't ask...

At this cluster of rock shops and small motels, the Kentucky Highway Department turns Kentucky 70 westward, and official highway signs point visitors to the left towards the main entrance of Mammoth Cave National Park. However, the visitor center lies along the shorter path on the straight road, Kentucky 255, the Old Mammoth Cave Road. Bob chooses the shorter route.

Five
First Sign of PharmARAMA

A short distance before we enter the park, we pass a bed-and-breakfast on the right. Out in the field beside the inn, the old ticket house stands alone, where for years, the landowner sold tickets and postcards to the folks who visited Sand Cave, where Floyd Collins died in 1925. No one I knew ever called him Mr. Collins. In an unwarranted sense of familiarity, we all referred to him as Floyd.

The chaos and tragic circus around the entrapment, rescue failures, and subsequent death of Floyd Collins created what historians call the first media event. It gave the landowner a macabre tourist destination on a direct route to Mammoth Cave—what he and Floyd hoped to do by developing Sand Cave, but without Floyd dying for it.

A rock rolled onto Floyd's leg and trapped him while he crawled out through a tight passage. The key point here is, he was heading out. His body blocked the one way in or out of the cave. The passage was too tight, and bent in a such a shape, he could not reach behind him to move the rock. Despite many efforts, no one could get around him. No one could dislodge the rock. Floyd died in Sand Cave around February 15, 1925, approximately three weeks after being trapped. A poem, a song, a play, a movie, and a novel recorded his tragic story.

When President Ronald Reagan visited Mammoth Cave National Park—the only president to visit the park—he sang the song "Death of Floyd Collins" from memory. We saw Bob's photograph of the park superintendent with President Reagan in the Frozen Niagara section hanging in the Museum of the Ranger in Yellowstone National Park.

* * *

Soon after we cross into the park, Bob stops at a small gravel parking lot and trailhead leading to the barred and locked entrance of Sand Cave. I experience a strong sense of having been here before. Bob grabs his camera out of the bag in the back.

"We should update your entrance sign photograph," says Bob.

There it blazes, pink and blue plaid, in the lower right corner of the standard national park entrance sign. Right beside the notice, "A World Heritage Site and International Biosphere Reserve."

My concerns over corporate domination of the cave combine with the contributions of my personal psychoses which, on tricky days manifest themselves in unpredictable ways, push me up on the anxiety scale. On good days, the psychoses show up in less obvious ways. My worst fears may not be true, but this pink and blue plaid logo on a Park Service entrance sign portends nothing good.

"They revealed the changes gradually. The money seduced the park management after the government had starved the parks for funding from one administration to the next. Well, you can understand."

"Yeah. I guess I do. But Bob. Pink and blue? Plaid? On a park entrance sign?"

"PharmARAMA has spent over three hundred and fifty million dollars here. Some good things have come from it. Some, I don't much care for. Zona won't come over here anymore," says Bob.

"But..." I pause. "The PharmARAMA billboards push the envelope of poor taste. On a National Park Service entrance sign, they are obscene."

Bob says, "You see what I couldn't describe on the phone."

"How serious though never dawned on me."

"Oh, yes. You'll see more over the course of the day. Everything in your nightmare hasn't happened. Yet. But a lot of it did. How are you doing?"

"Just fine."

I stand by the sign, and Bob takes a shot, looks at the image on the screen of his digital SLR.

"Stand still. I bracket my shots even though with this digital camera, some folks would say it's not at all necessary." He snaps a couple more exposures, and we walk back to the Sand Cave parking lot.

"Do you like the new Sand Cave sign?"

"I like it. Highly effective. You know, Mason Williams wrote a song with the line, 'Knickers that are pink and blue plaid…' In the sixties, those knickers evoked a terrible image. Now, with it on the park entrance sign, I don't know."

"It's ugly," says Bob.

"The Sand Cave sign came out of Harper's Ferry, not the sponsor, right?" At Harper's Ferry, the Park Service maintains a unit that produces interpretive aids for national parks.

"No. The park has a graphics guy who did nearly all of the signs. But the trail doesn't go to the mouth of Sand Cave anymore," Bob says.

"How far does it go?"

"Not far enough to see the geology, or anything. It stops short of the edge of the sandstone."

"I can't understand that. If the trail doesn't lead you to the cave entrance, why the new sign? I remember my first time back there alone. The forest canopy dimmed the light, and the setting spooked me, anyway. Before I reached the cave entrance, a great frog jumped off the ledge and hit me in the face."

"Sounds like fun," says Bob. "Most of the signs are being replaced, and they're making a good job of it. The trail being shortened is probably from resource protection."

* * *

Once we're driving into the park again, I settle down and enjoy the mixed hardwood forest on both sides. A doe and two fawns gambol across the road into the woods on the right.

"Excellent stage management, Bob. How did you cue the deer?"

"Funny," He says. But he doesn't smile.

Another pink and blue plaid sign explodes from the trees on the left. "Construction Entrance: A PharmARAMA Research Project!"

"Bob, help me here. This is where they blasted in the other entrance?"

"Yes, around the edge of the ridge," he says. "I saw the new opening soon after they blasted it and got it stabilized with concrete."

"There must have been protests," I say.

"Oh, yes. This road was closed off. FRC, Sierra Club, NSS, all those guys were out in force. They were at the park entrance and as close as they could get from the park side. Made my commute longer, but I understand their being upset."

"I guess so," I say. "So, what made the protestors back off?"

"Well, after PharmARAMA agreed to install airlocks at the other man-made entrances, the protests eased up. And a few other concessions. No pun intended."

"Did they do a good job on the entrance?"

"I went in again after they finished with the interior. There's a loading dock, large airlock, a meteorological station, and laboratory spaces. A double-wall, plastic barrier with a small airlock seals off the lab spaces from the rest of the cave. The way Denise, the shift supervisor, explained it, the sponsor cares about preserving the cave's atmosphere as it is — or was — sometimes."

"Sometimes, better than never," I say. "So, the three hundred and fifty million you mentioned covered actual park improvements? The rest they spent on research investment?"

"No. PharmARAMA spent the funds for this corporate entrance and their research facilities in addition to the park improvement money. No one has told me how much they've spent on research," Bob stresses his inflection.

"They spent a lot of time and money in the area behind Frozen Niagara. I don't understand why that area interests them because tourists, fluorescent lights, and being open to the surface atmosphere have changed Frozen Niagara more than almost anywhere else in the cave. Maybe."

"I remember the moss growing on a light fixture near the entrance," I say.

"There and in other places, too."

"What about the Industrial Entrance?" I say.

"It's well done. Airlocks, red and blue lights for controlling mold and algae, pressure monitoring, and meteorology. But what do I know? Still, they blasted a new hole in the cave, and who knows if they'll keep it up?"

"How close to the formations? Not Crystal Lake?"

"Too close, I'm afraid."

"September Morn!" My voice sounds a bit psychotic even to me. Perhaps more than a bit. "How did such a fragile, white stalagmite survive the blasting?" The formation stands on the edge of Crystal Lake on a lower level of the Frozen Niagara section. George Morrison's New Entrance guides would light the formation from a certain angle, making it resemble a nude girl—hence the name.

The statue took its name from a painting "Matinee de Septembre" by the French artist, Paul Chabas. He attracted little attention in France, but he garnered widespread free publicity in 1913 when a Manhattan gallery displayed the painting in the window. The vice police demanded the gallery owner remove the painting. They said, "There's too little morning and too much maid. Take her out!"

The same guides who lit September Morn also, as legend has it, built the dam and formed Crystal Lake into which the travertine statue stepped. They needed a lake for an underground boat ride as competition with the one on Echo River in the other, more well established part of Mammoth Cave. When I guided, Crystal Lake, enhanced with green lights under the water, sparkled when viewed from the Frozen

Niagara tourist trail overhead. Visitors on the trail could not see September Morn, and the tour route no longer included the lake. I saw her on an after-hours trip.

"From what I hear, and this may not be accurate, the sponsor's studies focus on microbes found at the edge of Crystal Lake. At least it keeps them off the trails. Mostly," says Bob.

"Are they studying the crystal elixir from my dream?

"Not that I know of, but they keep their secrets secret."

"Outrageous. Even with an airlock and the other stuff, how much damage have they caused?" I think I know the answer.

"I haven't been down to the edge of Crystal Lake since PharmARAMA moved in. So, I can't say, and I've heard nothing more. Besides this airlock, they funded installation of airlocks at Carmichael and at Violet City, Frozen Niagara, and New Entrance. They've done this balancing act all along. They spend a lot of money on good things for the cave, but there's a lot going on off the trails. You'll see what I mean."

"They've installed carnival rides, haven't they?" I'm anxious about cheapening the cave. "No gnomes?"

"No actual rides. Not yet. But still—lots of changes. Some from the sponsor, and some from the park prior to sponsorship. Fortunately, no gnomes. No smuggler's spaceships."

He drives below the posted thirty-five mile per hour speed limit, and I stare out the window. Not far along the two-lane asphalt, I glance left for the road leading to the Frozen Niagara entrance and the New entrance.

George Morrison, an investor from New York on holiday in Kentucky, fell in love with Mammoth Cave back in the early nineteen-twenties. He bought and leased property until he owned or controlled the land over the distant end of the cave which, under Kentucky law, gave him ownership of the caves below. He blasted the New Entrance to Mammoth Cave, built a hotel, and offered guided tours. His New Entrance guides explored and opened new passageways, including the

Frozen Niagara section which contained what Mammoth Cave mostly lacked—stalactites, stalagmites, and flowstone.

As we roll on, I remain alert for more changes. We drive by the building housing the top of the elevator for Snowball Dining Room.

Bob says, "The sponsor replaced the elevator right after they took over—moved in. Probably a sizeable chunk out of the three fifty. Until they closed the dining room, folks working in the Snowball Dining Room appreciated the new elevator more than anyone."

"I can't imagine how hard it was for the employees carrying stuff down a hundred sixty-seven steps. Then pulling those little wagons for a mile to Snowball. After lunch, pulling the wagons a mile and climb a hundred sixty-seven steps to go home."

The Park Service installed the original, open-cage freight elevator in 1956. The elevator clunked along, allowing time to enjoy the limestone. In the nineties, they installed a modern elevator like you would find in an office building. It failed within a couple of years. After that, the Snowball Dining Room crew pulled the wagons and trudged up-and-down the Carmichael Entrance steps.

Bob stops at the intersection with the main park road. Straight ahead the road circles around the Carmichael Entrance and the start of the Grand Avenue tour. They formerly called it the Scenic or Half-Day tour. Also, further along the same road the Lantern tour emerges from the Violet City entrance. The Park Service blasted both entrances. Though they sit side-by-side on the surface, a hundred yards apart, no convenient underground route between the two exists. A trip from one entrance to the other inside the cave would cover four or five miles, including a trip across Echo River.

Six
Surprising New Hotel

Bob turns right for the visitor center and follows the curve by the campground, concessions' service station and campground store, amphitheater parking lot, and the little locomotive, *Hercules*.

"They've restored the locomotive—not to running order—but for the steel and cosmetics, she's in good shape," says Bob.

"Where's the name plate for *Hercules*?"

"The name fell victim to historical research. This particular engine ran between Park City and the cave, but it never carried the name *Hercules*. Plain old Engine Number 4."

"I like the name better than the number."

"It made for a wonderful story. I used it for years and years in my evening programs. What can you do?"

As we turn left into the hotel parking lot, I don't see the building I expected. The redbrick hotel dating from 1961 and the program called Mission 66—the last period of major funding for national parks—gone.

The new hotel perches in the same spot along the western edge of the ravine leading to the Natural or Historic Entrance. A stone building in its place incorporates an interesting combination of arches, curving walls, recessed windows, and a flat green roof with small trees and shrubs—and people. Several visitors sit at tables on the roof, reading and drinking coffee. My dream included this scene.

Through some interesting architectural manipulations, the two-story building blends in well with the environment, giving the impression of a low, one-story structure. The exterior walls mimic the geology of the park where passages of Mammoth Cave lie beneath ridges of gray limestone capped with brown sandstone. It impresses me. I wonder if they quarried the rock inside the park.

"Believe it or not," Bob says, "In the lobby—it's two stories tall—they built a replica of Minerva's Dome." Minerva's Dome occupies the upper part of a vertical shaft on the Historic tour. The trail intersects near the middle of the shaft with the bottom being called Side-Saddle Pit. "Why they picked this dome for the lobby replica, who can say?"

"I'm impressed with the architecture."

Accommodations at the cave did not always impress. The 1844 history of the cave recorded in *Rambles in the Mammoth Cave*, says there was, as the author described it, "… an inn of sorts at the cave… But most overnight visitors, at least those with the means, preferred to sleep and eat at Bell's."

Bell's Tavern occupied what became Glasgow Junction with the coming of the railroad and then became Park City with the coming of the national park. *Rambles*, written before the railroad, said Bell's provided the closest stagecoach stop to Mammoth Cave on the Louisville to Nashville Road. The additional nine miles to the cave followed a rough wagon track.

In 1838, Franklin Gorin bought Mammoth Cave and began improvements, including a new hotel. During the same year, Gorin brought the enslaved 17-year-old youth, Stephen Bishop, to guide cave tours. Bishop became a world-renowned, cave guide. The guide to ask for when touring Mammoth Cave. He explored with enthusiasm, truly going where no man—not even prehistoric man—ever walked. By crossing Bottomless Pit, he opened up Echo River. Across Echo River, he found the gypsum wonders of Cleaveland Avenue.

Inside the lobby of the hotel, I stare at the small waterfall in the replica of Minerva's Dome. Astonishing. Similar to the position of the real dome on the tour, I stand near the vertical middle. You can look up at a dome or down into a pit. Here, the pit effect overwhelms—a complete and effective illusion created with mirrors. I attempt a three-hundred-sixty-degree view, which makes me dizzy. I stay upright, and Bob leads me toward the coffee shop. It's a standard park concessions coffee shop. Much better than a plastic kiosk in an airport concourse, but without the character of the old one from the seventies.

Three Park Service folks in NPS green and gray uniforms sit at a table, their summer, straw, flat-brimmed hats on a rack. People outside the National Park Service often call these Smokey-the-Bear hats, but their use by the Park Service predates Smokey, the mascot of the National Forest Service, and not the National Park Service. Bob speaks. I wave. We sit at a table by the window.

"I miss the old coffee shop and the L-shaped counter with the guides and rangers sitting in the corner. This place doesn't have the same atmosphere for me," says Bob.

"I agree. It's not the same."

"As for the cave, anything goes. Well, except displaying Lost John." While supervising the Civilian Conservation Corps building trails in the cave, a park employee found the body of a man from the Adena culture later dated at about two thousand years old. The body lay under a five-ton boulder on a ledge in a passage near the end of what later became the Lantern tour. The park guides of the time nicknamed him Lost John. He had not lost his way. A five-ton limestone boulder rolled over, pinning him underneath.

"Some influential locals want the cave as it was before federal ownership."

"What about the old guides?" I say.

"They don't say much. Some of them don't come out here anymore. Like Zona—not even for the guides' picnic. I keep coming. Well, I'm still guiding."

We finish our coffee, leave a tip on the table, and pay the check at the counter.

"Let's leave the car and walk over to the visitor center," says Bob.

Seven
Cave Guide Hijacked!

We cross the ravine on the concrete bridge and walk through a set of tempered glass doors in the side of the visitor center. The architecture differs from the hotel, but still pleases the eye. The rectangular, redbrick, Mission 66 visitor center, gone like the hotel. The new building stretches long and low with a hipped roof supported by sandstone masonry columns and buttresses. Glass walls surround the building. On the roof, shiny shingles. Solar panels. In the old building, the main level housed the lobby for the public, with the information desk, ticket sales, book sales, restrooms, and auditorium. The basement housed the guide lounge, locker room, and mechanical systems.

We enter an open, airy space lighted by daylight. The light-colored, structural timbers, supporting an open roof deck, rest on sandstone masonry columns. The gray slate floor provides the only dark element in the room. The ticket sales counter occupies one end, and a display area the other. The book-sales area occupies its own room near the main entrance. The breezeway separating the visitor center from the administrative offices, gone. The administrative wing, gone. They added a new exhibit area where the management offices were located several years after completing the new visitor center.

Two guides talk with a handful of visitors at the central information desk under what looks like a suspended chimney.

"Am I looking at a chimney?"

"Part of the natural ventilation system. It's involved in the green building certification."

"Impressive. Good for the Park Service. Why did they change the architecture from the hotel?"

"They built the visitor center before sponsorship got finalized."

"Looks like a lot of space. Nice. I like the lighting, too."

"Drafty in the winter-time," says Bob. "The information desk requires a coat."

Interactive displays at kid height provide information on cave flora and fauna and life on the surface. A pink and blue plaid sign screams out, "Mammoth Cave at War!"

As I stare at the sign, Bob says, "Microbes. The sponsor plays off the War of 1812 and the by-products of nitrogen-fixing bacteria leached from cave dirt. PharmARAMA ties it in with their present-day research and connects it with the War on Terror."

"How's the video program?"

"There's no auditorium, and therefore…"

"No video program," I finish for him.

"In the exhibit area, they put in a small alcove where they run a short video loop. For what it is, it's well done."

I ask, "Have you dealt with the order allowing weapons inside National Parks?"

"No gun incidents, yet. I know the Park Service had to accept it from on high," says Bob. "You saw the No Weapons stickers on the doors."

"Yeah, and I can understand why no one likes the new rule."

"No weapons in the cave either," says Bob. "Not by visitors anyway." I wonder about who else.

I start toward the Eastern National bookstore, but Bob interrupts, knowing how long I can browse in there.

"Let's check in with Denise and head on down the hill. I want to get there ahead of the nine o'clock Historic," says Bob.

"Shift supervisor, right?"

"Right. The park bureaucracy expanded. More of an explosion. The park made this back-of-the-house area secure. I guess it makes sense. No longer open to former guides like the old guide lounge," says Bob, leading me through an unmarked door to an area housing the expanded bureaucracy of the interpretation division. Bob crosses the hall and knocks at the open door.

"Bob! Glad you're here. Can you take a tour?" says a woman sitting in a tiny office across the hall from the door.

"Good morning, Denise. Why? Are you short on a Saturday morning?"

"Have you seen Bill?" I join Bob at the door and see a woman with short, gray hair sitting at a desk with a phone receiver resting on her shoulder.

"Bill Soonscen? No, not for a day or so. I guess I talked with him either yesterday or the day before. Why?"

"He's late for work. Can't get him on the phone. He has the eleven o'clock Historic. The one after Keven's. Do you have a uniform here?" She hangs up the phone and jumps up from her chair.

"I always keep a uniform here, but..."

"Right! I remember. You're bringing a former guide on Keven's tour plus some extra stuff. Am I right? Hi, I'm Denise." She extends her hand, and we shake.

"Excuse me. Let me introduce Walt," says Bob. "Walt, Denise."

"Nice to meet you, Walt. When did you guide here?"

As I begin with the dates, Denise interrupts, "Hey, Sarah, got a minute?" I see a woman in uniform, hat in hand, standing in the hall.

"Hey, Denise. Well, look who's here. Hello, Bob," patting Bob on the shoulder.

"Sarah, you got your vehicle here?"

"Sure do. It's how I get to work."

"Good. Run out to Bill's trailer—you know where it is, right?"

"OK. But why?" says Sarah.

"He's late, and I can't get him on the phone. See if his truck is there. Raise hell. Get him in here on the double. Hung over or not. Got it?"

"Sure, but why me?"

"You're here, and you don't have a tour until noon. Get going. Call me."

"Bye, y'all," waves Sarah.

"Sorry, Walt, but I am desperate for Bob to lead this tour. I've got no one else. We're skint otherwise."

"Denise, I would love to help, but we're going on part of Keven's tour and then scoot back to the Cataracts."

"I shouldn't pull rank or anything, Bob, but I'm in a jam. I would take the eleven o'clock, but I'm already doing the one o'clock Domes and Dripstones. Can't you help me out? Tell you what, let Walt go with Keven, and I'll give him a scientist ID and a cave key which will allow him access anywhere he wants. Then he can catch your tour at Great Relief Hall between twelve and twelve-fifteen and walk on out with you. How about it? Please, Bob?"

"I don't know, Denise. Walt, what do you think?"

"I was looking forward to our trip through the cave, but I don't want your leaving Denise in a jam because of me. I can entertain myself, but don't think I'm jumping ship."

"No problem about which tour you go on, although I'm not sure I'm up for a full-blown Historic. It's not what I planned."

"Oh, Bob, it would save my sanity, if not literally my life. Look at me!" Denise's appearance convinces us how pitiful she is.

"Walt, you're sure?"

"I'm on board. I'll go with you, and we can do the Lantern tour another time."

"No, you go ahead with Keven, walk the Lantern route by yourself, and link up with me later. Right, Denise?" Denise nods. "I'll go get dressed. Walt, you get your ID and come down the hall. I'll be in the locker room."

We leave Denise's office and go down the hall and enter a large work area. Bob continues down the hall.

"Stand on those two yellow feet and face me." Denise snaps my photo. At the computer, she asks, "You're a geologist, right?"

"Licensed professional geologist in Kentucky," I say.

"Excellent. Here's your badge." She hands me a plastic badge with my photograph and official gobbledygook regarding research in the cave, unlimited access, and associated weasel words.

"I'm double checking. It's OK to leave Keven's tour?"

"Absolutely. The trailer will check your badge, and you can leave the tour at Giant's Coffin. Here, sign this hand receipt."

I sign for the key, and she passes it over. Unchanged since 1978 when I last guided on an Easter weekend.

"Thanks for being flexible, Walt. If there's ever anything you want..."

"No problem, Denise. It'll be fun for me. Not sure about Bob. I'll go check on him."

"Right. Good thinking. Have a safe tour. See you, Walt."

"We *all* will. Thanks," I say.

* * *

When I met Bob and his wife Zona during the summer of 1976, the Ceteras had been spending their summers in Kentucky for several years. In the 1990s, they retired from teaching and school-nursing in Illinois, and they changed from summer-time to full-time Kentucky residents. Bob worked an eight-month schedule at the park with a furlough over the winter, a common term of employment in the National Park Service. Then, he landed a permanent position. Now, he works an intermittent schedule, filling in when someone gets sick or goes on vacation or whenever they think having Bob around would be a good idea. Which happens fairly often by the looks of it.

I walk into the men's locker room. Bob, off in a corner, tucks his gray shirt into green Park Service pants.

"I'm too old for this."

"You're in fighting trim for a man your age." I grin. "Seriously, I can come on your tour. Sort of personal backup?"

"No, no, I'm grousing. You would have to entertain yourself for two hours while I'm on the information desk. Barbara would never forgive me if you mortgaged your house in the bookstore while I left you unsupervised. Perhaps this will finally decide for me whether—"

"Whether what?" I say.

"Whether I hang up my hat."

"Mammoth Cave and the park administration are clinging to you, Bob. Despite your best efforts. How do you feel about our change of schedule?"

"I shouldn't let Denise down, and I'm worried what you will think."

"I would prefer to go with you, but, as you said, Mammoth Cave calls. And if you don't need me on your entire tour, I'll take a glimpse around. I'm disturbed more than I would expect by this dream. Don't alert the men in the white coats yet. Maybe later."

"Well, maybe you'll find some answers. All set? You're sure you don't mind my leaving you on your own? Because I will tell Denise she can find someone else."

"No, you can't do that. See this? I'm an official visiting geologist." Bob groans when he ties his boots. The groan does not come from his bending over.

"How long since you guided a trip?" I say.

"I almost quit, like we talked about. Some mornings I don't feel I can walk all those miles, much less climb all the steps and hills. That tower at Mammoth Dome threatens me with a heart attack every time." He looks at me with a sparkle in his eyes. "I guided two days last week. Domes and Dripstones, which is the New Entrance tour, paired with the Gothic–Star Chamber trip. I do like that tour. I grumble a lot. So, let's see this ID card."

I hand him the badge and lanyard.

"Not a bad shot either. I've seen worse." He puffs a little.

"You should see my Georgia driver's license." Bob looks at his watch.

"Hey, you better get going. Keven will head down the hill soon. He won't be expecting you by yourself. You don't have a pocketknife on you, do you?"

"No, why?"

"They're running metal detectors at the entrances," says Bob. At my questioning expression, he adds, "The war on terror."

"Did Denise ask about the same guy who told you about the baby owl?"

"Right. Bill Soonscen," says Bob.

"Why do you think she's that worried?"

"Bill's dedicated. He's worked here only a couple of years, but he loves the cave. Ex-military. Punctual. Reliable. Unheard of him not coming in early, much less not showing up at all. Denise takes the schedule seriously. I wonder what he's up to."

Eight
The Historic Entrance

On my way out of the visitor center and headed for the Historic Entrance, I notice a poster for an event called the IPD. Indigenous Peoples Day. A curved ramp along the right side of the bridge descends to a concrete path that leads to the road to the Natural Entrance.

As I consider the concrete bridge, the one built of redwood and cypress timbers from my dream pops up. Fake-cypress shakes covered the roof. I hope the sponsor added nothing that awful.

But my dream did not stop at the awful bridge, the sponsor replaced the Miss Green River II with a fake Ohio River flatboat. In my dream, Bob said it would make Walt Disney blush.

I can't believe the Park Service would have allowed redwood. Weird.

I stroll a short distance along the walkway. A large white sign bordered in red confronts me.

"WARNING!" it screams in huge, red letters at the top. It lists the items prohibited on cave tours, "All containers, including purses, fanny packs, backpacks, diaper bags, camera cases, firearms, knives, or other weapons, pepper spray, mace, or stun guns." Restricting diaper bags seems too much. I shake my head.

I continue along the path to the road. At the road, I stop and stare across the ravine toward the hotel. I turn right onto the one-lane road and amble down the hill to the Historic Entrance. I smile at the red faces of parents with young children, the elderly, and other visitors who ignored the guide's admonition to re-consider going into the cave. I recognize those visitors who clearly realize they should not have walked down the hill without advice from their cardiologist. Visitors who don't walk to their own mailbox will, with little thought, join a two- or four-mile hike underground. They expect a stroll around the mall. Or, at worst, Disney World. The cave is way cooler than Disney World. Especially in July.

As I stride along, I study the far side of the ravine. The old, irregular, limestone steps from the hotel still descend toward the entrance. Clark Bullitt, the pseudonym of the author of *Rambles*, described the Natural Entrance path as "…a lovely and romantic dell, rendered umbrageous by a forest of trees and grapevines; and passing by the ruins of saltpeter furnaces and large mounds of ashes, you turn abruptly to the right and behold the mouth of the great cavern and suddenly feel the coldness of its air."

Today the trees and vines still shade the ravine. Poison ivy mixed in with the grape. During the bicentennial year, the Park Service installed reconstructed leaching vats around the entrance and women in period costume tended a small fire. Not today.

Ahead, I spy a flat metal roof standing left of the trail near the entrance. Mist obscures the end closest to the entrance and flows down the ravine toward Green River. I feel excited as I approach. I consider the Natural Entrance one of my favorite spots on the planet.

A ranger stands at a security checkpoint equipped with a metal scanner. She's not busy. No one else is around. I introduce myself as a former guide. I explain how I'm waiting for Keven's tour. She inspects my photo ID.

"We didn't have these worries back in the seventies," I say. But I remember the law enforcement rangers warning us about the potential for incidents because of the bicentennial. And my having come from a security police group on a Minuteman missile base two months prior, I stayed wound a little tight on the paranoid side of things.

"No, I guess not," says the ranger.

"You must catch some stuff despite the warning signs," I say.

"We collected a lot of boy-scout knives before visitors caught on," she says. "The security scans for the other tours take place in the bus loading area, not at the cave entrances. It goes well now, but when we first started scanning, most of our tours got off late."

"I bet they did," I say. "And I take it the station over there disinfects for white nose syndrome." This disease of an unknown source causes a real problem for bats, including bat populations exposed to foot traffic in commercial caves.

"Right. Why don't you wait back up before the scanner where you'll be out of the way until Keven comes?" I step off the trail and uphill from the disinfection pans and the scanner. The shelter protects the scanning equipment and the visitors from the rain while they stand in line. With the shade from the trees, little direct sun shines on the entrance.

A wide, switch-back ramp leads down the slope into the Natural Entrance. Near the bottom, it passes under the overhanging roof of the cave. A small stream from the lip of the entrance splashes on rocks at the bottom of the entrance.

The ramp! The familiar feel is strong here, too. My dream had a ramp. Dream-Bob told me it made getting the oxen in easier for the War of 1812 re-enactment where folks portrayed the saltpeter miners. He said the re-enactment came in second ahead of the most popular day, Indigenous People's Day. That must have been the IPD on the poster. I walk back to the ranger.

"Is there a re-enactment for the War of 1812?"

"No, never heard of it. What? With the saltpeter miners and all?"

"Yes, and with oxen, and so on?"

"No, sorry. Good idea though."

I'm disappointed. The re-enactment kept the dream from being a total disaster. The re-enactment and the Indigenous People's Day celebration.

"Now, we have the IPD," she says. "Biggest visitation day of the year. The tribal people lead like a procession from here

to Violet City. Drums, flutes, dancing. Then they conduct
ceremonies like at Blue Spring Branch. The spiritual vortex
exists right at that intersection. Have you ever felt it?"

"I never identified it as a vortex, but I always feel a
presence, if you will, whenever I'm there," I say.

"I know, right? This cave puts out some radical vibes. If
you know what I mean?"

"Yes. I think I do. Thank you."

So, the IPD from my dream does takes place? And now, I
feel a powerful pull from Blue Spring Branch added to my
need to verify for myself the sponsor has built no hotel in
Wright's Rotunda.

"When is the IPD?"

"In October. You know. It's impressive. The ceremony
moves me a lot. Descendants of the Adena People begin here
in like a continuous dance back to that intersection with Blue
Spring Branch." she says. "I worked it last year. You should
come back for that. Big time!"

"Sounds interesting. Thanks." I move back out of the way.

Ferns, shrubs, and trees line the lip of the cave providing a
green wreath around the gray and black of the cave mouth.
Cool air flowing up from the entrance condenses the moisture
in the hot, humid air into a mist on summer days. The cool air
issuing from the cave flows down the ravine where deer—
including a big buck once—sometimes escape the heat of the
day and lay up mere yards below the entrance in broad
daylight. Daylight, but still almost invisible.

* * *

Within a few minutes, the chatter and tread of a hundred
visitors announce the Historic tour following their guide
Keven Neff down the hill. Keven wears the green and gray
Park Service uniform and the flat-brimmed straw hat.

"All right, everyone, line up here. Take all metal objects
out of your pockets and step through the scanner. The same as
at the airport. Once you're thoroughly scanned, step through

the decontamination pans and take a seat over on the concrete benches near the entrance. We'll be heading into the cave shortly." The visitors line up and empty their pockets. Keven walks over.

"Hello, Walt. Long time, no see." says Keven.

"Great to see you. I'm excited about your tour." We shake hands.

"Will you stay with my tour? Where's Bob?"

"Denise drafted Bob for the eleven o'clock Historic. Bill Soonscen hasn't shown up, and Denise grabbed Bob when we stopped by for our passes. We planned to walk back to the Cataracts and then come on out. Now, I'm alone."

"I see you have an ID. Impressive. Visiting geologist. Fine with me. What do you think of the changes?" says Keven.

"They're overwhelming. To tell the truth, I'm worried about what's ahead."

"Good. Healthy attitude. It'll come in handy. So, what's your Plan B?"

"I will leave you at Giant's Coffin and wander on back, see the Cataracts, Wright's Rotunda, Blue Spring Branch, and Mummy Ledge. I'll back track out and link up with Bob's tour in River Hall. Does all that sound OK?"

"Sounds good. I'd like to have you along for my entire tour. I could ask you questions. You could provide real audience participation. But, since you're all documented, use your cave key to go back up Pensacola and see Daran. He works for the sponsor. If he's not too busy, he can show the visiting geologist some science stuff." He chuckles.

"Great. I do have a key. I'll pay him a visit," I say. "I'll miss seeing the second part of your tour. Friendly group?"

"These folks are clearing the scanner quickly. I wonder if the darn thing works at all. Oh. Here's Randi bringing up the rear. Randi, step over here and meet a former guide." Randi doesn't belong to the guide force. She's a fully sworn federal law enforcement officer with a big, shiny, silver badge, not the standard gold badge of regular rangers like Keven wears.

She's tall, an obvious athlete, wearing her full equipment belt with a semi-automatic handgun, two spare magazines, handcuffs, radio, asp, mace, and a stun gun. At least, no guns for the visitors.

"Randi, nice to meet you," I say.

"Same here, Walt. You're a former guide?"

"In the seventies. Trailed mostly."

Keven steps in, "Got to go, Walt. See you later this evening?"

"Sure, I guess."

"At Bob's. We're coming for supper. Come on, Randi."

Keven steps onto a little inset in the rock wall surrounding the entrance and addresses his tour. He covers the standard material. Stay on the trail, touch nothing but handrails. Keep up.

As Keven ends his remarks, he says, "Along our path through the cave, you will see small plastic domes, pipes, and roped off areas. The park's sponsor conducts research in the cave for microbes they may develop into alternative medicines and vaccines. Don't worry, but please respect the research and avoid the domes. Now, before we enter *The* Mammoth Cave, does anyone have a question?"

"Will we see any monsters?" squeaks a small voice.

"Good question, young man," Keven says. "Monsters inhabit the surface world. Mammoth Cave provides homes for bats and crickets and other small creatures. However, we will not see many bats on our tour today. We may see a single tricolor bat, a tiny bat, hanging from a rock ceiling. Possible, but rare. Tricolor bats don't gather in colonies. Some of you may have known those little winged mammals by their old name, pipistrelles. Mammoth Cave does not harbor large populations of bats like it used to, but we have some.

"The biologists have engineered the entrance gate to provide a friendlier opening for bats flying in and out. At this time of the year, the Indiana Brown Bat lives outside the cave in trees and barns and people's attics. Other projects in progress will restore the Natural Entrance area to an even more bat-friendly environment."

Keven did not mention one reason large numbers of bats no longer hibernate in Mammoth Cave. Early naturalists trapped them by the hundreds. Dr. Call reported in the revised edition of *The Mammoth Cave of Kentucky* how in a single catch one night, he netted six hundred and seventy bats. He sent most of them to the U.S. National Museum. What did the National Museum do with hundreds of bats? Probably not much.

I know the Smithsonian collection still includes unopened boxes of plant and animal specimens from the Hayden expedition to Wyoming in the eighteen fifties. I imagine Doctor Call's bats lie in their original shipping container in a Smithsonian warehouse. How would they have packed six hundred and seventy bats back at the beginning of the twentieth century? It's obvious. In whiskey barrels.

"Let me remind you, Mammoth Cave's status as a National Park means that all wildlife, all plants, and all rocks are protected. If you encounter a bat, do not disturb it, and under no circumstances pick it up. Thank you for your interesting question."

"Any other questions? No? Get ready to follow me deep into the Earth."

"Randi, are we ready?"

She signals with a wave of her hand.

"Follow me!" says Keven.

Randi stands at the top of the steps and takes tickets. I fall in and flash my ID.

"Thank you, Walt. I'll be right behind you."

"Nice ramp. All this for wheelchair access?"

"No," she says. "The sponsor built it for their electric jitneys, like cargo golf carts."

"Not for oxen?" Randi shakes her head and grins.

Nine
Into Mammoth Cave

At the bottom of the steps, I turn and glance back at the rough oval of the bright green world surrounded by the gray limestone of the twilight zone—not the old television show—but the zone between the drip line at the mouth and where full-time, total darkness reigns.

The gate defines the man-made, twilight zone. We scoot in past the gale of cave air rushing out. Randi locks the gate. The tours exit here through an unlocked, one-way, ceiling-high turnstile. The twilight extends along Houchins Narrows through the miracle of LED lights.

We enter through the historic, natural entrance of the world's longest known cave system. The Park Service properly calls it a system because dedicated, sometimes obsessed, cave explorers discovered cave passages that connected Mammoth Cave with other, previously thought independent, caves in Flint Ridge. And, through years of enormous effort, they discovered connections to other ridges. The mapped cave passages total over four hundred miles, but the mileage continues to increase as exploration pushes out to distant limits.

The system comprises six ridges, five of which lie mostly within the boundaries of Mammoth Cave National Park. Extensive newly connected cave passages require travel through complex and difficult passages in Toohey Ridge, which Bob and I crossed over on our trip from Cave City. Nevertheless, the question pops up on tours, "How much of Mammoth Cave is unexplored?"

* * *

On the right beyond the gate, lie two wooden pipelines from the War of 1812 saltpeter leaching operation. I'm glad they remain in place. I breathe deeply and savor the cave odor. Not offensive, but characteristic. Like a clean, but damp basement. Surrounded by limestone again feels good. Like home.

Helen Fitz Randolph, in her *Mammoth Cave and the Cave Region of Kentucky,* waxed classical about the age of the cave when she wrote, "The Grapes of Proserpine, forever ripe and forever unplucked, were hanging in the underworld of Mammoth Cave before the myth of Demeter's daughter and the pomegranate inspired Greek poets or Orpheus sought Eurydice." Her *Grapes of Proserpine* probably refers to some gypsum formations in Cleaveland Avenue between the Rocky Mountains and Diamond Grotto. The first mile of the Grand Avenue Tour goes through Cleaveland Avenue, which enters through the Carmichael entrance, an area of the cave I won't see today.

I follow right behind the tour because I want to hear Keven's talk at the Rotunda, the location of the first saltpeter leaching vats. The lights show the cave in a new aspect. New for me, anyway. Not disorienting, but a whole new look for a familiar place. I walk along Houchins Narrows, the passage between the gate and the first big room.

Mammoth Cave lore says a man called Houchins became the modern discoverer of Mammoth Cave in 1798, when he shot and wounded a bear. He tracked it to the entrance of the cave and followed his quarry inside, thus discovering the Natural Entrance to Mammoth Cave—again. However, word of mouth among cave guides says the Houchins legend didn't appear until the 1870s. Even if he did chase a bear in here in 1798, Mr. Houchins came late among discoverers of the entrance. The original human—thousands of years in the past—an indigenous person during the Late Archaic Period entered through this same entrance approximately five thousand years ago. Approximately the same as it exists now, or so geologists and archaeologists think. The folks from then and from the Early Woodland Adena culture were in and out of the cave for approximately three thousand years. To put that in perspective, in 2016 Mammoth Cave celebrated two hundred years of guided tours.

The last time I walked through here, eight-foot fluorescent lamps mounted on the floor lit the passage. Rocks, or concrete valences more or less resembling rocks, shielded the direct view of the lamps from the trail. They bounced cool fluorescent light off the limestone walls. The new light fixtures diffuse more even light, without the bright spots marking the old luminaires. The light appears gray because of the surrounding gray limestone walls and ceiling.

Once I'm through studying the new lights, I turn to the pavers lining the path.

"How far do these pavers go?" I ask.

"From the gate to the boardwalk on the other side of the Rotunda," says Randi.

"Right, the boardwalk," I say, hearing the gloom in my voice. After the nightmare, I worry about any damage to the cave. Sponsor or not.

As we near the Rotunda, I scan the left wall for a rocked-up opening. When we reach the spot, an open stone lattice occupies that space. The lattice admits cave air that enters a man-made shaft topped by a manhole in the little plaza close to the visitor center. A lateral branch of ductwork conducts the cave air to the building's air conditioning system.

"They're conditioning the visitor center with cave air again?" Randi waves her hand forward urging me on. We have lagged behind the tour. In 1976, the Park Service discovered radon—a naturally radioactive gas which can cause cancer—in the air on tour routes. Because of the radiation emitted by radon, the Park Service stopped using cave air for the buildings on the surface, and they prohibited smoking on cave tours. We recorded our time when we entered and exited the cave each day to calculate our exposure. A full-time employee monitored radon levels on the tour routes. Now they're using cave air again. I knew science had declined under the administration, but I never imagined how far. Apparently, the depth of the cave forms no bottom to science's descent.

Emerging from Houchins' Narrows into the Rotunda, the view never fails in its drama. With the old lighting, a bright spot on the right wall where you emerged reduced the overall sense of space. Now with the bright spot gone, the Rotunda overwhelms. I suppose some cave guides, with much longer service than I, grew accustomed. Not me. And today, long absence and the new lighting amplify the experience. The 140-foot span of the limestone ceiling impresses.

The underground stations of the Washington Metro, with their even, gray light reminded me of the Rotunda. The new lights show the Rotunda in soft, gray light that is more even from the first moment. Another new look for a familiar place.

"Amazing," I say out loud.

After taking in the sweeping width of the chamber, I shift my attention to the leaching vats at the center where the miners leached the cave dirt for calcium nitrate. Other microbes must toil in the cave dirt to drive such intense interest from PharmARAMA.

I can hear Keven clearly across the great chamber. He describes the leaching operation. The trail splits left and right around the pit containing the wooden leaching vats. New stainless-steel guardrails surround the edge preventing visitors from falling in and trampling all over the artifacts that have remained in place since the War of 1812.

I stand at the threshold of the Rotunda and look down Audubon Avenue fading away on the right into the dark. Six-inch to two-foot-thick strata of limestone subdivide the walls. The layers extend from Audubon on the right, around the curve of the Rotunda's far wall, and down Broadway on the left. The strata appear horizontal to the unaided eye, but the layers dip, or tilt, two or three degrees to the northwest caused by ancient tectonic forces.

The colors span various shades of gray on the walls and ceiling. The shadows, black. The cave dirt, a dull orange. The wood of the leaching vats, gray or brownish gray. The bright things, besides the new rails, include bits of white PVC pipe protruding from mounds of earth. And white plastic tents.

My dream had a reconstructed pump tower for the re-enactment. The light fixtures sat on top of the tower. The light fixture from that position distributed the light in an even pattern. No reconstructed tower today, only the lower parts of two original tower legs, but the lighting still impresses.

Progressive breaking away of top layers of limestone forms a circular pattern. Like a dome. It leaves the natural rounded, rotunda. The beds of limestone thin as they near the ceiling, and they contain more shale, providing less strength for spanning large distances. Professor Art Palmer, in his *Geological Guide to Mammoth Cave National Park*, suggests Broadway and Audubon represent the upper portion of what may be an eighty-foot high passage, the bottom part of which consists of breakdown and sediment filled over time to the level of the trail.

Perhaps fifteen or more years ago, one of the permanent guides led a small group into the Rotunda on a frosty January morning. Fine dust lingered in the air magnified by the fluorescent lights. An eight-inch-thick slab of limestone covering half the size of a tennis court lay on the cave floor on the far side of the leaching vats. Early that morning, the falling slab crushed part of the guardrail, and some rock tumbled into the pit. No one was present to hear the thundering crash when the slab all in one piece dropped over forty feet to land on the floor. No one lay underneath it. The guide gathered his tour on the trail leading down Broadway, the way the tour would walk.

The guide explained rocks do fall in caves, and this slab allowed them the first view of how they can fall. He discussed the leaching operations and previewed their walk down Broadway. One visitor asked when the slab fell. The guide said, "We don't have an exact time when it fell." No one asked about leaving the tour.

Barbara and I photographed the fallen slab with Zona and Bob within a month of its falling. Keven modelled in those photographs, as he had posed in uniform in many of Bob's Mammoth Cave photographs.

The guide leading the first trip into the Historic Entrance after the rock fall did not leave his group running from the cave screaming, but only because the Mammoth Cave guiding experience instils in its members enormous self-control. What did the guide think? I wish I could have seen his face.

I pause for a more careful look down Audubon, and I spot the edge of a Plexiglas dome behind a rock, and parts of white PVC pipes sticking out of the cave dirt. They're not hidden. Their presence tells me the sponsor is conducting something against Mammoth Cave's nature. But is it more alien than the leaching operations because it is more modern? An uncomfortable thought. At the end of questions, Keven introduces a woman from the sponsor.

Ten
PharmARAMA in Mammoth Cave

"This morning, we have an extra treat. We'll hear from PharmARAMA's deputy director for research, Dr. Hilda Floren."

The tall, thin, blonde woman dressed in a starched, white lab coat, with the pink and blue plaid logo steps forward, breathless because she rushed to the Rotunda from down Broadway on our left. She grimaces at Keven and turns to the visitors gathered at the handrails. After a moment for catching her breath, she delivers a brief speech with an odd mixture of pharmacological poppycock and talking points about the War on Terror. No hint about their research. Or what it has yielded.

I recall a passage from "Standing by Words," an essay by Wendell Berry, "…their obligation to inform becomes a tongue-tied—and therefore surely futile—effort to reassure."

Dr. Floren stares at me. At this distance, I can't see her eyes clearly, but her stare feels glinty. She must wonder who I am with an ID badge she knows nothing about.

Eleven
From Church to the Prince of Denmark

Keven leads the visitors along Broadway, the age-old trail for the Adena people, the peter dirt miners, tours from the early 1800s on up till now. The Civilian Conservation Corps reworked the trail with back-breaking thoroughness in the 1930s. Shovels and picks and wheelbarrows. The trail takes up only a part of the passage's sixty-foot width. We step up from the pavers onto a wooden boardwalk elevated above the clay beneath. We tread boards made of composite materials, but they used actual wood for the handrails and the foot boards on either side. Bob told me they used Florida cypress for the lint rails. He thought they built with reclaimed wood.

He also told me about the lint rails. "It drives the whole thing," he said. "The rails help keep the visitors on the trail, and the volunteers collect a lot of lint on a quarterly schedule. Lint from cave visitor's clothing somehow presents a hazard to cave life."

I wonder what in the world they do with it. I don't remember a lint ball on display in the visitor center. I can hear Bob's response, "Don't say that out loud. They may not have thought of a displaying a lint ball, yet."

* * *

I walk along the edge of the elevated boardwalk and peer down at the trail where we would have wound our way up and down small hills of breakdown. The boardwalk diminishes my sense of walking in Mammoth Cave. After almost two hundred years of cave visitation, what does the boardwalk accomplish? Even with its lint rail. It accomplishes one thing. A quiet walk through a large passage with only the murmurings of visitors becomes a thundering stampede of Cape buffalo.

At the top of the small rise, I pause. I stare at the narrow ledge in the Kentucky Cliffs that conceals the top of the

Corkscrew. Prior to the installation of the steel tower at Mammoth Dome, tours used this steep, torturous passage equipped with ladders as a shortcut return up from Echo River and River Hall. They quit using the Corkscrew long before my first summer of guiding.

Reverend Hovey quoted one of the oldest published descriptions of Mammoth Cave–but did not identify the author when describing the Corkscrew,

...among the Kentucky Cliffs, just under the ceiling, is a gap in the wall into which you can scramble and make your way down a chaotic gulf, creeping like a rat, under and among loose rocks, to the depth of eighty or ninety feet—provided you do not break your neck before you get half-way.

The books and other publications of Reverend Horace C. Hovey, the noted late nineteenth-century minister and enthusiastic promoter of Mammoth Cave, provide an important record of cave history. While some cave-guide lore says a lost visitor discovered the way through the Corkscrew from River Hall following his cigar smoke, the formerly enslaved William Garvin discovered it when employed as a guide. Cave guiding came after Garvin served in a Black Army unit, Company M, 12th Heavy Artillery. Joy Medley Lyons, in her book *Making Their Mark: The Signature of Slavery at Mammoth Cave*, reports that because of Garvin's enlistment, his life history is more complete than others who did not enlist.

Older guides said the scrambling over boulders and climbing ladders made the Corkscrew a challenge, focusing the Park Service officials on the break-your-neck aspect in discontinuing its use. Installation of the tower at Mammoth Dome in 1953, eliminated the need for tours to backtrack their way to the entrance. Even through the Corkscrew. To get out, they had to climb the tower steps.

As the tour moves beyond the Corkscrew and crests the hill, the boardwalk changes to steps and descends to more concrete pavers at Methodist Church. The pavers disorient me even though they represent a minor change when set against the vastness of the great Mammoth Cave of Kentucky. They desecrate these age-old passages. Unreasonable, I know. To me, the pavers present a surface more slippery than the clay trail, but the guides say the pavers are skid resistant.

When we step off the stairs at Methodist Church, near absolute silence returns. Two wooden pipelines elevated one above the other, hold my attention. Pilasters of cave rock support the pipes. The saltpeter miners converted tree trunks into pipes by boring out the center wood using a spoon-bit auger. They used tulip poplar most often because the trunks grew straighter, and the core bored out easier than oak. They tapered the wood pipes on the ends with what resembled a giant pencil sharpener to form a "spigot and socket" type of joint banded with an iron collar. They joined the ends of the pipes to form pipelines.

The first pipeline transported fresh water, which came from the spring at the cave entrance to the second set of leaching vats yet ahead of us at Booth's Amphitheater. The second wooden pipeline returned the leachate to the Rotunda where men hand-pumped it into a tank on a tower. From there, it flowed by gravity to the entrance for further processing. I am glad the pipes remain undisturbed.

Burton Faust, in his *Saltpetre Mining in Mammoth Cave, KY*, describes the saltpeter leaching operations and the construction of the wooden pipelines. Including a sketch of the giant pencil sharpener.

I catch up with the tour as Keven addresses them at the Church, a medium-sized chamber formed by the intersection of Broadway with a short passage coming in from the left. Hovey identified the side passage as Archibald Avenue.

"Welcome to Methodist Church," says Keven. "You are looking at a side passage shortened aeons ago by breakdown—the complete collapse of ceiling layers into the passage. No path exists beyond the top of the breakdown yonder." He points out the top of the breakdown with his high-powered flashlight.

"Legend tells us local clergy held church services here for the Black enslaved men mining saltpeter during the War of 1812. Whether the miners worshiped here, we aren't sure. Area ministers conducted church services here on an irregular basis after Mammoth Cave became America's second major tourist attraction." No one asks about the first tourist attraction. Maybe they're all from Niagara Falls and already know.

On the left, a ledge called the choir loft juts out about twenty feet above the floor. Today, no choir. No singers dressed in royal blue robes spring from the blackened loft as in my dream. Across the mouth of Archibald Avenue and at the same elevation, hangs the pulpit. Today there's no preacher either.

The deep black of the choir loft and pulpit results from uncounted torches made of cotton rags soaked in kerosene tossed by cave guides through the darkness of this chamber leaving layers of greasy soot undisturbed over many decades.

The highlight for the guides of the self-guided tour included throwing a torch or two at Methodist Church. During the decades before the park installed electric lights, guides threw torches to light the more distant recesses of a chamber or to highlight a particular feature. Throwing the light instead of carrying it allowed the guide to stay on the trail and not clamber over piles of breakdown with a lantern. After electrification, cave guides continued throwing torches to amaze visitors, display historic lighting methods, and not least of all, to entertain the guides.

Years later, park management ended torch throwing because of its effect on the biology of the cave. When torch-throwing originated, I never learned, but Reverend Hovey does not mention it. He writes about burning magnesium or "red fire."

An early report of a trip to Mammoth Cave published in an 1861 issue of *Dublin University Magazine* describes Bengal lights. These signal-flare types of fireworks produced a "blue, sulfurous flame casting a lurid glare on the rocky walls like lightning."

The choir sang "Rock of Ages" in my dream. I've not heard anyone singing here or elsewhere in Mammoth Cave. The park invites the public for an annual Christmas sing in the Rotunda, but I've never been at the cave during the holidays.

I amble up the next hill with Randi right alongside. No one's getting behind her on this tour. At the top of the hill, the visitors crowd the wood guardrails keeping them from tumbling into the second set of leaching vats. Across the trail, mounds of leached cave dirt lie where the miners left it—or where the CCC crews left it.

Plexiglas domes, white PVC pipes, and monitoring wells crowd this area. Sampling pumps emit low buzzes. The sponsor's scientific equipment stands out in the open. They've made no attempt at hiding or disguising them. No sponsor employees lurk in the shadows off the trail.

The Reverend Hovey wrote about these piles of dirt.

And now we pass along the great piles of dirt, and when we remember much of this material was brought to this locality in sacks, on the shoulders of slaves, from points often two or more miles away... we are impressed with the toil needed to procure materials for leaching.

Some guides have described the miners' work in the cave as pleasant because it was cool. And reports say the enslaved men experienced good health. Hauling bags of cave dirt—and mud—was back-breaking work, not to mention sloppy and slippery. The work may have been pleasant enough when compared to chopping weeds in a Mississippi cotton field. But it wasn't pleasant.

After discussing this second set of vats, Keven directs the visitors' attention to Stage Rock, where a figure in shadow slumps.

"Randi, go ahead and turn on the spotlight," says Keven.

"It's not working," says the trailing law enforcement ranger.

"Folks, the wax figure there represents Edwin Booth, the famous Shakespearean actor of the late 1800s, and brother of John Wilkes Booth. When his career had somewhat recovered from his brother's assassination of President Abraham Lincoln, Edwin Booth delivered Hamlet's soliloquy from there on Stage Rock in 1876. He reported a satisfactory test of the cave's acoustics. I'm sure his fellow cave visitors enjoyed the extra treat."

With Keven's cue, Randi pushes another button, and we hear a scratchy noise, and then silence.

"Well, folks, it looks like our technology has failed in both light and sound. I don't suppose we have any Shakespearean actors with us today?" Keven says, smiles, and scans his group. A hand goes up. "Yes, sir. You are familiar with Hamlet's soliloquy? Come on up."

A man of some presence makes his way through to where Keven is standing. They confer, and Keven signals Randi to join them.

"Folks, we are in for a rare treat today. Mr. John Ammerman from Emory University is with us. He has written and starred in a one-man show, 'Booth, Brother Booth' and will perform for us today from Stage Rock." Randi escorts Mr. Ammerman up the stairs and onto stage rock, but not near the figure in shadow.

"Thank you, Keven. I have researched Mr. Booth extensively. I will perform this soliloquy as I interpret he would have done so in 1876. From William Shakespeare's

'Hamlet,' act three, scene one." A pause. John looks up, raises his hand to his temple.

"To be, or not to be…"

"John Ammerman! This coincidence is even more spooky than my dream. This is fantastic! Barbara and I know John from his work at the Georgia Shakespeare Festival, and specifically, 'Booth, Brother Booth.' His voice resonates in this limestone amphitheater.

He concludes, "… Soft you now, The fair Ophelia! — Nymph, in thy orisons be all my sins remembered." He pauses and takes a bow. It's his audience now, overwhelmed. Enthusiastic applause breaks out with cheers. Randi escorts him back to the tour.

"Mr. Ammerman! What a fantastic performance. Congratulations. Thank you."

Keven heads off the inevitable question by explaining that the set of shiny steel steps that John used to ascend the stage leads beyond Stage Rock to Gothic Avenue. He identifies the Star Chamber tour for those who desire a trip into Gothic Avenue. Murmurs ripple through the group. The visitors around John are shaking his hand and clapping him on the shoulder. He's signing cave maps that some visitors have brought with them. I work my way toward them with my map.

Gothic Avenue occupies the highest, and thus, oldest level in the cave. The last tour I knew to include Gothic was the Bicentennial Tour in 1976. Now the Star Chamber tour takes visitors there by lantern light. In 1976, a guide dressed in period costume took fifteen visitors on an evening tour using simulated lard-oil lanterns and no electric lights. The Park Service provided realistic replicas of the lanterns, but the lanterns burned kerosene in place of bacon grease.

Barbara and I walked back in Gothic with Bob and Zona on a couple of photography trips. Barbara likes Gothic more than any other area of Mammoth Cave. Keven takes a few questions and moves the group on down the hill and around several curves toward the next stop at Giant's Coffin.

I stare at the still figure standing in shadow on Stage Rock, high above the leaching vats. The outline stands in clear contrast with the back-lit limestone, but the details of the figure blur in shadow. Why doesn't the figure resemble the Edwin Booth of my imagination? It doesn't resemble John Ammerman at all. Bob's description made it sound more dramatic. This figure hangs too loose. A renowned Shakespearean actor with a slouch? And here, Booth portrayed Hamlet, not neighbor Verges.

I catch up with John as Keven leads the tour onward.

"John, I'm Walt. I met you at Georgia Shakespeare. I'm Barbara's husband. She volunteered in the office. Fantastic to hear you perform here. What a coincidence!"

"Hi, Walt. Of course, I remember you. What are you doing here?"

"Let's walk along," I say. "Well, I used to work here in the seventies, and we're back to see some old friends including Keven. My other guide friend, Bob, would have been here, but he had to work. We brought him and his wife Zona to see your show at Georgia Shakespeare when they were still in the tent. Absolutely flabbergasted!"

"Thank you. It was hard to resist when Keven asked about actors. To stand where I know Edwin Booth stood and deliver the soliloquy was too tempting. It was thrilling."

"Are you here alone? Where's Kathleen? How did you come to be here today?"

"Yes, alone. Rehearsals kept Kathleen tied up at home. I'm running a series of workshops for some colleges in the area. I remembered something about Edwin Booth having been here, so I took a day and drove over. Did you tell me he performed here?"

"Yes, I think so. We talked after Barbara and I saw 'Booth, Brother Booth' the first time. Outstanding." On the way down the hill, I say, "I had a dream recently about Mammoth Cave, and in that dream, I questioned the abrupt transition from total faith at Methodist Church to the existential questioning of Hamlet."

"It is quite a leap, isn't it?" says John.

We pass more white plastic domes, tents, and vertical sections of PVC pipe.

With large numbers of visitors, guides don't have time to stop at all the features along this trail. I point some out to John including the bear reared up on Houchins outlined on the ceiling in black-stained gypsum crust against bare, white limestone. Wandering Willie's Spring, a brief pause at hearing the drip of water heading down to Richardson's Spring in the passage below. Cyclops Avenue on the left. I amble along enjoying the cave with John until Randi urges more speed.

Twelve
Giant's Coffin and Separation

We turn the bend and behold Giant's Coffin. A large block of limestone separated from the right wall aeons ago, lists to port. The rock carried its first English name *Steamboat*, but later guides adopted Grant's Coffin, after which it received its current name with fewer political overtones.

Keven stops the tour and tells them about indigenous people who visited the cave on a regular basis and then stopped about two thousand years ago, which times come from carbon dating of artifacts.

"The people of the Adena culture came into Mammoth Cave over three thousand years during what archaeologists call the Late Archaic and Early Woodland periods. They left behind enormous numbers of cane-reed torches, moccasins, breach clouts, gourd bowls, and ladders made from cedar trees. They reported these artifacts in incredible numbers. The early visitors to Mammoth Cave built bonfires from them." A collective gasp comes from the members of the tour. "Such actions today seem incredible vandalism to us. These early cavers scraped sulfate salts, primarily gypsum, from the walls. We know no more than that. We don't know what they did with the gypsum."

I miss the statue of the Adena man from my dream. New glass cases along the wall opposite the Coffin display a handful of artifacts left in the cave by these early visitors. Evidence of their activity stretches at least two miles from the natural entrance.

These visitors are enjoying the tour. Some groups can't manage a response to "Good morning." This group asks good questions and listens respectfully to Keven's answers.

"Was that figure at the Amphitheater intended to represent Booth?" says John.

"Well, I think so, but it's not very impressive, is it?"

"No. I'm not sure he would pass even for Richard the Third. Maybe Caliban. But not a role for Edwin Booth. Strange."

Keven concludes his talk, and he waves me forward.

"John, excuse me for a moment." I walk up to Keven.

"Be careful back there in the dark. The nine-thirty lantern tour will be right behind you. You should get to Blue Spring Branch before they catch up. Hide in there until they go by."

"Did you realize I know John Ammerman? He blew us all away. We saw his production of 'Booth, Brother Booth' at Georgia Shakespeare."

"I saw you two talking. Do you think this ties in with your dream at all?"

"Who knows at this point? Thanks for letting me tag along."

"No problem. I'll chat with Mr. Ammerman at the end. Be careful."

I walk back to John, "I'm leaving you here and going off on my own. Enjoy the rest of your tour. It was great to see you on Stage Rock. Say hello to Kathleen."

"Thanks, Walt. Good to see you and all my love to Barbara."

I walk back to Randi. "I'm going to walk along Main Cave probably back to Mummy Ledge."

"Well, you have the authorization. Be careful back there by yourself. Nice to meet you."

"You bet. See you later."

She moves off and herds the tour behind Giant's Coffin. When the last visitor disappears behind the rock, Randi looks back, hesitates, then salutes and disappears.

The lights click off, and I pull out my flashlight.

Thirteen
Main Cave to the Cataracts

When I worked the self-guided Historic tour, we made a loop with six stops counting the entrance where we collected tickets from visitors. One loop in the morning and another after lunch. After twenty minutes, my replacement bumped me along to the next stop where I bumped the next guide in line. The guides made their fourth stop at Giant's Coffin.

A chain across the trail leading farther down Main Cave stopped most folks from continuing, and they kept the lights off on the first part of the trail taken by the Lantern tour. Most guides working the self-guided tour jumped the chain and sneaked back for a gander at the TB Huts during slow periods in their stint at Giant's Coffin. I never ventured back there while working. Too afraid of someone catching me away from my post. Too fresh from the Air Force.

In 1842, Dr. Croghan moved some patients into the cave for full-time residency in the first consumption sanitorium. Later they renamed the disease tuberculosis. He began with wooden huts in 1841 and built several stone huts in 1842 when the first patients arrived. The experiment failed. Two of the stone huts survive and visitors see them on the Lantern tour and the Star Chamber tour. A short way past the TB huts, the electric lights end. The park never installed lights beyond the huts along the Lantern tour route.

The Historic tour lights reflect off the ceiling, lighting my path as I stroll around one of the TB huts. How did living here full time affect the patients? Dr. Croghan based his idea for the hospital on the theory that the disease caused a rotting, a consumption, of the lungs. Since material such as wood, fibers, and bodies didn't decay in Mammoth Cave, he assumed the air would arrest the rotting of lung tissues. The patients spent their lives in total darkness and fifty-four-degrees. They depended on fire for light, heat, and cooking. Visitors reported smoke in Main Cave as thick as a London fog.

Few patients left the cave alive. Dr. Croghan buried the others in a little cemetery accessible on the Heritage Trail west of the hotel. The good doctor died of TB, and some historians think Stephen Bishop may have died of it. The estate buried him in the same cemetery as the patients. Some years later, a charitable visitor donated a granite headstone for Bishop. Has PharmARAMA found TB cysts in their soil samples from this area?

And what about fungi in the cave soil? Research has shown that fungal networks in forests provide a communication network that allows trees to communicate with each other. Why not a fungal network that allows Mammoth Cave to communicate?

* * *

The Lantern tour continues along Main Cave illuminated by kerosene lanterns carried by guides and visitors. My route will be much the same, except I will turn and retrace my steps instead of continuing through Ultima Thule, Elisabeth's Dome, and exiting Violet City.

I check my pocket for the small LED light I always carry. A backup to the flashlight. Both have fresh batteries.

Once through the second chain gate, I go round the Acute Angle and beyond. My limited solo experiences in any cave makes me anxious doing this trip alone—in the dark. *Try not to run.*

The maintenance employees travel throughout the tour routes alone. The maintenance person who works at Mount McKinley on the Grand Avenue tour spends most of their day alone. Except for a few fifteen-minute periods when the tours stop for the restrooms. When I guided tours in the seventies, four Scenic Half-Day tours climbed Mount McKinley every day in the summer.

The passage continues wide and high. Gypsum covers the ceiling and upper walls. As Keven mentioned at the last stop, the Adena cavers scraped the lower walls free of gypsum as high as they could climb on their single-rail, cedar-pole ladders. A few of the ladders remain. Earlier visitors and others collected them as souvenirs, scientific samples, or as firewood.

Beginning well over a hundred years ago, when the visitors arrived at Star Chamber, they sat on cold, limestone benches on the right side of the passage. The guides collected all the lanterns, leaving the visitors in total darkness. With the indirect light from three lanterns, they illuminated the "stars" on the ceiling representing the night sky, including the Milky Way according to Reverend Hovey. A guide grouped the remaining lanterns in his two hands and slowly walked from behind a small hill, simulating sunrise. The talented Lantern-tour guides accompanied sunrise with the crowing of roosters and sounds of assorted barnyard animals.

Hovey wrote that the Star Chamber display inspired Ralph Waldo Emerson's essay *Illusions*. Emerson called it a theatrical trick. But he also wrote, "We should be content to be pleased without too curiously analyzing the occasions." I'm having trouble with being content. I am far enough away from the Historic route that any sound is one I make. Any light is light I bring with me. Any monsters come from my imagination. I hope.

Hundreds of years of lanterns and thousands of years of torches have blackened the cave walls with soot. The soot sticks to gypsum, a mineral of calcium sulfate, precipitating out of the water in the pores of the limestone rock. The precipitate accumulates over enormous stretches of time and forms crusts inches thick. The torches of the early cave visitors deposited soot on the gypsum. The contrast of the soot-coated gypsum with limestone scraped bare of the mineral marks the limit of their reach up the walls.

Most of the light that ever brightened this section of cave came from burning cane-reed torches. The soot from more modern man's two hundred years in the cave is insignificant to that of the Adena folks who were in here for approximately three thousand years.

Archaeologists have not determined why the Adena people wanted gypsum. Gypsum and other salts forming on the walls and ceiling, being soluble in water, haven't survived outside the cave. No archaeologist has reported any site with gypsum artifacts in the park. Did the Adenans use it for paint? Medicine? Gypsum and some other salts found on the cave walls have a laxative effect. Particularly mirabilite and epsomite, which are also found on walls of the cave. Or did it have a ritual significance beyond our limited imaginations? No one has reported any evidence.

Today, we mine gypsum from bedded deposits buried deep underground and use it for making gypsum wallboard, one brand of which is Sheetrock™. No one has suggested the Adena folks ran a side-line in wallboard contracting.

In small spots, the blackened gypsum flakes off, revealing a layer of gypsum untarnished by soot. If the entire crust of gypsum falls off, the gray limestone underneath leaves a bright spot against the sooty blackness. These areas stand in sharp contrast—like stars against the night sky.

* * *

I enter the Snow Room where heavy deposits of gypsum along with another sulfate mineral, mirabilite, encrust the walls and ceilings. Mirabilite crystals cover the breakdown and non-trail areas, giving the appearance of snow in the limited light. The guides named this room for the crystals of this salt that fall from the ceiling even if excited by only the heat from lanterns. The ceiling here is not black because soot does not stick to this mineral.

After Star Chamber and the Snow Room, I walk on toward Wright's Rotunda. I pass through the *S* Bend, which Hovey called the Sigma Bend, and look for the glow of blue light that signified the hotel's proximity in the dream. The blackness of the cave remains uninterrupted. No left turn with a steel gate.

In Wright's Rotunda, the rocks and the trail have not changed. No light, save my flashlight. The trail goes close along the right wall. My lone flashlight illumines little of the soot-blackened walls on the far side.

The room measures one hundred seventy-five feet in width and five hundred fifty feet in length. Hovey described this room in terms of a subterranean Nile River with the side passages looping back to the main passage equivalent to side streams flowing around islands in the *Nile River*. My flashlight, puny in such a space, fails except in lighting a small part of the ceiling. I see enough to determine the sponsor has committed no desecration here. Piles of breakdown cover the floor of the chamber. No hotel, no restaurant, no wine cellar exists as in my dream. The weird parts of my dream leave me unsettled, but the accurate parts make me worry for the safety of Mammoth Cave.

As I leave Wright's Rotunda, I scan the trail more than the passage itself. Tire tracks from one of the sponsor's battery-powered jitneys show in the clay. How did they get them across the steps at Methodist Church? PharmARAMA must have one cart for this side, and another for the Rotunda side. They can't come in through Violet City. Impossible.

* * *

At a sharp bend in the passage, water from the surface enters through a vertical shaft that intersects the cave. It falls through the height of the passage, and once more enters the rocky bottom of the void where it discharges into Echo River, the main underground river in the cave, and from Echo River Spring flows into the Green River, thence to the Ohio, the Mighty Mississippi, and down the Mississippi to the Gulf of Mexico.

With no artificial light in this part of the cave, illuminating the falling water challenged the ingenuity of cave guides. Over the years, they devised a variety of ways of doing it. Magnesium flares, Bengal lights and, in more modern times, cotton torches soaked in flammable oil thrown from a stick. The guides on the Lantern tour threw about 40 torches per tour. The guide flung torches onto distant ledges and lit up features or emphasized the size of a large room. Long-ago guides arranged handy pieces of breakdown rock at most stopping places on tours where the guide could stand "on the rock" above the crowd and *fill their buckets* with facts and tales about Mammoth Cave—and fling their torches.

Guides twisted strips of cotton cloth—undershirt material from a nearby garment factory worked the best—to resemble a twist of tobacco, which the Kentucky-born guides raised on tobacco farms knew all about. Because four Lantern tours per day required a lot of torches, the Lantern tour guides recruited new employees, including me, to help make them. We spent time in the guide lounge making torches and learning cave lore. Guiding at Mammoth Cave marked a golden time in my life.

The twisted torches included a loop at one end and a thick body of wound cotton at the other. The guides soaked the torches in kerosene, wrung them out, and placed them in a metal can. The lead guides wore the cans at their sides on leather shoulder straps. They carried a special, carved, hickory stick tapered from a comfortable handle to a slender end with a metal tip.

At the place the guides wanted additional illumination of some feature, they hung an unlit cotton torch on the metal tip of the stick and, holding the handle with one hand, ignited the kerosene-soaked cotton with a cigarette lighter. Then, they twirled it several times for dramatic effect. Once the flame was ready and the audience silent, rearing the stick back like casting a fishing lure, the guide flung it up onto a ledge or other suitable location. The twirling torch, first on the end of the stick, and then in flight, gave off a fluttering roar, adding to the drama. It burned for several minutes, depending on the amount of cotton and kerosene. An experienced guide sometimes overlooked clearly stating to the novice an important tip. Hold on to the stick.

The Lantern tour guides threw forty or eighty torches a day, and that made them proficient and accurate. The genuine test of ability lay on a small ledge here at the Cataracts. If they could hit the spot regularly, they achieved a sort of master status, though never acknowledged to their face. The difficulty of landing the torch at the Cataracts lies in the ledge's smallness, the presence of extinguishing water, and the proximity of the wall that conceals the ledge. When guides missed this and other tough targets, cave rats caught the blame for kicking the torch off the landing spot.

Reverend Hovey wrote that he and Dr. Call crossed the Cataracts on a narrow ledge, describing this achievement with praise for themselves. They reference Dr. Bird—an earlier cave chronicler—who pronounced this point, "…the termination of the Grand Gallery." The end of Main Cave. The passage continues in reduced width and height, and without the grandeur.

* * *

With water falling through the passage, sounds emanate from the cascade. I strain to make out voices. Guides have reported voices in the cave from here at the Cataracts and in more remote reaches away from the visitor trails. I hear through the water, "Help." A faint whisper riding the falls. I turn out my light. No light remains. Only the sound of the water. The voice is stronger. I switch on my light and point it toward the trail. A man sporting a full beard and wearing green coveralls stands in the middle of the trail. He grins.

"Howdy! I'm Orville. I'm with maintenance. Who might you be?"

I explain who and what and why.

"Well, good for you, Walt. Nice to meet you. I don't run up on folks all by their lonesome out this way very much."

"No, I guess not. Hey, Orville. That was you calling for help, wasn't it?" I say.

"Hah! So, you heard it, too. I hear it every time I come by here. Weird. First couple of times, I have to admit, I trotted right up to the edge and looked in to see if anyone had fallen over. Then, after a while, I guess I kind of got used to it."

"That's really something. I've never heard of a voice here."

"The tours don't hear it. All those bodies must dampen the acoustics. You have to be alone to hear it. Leastways, that's when I've heard it."

"Thanks, Orville. I appreciate your coming by right now. Does anything else ever make you nervous while you're in here by yourself?"

"You know Blue Springs Branch, don't you?" says Orville.

"Sure. I'm headed back there now. What about it?"

"Well, there's generally something happening around there and on over at Mummy Ledge. You sit still in the dark, there's haints galore will come out to mess with you. I kind of like them now. But, man, when I first started. No sir. I paused for a little, felt that breeze on the back of my neck and trotted right on toward Violet City. Yes sir. Whether I was coming or going."

"I'll keep that in mind when I'm back there. I guess I better head on out or the Lantern tour will catch up with me. Nice talking to you, Orville."

"Walt, you watch your step. Remember nothing back there will hurt you but yourself. I'm living proof of that. Take care."

"You, too."

Courtesy of the men who worked in the Civilian Conservation Corps, I cross the edge of the pit with ease and safety as have thousands of visitors before me. Three passages connect at the Cataracts, and I follow the center one.

* * *

When I walk into a large room in the cave like the Rotunda, and provided the lights are on, I become aware at once of the large underground chamber. With lanterns, and to some extent with a single flashlight, focused on the trail at your feet and no other lights, awareness of entering a large chamber like Chief City relies mainly on noticing the passage walls no longer run along either side.

A kerosene lantern or a lard-oil lantern—a cane-reed torch for that matter—projects a circle of light. A small circle of dim light. The light from those devices project little beyond the reach of the person carrying it. I travel in the relatively small circle of light of my flashlight, and beyond the light, only darkness. And so, I enter Chief City.

Without the cloth and kerosene torches, guides threw around lighting up the larger chambers, much less Bengal Lights or Red Fire, I miss the drama, but I push my flashlight beam towards walls that absorb most of the light and reflect little. A visitor here asked a Lantern tour guide, "I guess you go through a lot of batt'ries shining across these big rooms?"

The trail runs the long axis of Chief City, which at two acres, give or take, forms the largest chamber in the cave. Near the center a large mound of broken limestone slabs, called The Mountain, climbs near the ceiling. I flash the light left, right, forward, and upward. I whirl around. No one. No thing. No breeze. No voice calling for help. I'm bringing it all with me.

Here at Chief City, the art of torch throwing achieved its highest drama. The Lantern tour visitors saw the orange arcs of six or seven torches' long flights and the flames at the landing spot. The lingering flames of the torches illuminated the vastness of Chief City. With an open camera shutter, Bob captured these arcs of light. In one sublime view, he painted this primitive underworld with flame and shadow.

Near the center of the big room, I switch off my light. The room goes dark. Total darkness. No star shine, no over-the-horizon glow of city lights, no reflection from low clouds. No light. None. In this extensive area, deep underground, surrounded by dry, solid rock, no sound intrudes on the solitude. Reverend Hovey described it in this way:

> *The impressiveness of Chief City is enhanced by the utter solitude, as the writer can testify, having been, on a certain occasion, accidentally forsaken by comrades and guides, and left alone on the subterranean mountain at the solemn midnight hour. Sitting solitary, with no better light than that given by a single lamp, and even extinguishing that faint luminary in order to enjoy the luxury of absolute silence and Cimmerian darkness, it was strange what a rush of imaginary sounds filled the place, and how the fancy peopled the dome with uncouth and mysterious shapes. What a relief it was to break the spell by the simple method of striking a match, and what company was found in the cheerful flame of my freshly trimmed lamp!*

I stand still and hear the ringing in my ears—the sound of blood moving through my eardrums. No other noise. No light. Perfect still and calm. Then, a faint rumble disrupts my reverie. No light, but a definite rumble. The tread of 40 visitors and their guides headed my way. The flare of my flashlight penetrates my wide-open pupils.

Fourteen
Blue Spring Branch

A sense of presence at the intersection of the continuation of Main Cave with Blue Spring Branch and Blackall Avenue makes it, for me, one of the more interesting places in the cave. Reverend Hovey said neither of these passages would reward the regular visitor. He mentioned a good trail in Blue Spring Branch. Of Blackall Avenue—then called Symmes's Pit Branch—he said that it ended in a "funnel-shaped pit, called a 'well' but dry…"

Cave guides in the early years described the Pit as a portal into the Hollow Earth theorized by Captain John Symmes in the years following the War of 1812. However, Symmes's theoretical portals existed at the poles of the Earth, not in Kentucky. Guides enhanced interest in their tours with other names such as Bottomless Pit, Devil's Looking Glass, and Giant's Coffin. Hovey omitted the story about the portal from his account and renamed the passage Blackall Avenue. Ghost stories I heard about this intersection, derive from events since the cave became a national park, not from the more distant past.

I climb the slope into Blue Spring Branch and stroll along the well-worn trail while waiting for the Lantern tour to pass.

The ranger at the entrance mentioned a vortex here. A spiritual vortex. I feel a strong sense of presence. Of what? No idea. A group of guides in here after hours heard three knocks, and then three tragedies struck members of the group within three months. Carlos Castaneda wrote about three knocks and three signs being associated with a vortex. The shaman, Don Juan, told Castaneda about three knocks in the book, *The Power of Silence*. Three knocks, three coincidences, or three events appear often in spiritualism. In that case, Don Juan said the person's spirit signals with three knocks for an important message.

In the eighteen nineties, the Right Reverend Hovey variously ascribed the trail to the work of the aboriginal cave explorers or to the saltpeter miners. It predated the CCC of the 1930s. Archaeologists confirmed middens in this passage, where the people worked flint and stone. Shards of flint left behind in worn, circular areas characterize sites where they knapped flint. Inside and outside the cave. People from the Adena culture—and from earlier groups—came in here in large numbers over long periods of time, if we can believe reports of the vast quantities of artifacts found all over Main Cave. And I think we can.

I can't help but wonder, did the Adena cave visitors sense a presence or energy in here? Did they come this far into the cave because of some special quality this place possessed? Another possibility occurs. Did they, by what they did here, impart the special quality? Those ancient cavers walked long distances to get here with no more light than that provided by cane-reed torches. And not on CCC-groomed trails. The present-day Indigenous People's Celebration follows the path of those ancient pilgrimages.

Some archaeologists have suggested the Adena people did not have to walk two miles to get here. Their theory says the early cavers came to Blue Spring Branch from a second natural entrance through what is now the end of the passage. The break down corresponds to Double Cellars on the surface. No one has developed any evidence, and it remains a theory. Still, it's interesting. I can speculate on how they got here but can produce no useful answer. They came here, whatever *cave tour* they took.

The Lantern tour shuffles by on their way to Mummy Ledge. The guide will make a stop there. After about fifteen minutes, I will poke my head out.

* * *

What did the saltpeter miners who worked back here, far away from the light and activity of the leaching vats, feel? Did the early guides feel any presence here? Stephen Bishop explored Mammoth Cave with intrepid dedication. But did some power or presence beyond his explorer's curiosity and imagination draw him on in his feats of discovery?

What about The Reverend Hovey? His remarks about this passage, beyond the origin of the path, consisted only of, "Neither of these branches will repay the ordinary visitor for exploration." His fancy populated the darkness of Chief City, but of Blue Spring Branch, he makes no spiritual report. Does the Reverend perhaps protest too much? Did my dream leap complete from my mind, or did Mammoth Cave exert an influence over me? Bob was being facetious when he said, "The cave calls, and you must answer." I wonder.

* * *

Farther up the passage, I spot what must be another midden. Around the next curve, I stop again. Turn out the light. What if I came here and sat with the darkness and the stillness? Jack Turner wrote, "...go into a great forest at night alone. Sit quietly for a while. Something very old will return." What would come to Blue Spring Branch in the total darkness and the quiet of Mammoth Cave's eternal night? How old would it be? Did Oliver's *haints* exist in the cave, or just in his mind? A former cave guide planned to spend the night at the mouth of Sand Cave on the anniversary of Floyd Collins' death. Did he ever do it? Probably the weather turned nasty, as it does in February.

I'm surprised I'm not more nervous being alone this far back in the cave. No reason to fear. Keven did say there are no monsters. And, Orville said, "Remember nothing back there will hurt you but yourself." The problem with those reassurances lies in the psychological load one carries.

Around a bend in the passage, I see no Plexiglas domes. No white PVC pipes. How easily I let them blend into background. There have been none here nor any since I entered Wright's Rotunda. I saw none in Chief's City, but I did not mark their absence until now.

I find one more midden someone once pointed out on a photography trip. The passage goes on back where it ends at the inevitable breakdown. I detect no air currents. See no light. If there was no entrance here, those folks walked a long, rough trail to knap flint in the light of cane reed torches.

Over ten years have passed since we came here taking cave pictures with Bob and Zona. We came in through Violet City with another cave guide, Alma, her kids, and a couple of others. Keven, too.

Back then Keven's son Daran worked with a pay-for-a-working-vacation group conducting an archaeological survey. Barbara watched one of the crew find a gourd bowl *in situ*. She still talks about their find. I step with care out into the larger trunk passage. No sound from up ahead. The tour finished at Mummy Ledge and moved on.

I stroll down the hill and shine my flashlight along the tracks of the jitney continuing past Mummy Ledge headed toward the Violet City entrance.

I stare at the steel cradle wrapped around the five-ton boulder that crushed the life out of a man about two thousand years ago. The body was almost whole. Skin, hair, internal organs, all preserved by the salts in the soil and the particular atmospheric conditions of this dry, upper-level passage. The National Park Service took the body off display in the spring of 1976 before I started work, part of the new policy of not displaying human remains.

At Mummy Ledge, another blackout holds additional promise. Flashlight off. The darkness does not rush in. It is there. No lingering light. All dark. No sound except my own breathing and the blood in my eardrums. A faint current of air brushes the back of my neck. Hair springs up there and on my arms. Barely there. I swing the flashlight behind me and turn. Nothing. Footsteps seem to echo in my head. Rapid. More than two feet. Running away. How did a dog get into the cave this far? How did a dog get in at all?

Several guides have reported the feeling of someone brushing past them. They saw no one. Was this breeze the same thing? My flashlight now seems a more meager light against the darkness. But, in its faint glow, I occupy the same space, but no longer the same state of mind. I have seen for myself the real and unreal changes. Yes, it's time to head toward the Historic entrance. *Walking, not running.*

Back up the hill and past the intersection with Blue Spring Branch.

* * *

At Giant's Coffin, the lights are off. My timing has been good as I am ahead of Bob's tour. Again, long years have passed since I visited the lower chambers beyond the Coffin. I look forward to treading the trails of that narrow, serpentine route of pits and domes. And I'm curious about what Daran works on out Pensacola Avenue.

Known by various names over the years, the guides have called the route going forward, the lower regions, the nether regions, Route Number One, and Dante's Gateway. The gates of Hell. If you're going downhill underground, you must be going toward Hell. The Echo River tours followed this route to the lowest level of the cave at 360 feet below the surface. The Echo River trail, some of it now on metal bridges, passes Lake Lethe and then the River Styx, two bodies of water from the classic underworld of mythology. Greek mythology, that is.

At the river, some old guides quoted Charon's speech at the River Styx. Charon, the boatman, ferried the souls of the damned across to Hades. The speech ended with the line, "Abandon all hope you who enter here." A cheery send-off. Since I am alone, I recite the passage aloud. No response.

I pass through Dante's Gateway leading down behind Giant's Coffin to the Wooden Bowl Room. Even in 1844, the author of *Rambles* gave no explanation why the guides named this chamber for a wooden bowl. I face toward Ganter's Avenue, a gated-off, long, rough passage leading to a cliff called Rider Haggard's Flight where a climb down a pile of rocks connects to the far side of Echo River. H. Rider Haggard wrote *She*, *King Solomon's Mines*, and *Allan Quartermain*. I do not understand why this was his flight.

Ganter's provides the only route to the other side without a boat ride on Echo River. It's neither easy nor short. The steep cliff had stopped exploration by the Adenans. No one has reported artifacts from beyond the cliff.

More modern guides piled up rocks from the farther side to make it accessible. When returning tours got trapped by a rising river, they could come through Ganter's—difficult for visitors but better than staying trapped in a cave with no exit until the high water receded. Several times in the 1920s and 1930s, the water backed up from Echo River and River Styx as high as the top of River Hall. Someone nailed little disks to the rock to mark the high-water levels.

I stop and listen. It sounds like someone yelling. Then it fades out. What could that have been?

From the Wooden Bowl Room, I descend the Steps of Time. Backwards like it says in the book. Some guide found out early on that wearing a flat-brimmed hat presented an obstacle when descending this short flight of steps. Backwards works better. And it makes a good joke.

I pause at Richardson Spring in Blackhawks Avenue. Plexiglas domes, white PVC columns, and the eerie glow of green instrument lights clutter the area. The water dripping through this passage comes from Wandering Willie Spring in Broadway directly overhead, separated from this spot by many feet of less than solid limestone. Big pores. The first summer I guided, a small aquarium held two eyeless fish transplanted from Echo River. Water from the spring dripped continuously into the tank. The fish prospered. They didn't survive when management moved the display to River Hall. Forward to the pits and domes.

After a short walk beyond Richardson's Spring, I stand at Minerva's Dome, which stretches thirty-one feet high and Side-Saddle Pit dropping fifty feet below. Careful examination compares well with the replica in the lobby of the surface hotel. Hovey described the vertical fluting along the sides as intricate. More water in the lobby version. More of a fountain. Farther along the path, I reach the edge of Bottomless Pit.

Stephen Bishop, the bold cave explorer, led a visitor named Stephenson across the pit in October 1838. Legend says they crossed the pit on either a ladder or a slender cedar pole. The Pit measures one hundred five feet deep, not bottomless. Overhead, Shelby's Dome reaches about sixty feet. Stephen Bishop wouldn't have crossed anything this wide on slender cedar poles, nor should he have. The pit had to have been terrifying enough. Crossing it on a slender cedar pole would have been crazy.

Once across the pit, Stephen Bishop opened vast reaches of the cave, including Mammoth Dome and Echo River. After Bishop crossed the river, he discovered a passage filled with spectacular displays of gypsum formations. They called it Cleaveland Avenue after the famous mineralogist. The formations seen on the tour today, spectacular though they may be, merely remind us of what Bishop first saw, which must have been glorious indeed.

With the self-guided Historic tour, the visitors roamed on their own through these passages between Giant's Coffin and River Hall. On one of my passes across Bottomless Pit, I saw a white brassiere hanging on a projecting rock across the pit from the bridge. No one ever reported it missing.

On the Bridge of Sighs, I gaze into the abyss. I continue across unimpeded. The trail divides. The larger passage, Pensacola Avenue, goes straight, the left leads to Scotchman's Trap and Fat Man's Misery, a tiny passage as implied by the name. A chain-link fence and gate block Pensacola Avenue. The tour route goes left.

Fifteen
PharmARAMA in Pensacola Avenue

Light beyond the first bend of Pensacola glows through the chain link. In the early part of the twentieth century, Hovey still called it Pensico, an abbreviated name, but Max Kaemper labelled it Pensacola on his 1908 map. After unlocking the gate with my cave key, and relocking behind me, I enter the passage. During my walks through here to the next stop at River Hall, time always seemed far too short to allow more than a glance in Pensacola. I got nowhere near the dry flowstone formations of Angelica's Grotto at the end.

I enter Wild Hall and find where the sponsor has concentrated their research. Three large white tents glow with internal lights along the left wall. The lights inside cast rectangular shadows of equipment and cabinets on the translucent walls. A few hundred yards farther, the shapes of two humanoids—a male and a female—dressed in white coveralls, wearing white hardhats and headlamps. Holding clipboards.

"Hello, Daran." He jerks up, not having heard me approach. "You remember me, don't you?" Daran accompanied us on many cave photography trips.

"Walt. So, you're in here by yourself?"

"Yes. Strolling and looking. I came in with your dad's tour, then wandered back to Mummy Ledge. Denise gave me this ID and a key when she Shanghaied Bob for the eleven o'clock Historic."

"Dad mentioned Bob might bring you by here. Are all these changes new to you?"

"Barbara and I haven't been to Cave Country in years. Bob dropped hints, but I'm overwhelmed."

Daran shakes his head and says, "It's amazing all right. This is our busiest area right now. And Crystal Lake over in Frozen Niagara."

"How do you like the work?" I ask.

"It's cool working in the cave—well, fifty-four degrees to be exact." He pauses, "I'm sorry. Walt, meet Courtney." I exchange greetings with Daran's colleague, a petite young woman with short, dark hair. She seems uncomfortable—maybe she doesn't like strangers in her research area. After clearing my plan with Daran and Courtney, I move on toward Angelica's Grotto.

"Don't kick over any experiments," says Courtney. "Please don't take any pictures."

"No problem. I'll be careful. Why did they call this Wild Hall?" I ask.

"I've heard they named it *Wild* because of the scattering of the rocks," says Daran. Even Hovey offered no reason behind the name.

The passage runs almost straight and remains wide. If my memory of the Kaemper Map is accurate, Pensacola parallels Broadway on the north side, but deeper in the rock.

"Well, they had to call it something," I say and stroll on. More Plexiglas domes and more tents. A weather station with glowing green and amber lights mounted on an aluminum tripod sits on the left side of the trail. The passage walls and ceilings run to grays and little but bedding planes and joints to distinguish one area from another. The orange of the dirt contrasts with the gray.

Pensacola presents a pleasant prospect, but it's not thought interesting enough for today's visitors. Turning a group around in this passage and leading them back out to continue through Scotchman's Trap and Fat Man's Misery might confuse the visitors.

At the end of the nineteenth century, the Route of Pits and Domes stopped here. The guide turned the group around, and they walked back the way they had come. Hovey describes several attractions here. Resonator Hall, the Grand Crossing, and Angelica's Bower. At the end, stubs of the stalactites which once earned the names of Bower and Hanging Grove and the Pineapple Bush, provide evidence of decades of vandalism.

In three-dimensional space, thick sections of limestone separate me from Houchins Narrows and the Historic Entrance. From the dead end, I retrace my steps back toward the tourist trail.

As I pass the tents on the way out, Daran hunches over an instrument inside one tent. I call to him from the tent opening.

"Thanks, Daran, for your hospitality." He comes out.

"You're headed back?"

"I guess you get a lot of guides back in here," I say.

"No, not much," says Daran. "Since the new wore off, they seldom come back here. Bill drops in and chats."

"Bill Soonscen?" I ask. Courtney joins us.

"Yeah," says Daran. "He often stops in at the end of the day. He stopped by here at quitting time last night."

"How late do y'all work down here?" I say.

"It depends on how our projects go and how much trouble we've had with the instruments," says Daran. "Remember how sensitive camera gear is to dust in the cave? Analytical instruments require tents, and even they don't always block the dust. That's how it is. Last night, we left about six or six-thirty. After the last tour got through Scotchman's Trap. We always wait until they pass. Less confusion for the visitors." And fewer questions for Daran.

"So, Bill waited here with you until the trail was clear?" I say.

"Yeah. We walked together up to the mouth of Pensacola. He left us to finish his sweep, and we walked back past Giant's Coffin checking instruments," says Daran.

"Bill didn't come to work this morning. We stopped in for our passes, and Denise said she hadn't heard from him. Not like Bill she said. So, she hijacked Bob for the Historic."

"No, Bill doesn't malinger. He may have caught a summer bug or something," says Courtney, a frown on her face belying the casual tone of her voice.

"Probably, but I'm surprised he didn't call," says Daran.

"Are you coming for dinner tonight at Bob's?"

"Yes, I am. Wouldn't miss it."

"I don't think I would be out of line with Bob or Zona, if I invite you, Courtney. Why don't you join us? We'll wind up talking about the cave, but you're welcome. Bring a friend if you like," I say.

"Thank you. I may," she says, her frown turning into a faint smile.

"Good. See you at eight."

"Come back and see us," says Courtney, her voice devoid of feeling. Perhaps the lighting affects her expression, but she looks pale. Paler than when I came in.

Sixteen
Vanderbilt Hall and the Corkscrew

When I emerge in a duck walk from the other side of the Misery, I take advantage of the only set of restrooms on the Historic tour, and then amble through Odd Fellows Hall to River Hall.

I pause at the top the stairs leading into River Hall and glance back. Bob, ahead of his Historic tour, pops out. When he looks my way, I wave and signal I'm going on. He gives me a thumbs-up. I don't push the button at the top of the stairs for the next section of lights.

I cross along the top of River Hall. Down the slope, my flashlight beam reflects off the gate that secures the muddy passage leading to Echo River. To the right, I spy fresh disturbances in the cave dirt leading from the visitor trail up toward Vanderbilt Hall. I follow them to the bottom of the Corkscrew. Vanderbilt Hall housed the predecessors to the restrooms in Great Relief. The olfactory evidence of those older facilities lingers. The eleven o'clock tour's footsteps sound their approach, and Bob turns on the lights. I remain in the blackness of Vanderbilt Hall to blend with the tour without creating a disturbance.

As Bob stops near the entrance to Sparks Avenue on the way to Mammoth Dome, the visitors, refreshed from their time in Great Relief, assemble near him.

"We stop here at River Hall to talk about Echo River and life in the cave," says Bob. "We will make our last stop at Mammoth Dome. Now, the route to Echo River goes down through the gate behind you. From here, the All Day tour continued down to the river, took a boat ride, and after a short walk, came to the Snowball Room. Here stand almost directly beneath Methodist Church…"

As Bob continues, I slip out of Vanderbilt Hall, and ease around toward Darryl, the ranger trailing the tour, a tall, Black man with a thin moustache.

"Who are you?" A flashlight beam hits me in the eyes.

With my left arm lifted to shield my eyes, I spot a flashlight held by a cub scout. I turn to Bob and shrug my shoulders.

"I see one of our intrepid scouts has spotted a special visitor. Walt, wave to everyone. He's a visiting geologist who has joined our tour here at River Hall." Bob acknowledges me with a nod. I wave.

"Good timing," the trailer says.

"Yeah, I'm lucky."

"What I've heard is *once a guide always a guide.*" He smiles.

"Thanks. How's the trip?"

"It started out like you see it. Bob's a great guide. But you met our cub scout."

"Trouble?"

"He's been everywhere with that flashlight. His dad isn't paying attention. I think he has a girlfriend with him. Not sure."

"I guess Bob is handling it well."

"Bob's a natural."

"Darryl, are we all ready to move on to Mammoth Dome?" says Bob.

We flash our lights.

"Excellent. We are all ready. Let's move out." He turns and lead us up into Sparks Avenue. I trail at the back with Darryl.

* * *

As we enter the bottom of Mammoth Dome, several spouts of water shoot out from the walls.

"Must be raining on the surface," I say. Bob's weather forecast has proven accurate. Several times on the self-guided tour, sudden, torrents of water shot from the walls of the dome where before the water dripped. Rainwater falling on the surface takes a short route into the cave through Mammoth Dome sinkhole. An afternoon thunderstorm can put on an impressive display here. Mist and darkness obscure the top of the dome, over one hundred feet away.

"It's kind of noisy when it rains," I say.

"Let's move on up," says Darryl.

While climbing the concrete steps to the main floor of the dome, I focus my flashlight beam on the fossil remains of a colonial coral etched in relief from the limestone. When I guided in the seventies, geologists called the coral by its then-scientific name *Lithostrotion harmodites*. As things happen in geology and in other sciences, paleontologists reclassified the coral and changed the name to *Schoenophyllum aggregatum* Simpson. Whatever the name, this coral has long formed a touchstone for me. It marks an important horizon in the limestone stratigraphy of Kentucky.

At the top of the concrete steps, I walk out onto the concrete floor and gaze at the Ruins of Karnak. Motors whir, and I spin around looking for the source. A big, bright yellow, open-cage, mine elevator stands in sharp contrast to the brown, steel tower of steps and everything else in the cave. *What the hell?* The sponsor must have a side-line in mine elevators. It looks big enough for ten or twelve visitors.

Bob stands on the second landing on the tower.

"Welcome to Mammoth Dome. Mammoth Dome Sink, above us, lies downhill, behind the hotel, and we stand several hundred feet below that sinkhole." He explains how the columns carved out of the walls called the *Ruins of Karnak* have nothing to do with a late-night television show but come from the name of a ruined temple in Egypt.

"Darryl will assist you with loading and timing the elevator. I am going on up. When you get there, follow the trail through Little Bat Avenue out into Audubon Avenue. I will wait for you there." Bob finishes up here at the last stop, thanks them for visiting Mammoth Cave and hope they enjoyed the tour. Applause and cheers bring a smile to Bob's face. The visitors split about sixty-forty, with the sixty percent going up the tower. The elevator moves the remaining visitors in three rapid trips. Darryl brings it back down for the next tour and follows me up the tower.

"I like it better than the stainless-steel coal skip with flashing red lights."

"Coal skip?" says Darryl.

I explain my nightmare, and how it included a coal skip provided to bypass the tower here at Mammoth Dome.

"No kidding. Better this, right?"

"Yeah, I guess. But why yellow?"

"It doesn't exactly blend in with anything, does it?" says Darryl.

"Well, it beats pink and blue plaid."

* * *

Little Bat connects to the passage formerly called Big Bat Avenue. The Reverend Hovey said Kentucky's eccentric "Professor Rafinesque…renamed it for his rival naturalist." Thereafter, the guides called it Audubon Avenue. Did Rafinesque name the hall after Audubon for its grand appearance or for all the bat droppings present in his day?

The grandeur of Audubon Avenue always takes my breath away. At the exit from Little Bat Avenue, I take in the high limestone wall in its majestic sweeping curve to the right towards the Rotunda. We also catch our breath from the climb. In theory, climbing the tower steps presents only a minor obstacle—depending on your cardiac and respiratory health. And with Bob beating everyone up here, he must have already caught his second breath.

Darryl flashes Bob with his light, and Bob turns and leads the tour across the Rotunda and out through Houchins Narrows. I trail at the end with Darryl.

"It's still one of the more amazing views in the cave," I say.

"Right you are."

More Plexiglas domes fade away into the darkness on our left. Darryl stays close behind the last of the visitors. He doesn't want to chase after someone down Broadway. Namely a cub scout with a flashlight. The visitors line up at the turnstile, but they soon pass through, and we climb the stairs going out of the cave. No elevator here. I wonder if the sponsor has considered enlarging the air shaft and installing an elevator for the Natural Entrance. Probably better to leave that alone.

* * *

"Well, how was your tour—or should I say tours?" asks Bob.

"Fun. I found it interesting being alone in the dark on the Lantern tour. I held several blackouts. Nothing spooky—well, almost nothing."

"Tell me about *almost nothing* later. What about the yellow monster?"

"I told Darryl I liked it better than the big, shiny, stainless-steel coal skip from my dream. The cab doesn't swing. How did they get it approved?"

"Money talks. That elevator answers a lot of complaints visitors have made about getting near the end of the tour and finding a fire lookout tower to climb, never mind the walk back up the hill. Park management found that agreeing was too damned easy."

"OK, simple decision. But you said no rides."

"That monstrosity is no ride. Nor entertainment either. It's vertical transportation." A twinkle appears in his eye.

"What else? You're hiding something."

"They have installed aluminum ladders in the Corkscrew for some sort of study. Denise says it's a cave weather study or something."

"They can show that the air flows up through the Corkscrew with cigar smoke," I say. "They don't need ladders for that."

"Well, the guides joke about a super slide," says Bob, chuckling.

"Oh, great. Gnomes will be next, right?"

"PharmARAMA is funding a wax re-creation of Houchins and the bear to be installed in the Narrows." He laughs.

"We can't win, can we?"

"Resistance is futile."

"One more thing."

"Go ahead."

"You won't believe who was on Keven's tour. Remember when you and Zona came to Atlanta and saw 'Booth, Brother Booth' with John Ammerman at Georgia Shakespeare?"

"Sure, he was great. Zona and I enjoyed the show," says Bob.

"Well, he was on the tour. The spotlight failed, and the audio didn't work. Keven asked about Shakespearean actors, and John raised his hand. He delivered Hamlet's soliloquy from Stage Rock. It was amazing!"

"Denise owes me so much. She can't begin to understand. Did you talk to him?"

"Yes. Here. He signed a cave map for you and Zona."

"Holy cow. Thanks. That's great."

"The spotlight didn't work," I say. "And the figure didn't look right either. John commented on it. Said it looked more like Caliban from 'The Tempest' than a role for Edwin Booth."

"What do you mean? The light worked when we stopped there. The figure of Booth stands there with his right hand raised. Isn't that Shakespearean enough for you?"

"Yes. Very Shakespearean. The figure I saw sported a beard and held his hands at his sides. He slumped. Not like my idea of a great Shakespearean actor at all."

"How strange."

"Do you have time for another look?" I ask.

"Let's go. I have nothing to do except lunch until the five-fifteen Frozen Niagara."

Seventeen
Checking Up on Edwin Booth

In the Rotunda, we turn left and walk back along Broadway. We see neither Dr. Floren nor any other sponsor employee. We cover the distance over the boardwalk, down the hill to Methodist Church, and up to Booth's Amphitheatre.

When we climb the steel ramp, the spotlight shines on a decent representation of my idea of Edwin Booth, but not the figure from this morning. This figure stands erect, with an outthrust chest, right hand raised in a dramatic gesture. No beard.

"More like Booth," I say.

"What do you mean?" Bob asks.

"I didn't see this figure on Keven's tour. Like we talked about, the other figure had a beard, and he stood shorter, slouching. Not like this one. This guy could have played Macbeth or Lear—not the one from this morning. As John said, better suited for Caliban."

"All the images of Edwin Booth I have seen show him clean-shaven. Mary Ann said they based this wax figure on extensive research. Well, there are photographs. You say the figure you saw had a beard?"

"And his hands where limp at his sides. Mary Ann?"

"She's the manager of visitor services. Sort of like the chief guide of the old days."

"I knew three women named Mary Ann who worked here the first year I guided."

"This particular Mary Ann has never worked at Mammoth Cave until this assignment. I have no explanation, but someone seems to be running a variation on the theft of Floyd Collins' body," says Bob.

During the cave wars in the late 1920s, after the then owner of Crystal Cave arranged for the wax museum to tidy Floyd up, they displayed him in a glass-topped coffin in Floyd Collins' Crystal Cave over on Flint Ridge. One night, competitors broke into the cave, stole Floyd's body from the coffin, and threw it off Green River Bluff. They recovered Floyd's body, but also arranged for additional wax restoration before returning the body for display. The search party failed in its recovery of one of his legs.

"Well, this fellow has all his limbs?" I say, thinking we still need an explanation.

"The spotlight may have failed because whoever substituted the other figure didn't want it too obvious. Why swap them out? And, who had the opportunity? If it's a joke, the joker risks their job," says Bob.

"Then, why do it at all?"

"If Wolfgang finds out, he'll fire them," says Bob. "Seriously. He's more paranoid about observing Park Service rules than anyone in the Park Service."

"Who's Wolfgang?" I ask.

"Project director for PharmARAMA. His full name is Warren Gamaliel Anderson. He wants everyone calling him W.G., but behind his back, they call him Wolfgang. Wolfgang enjoys enforcing rules. The more arbitrary the rule, the better he enjoys enforcing it."

"Gamaliel? A Kentucky name?" I ask.

"Named after President Warren G. Harding," says Bob.

"Someone named their son after President Warren G. Harding?" My reserve of credulity pings on empty.

"Oh, he's proud of it."

"You can't make up stuff like this, can you?"

"No." Bob shakes his head, looking sad.

"Speaking of PharmARAMA, did they give their staff the day off?" I ask. "I saw no one since the Rotunda except Daran and Courtney."

"They move around a lot, but they always post someone here. They run interference with the visitors twisting knobs on instruments and dropping candy wrappers down the pipes."

"No one was working here this morning. I saw no sponsor folks after Doctor Floren until Daran and Courtney. Some kind of stand down?"

"Unusual. Since you mention it, I've never been through the Historic without tripping over them all along the way. I don't have a clue."

"Getting back to our wax figure mystery, who would have seen the replacement figure?"

"Well, Keven's nine o'clock—you tagged along on that— and the nine-thirty Lantern. For my eleven o'clock Historic, everything was like you see it here. Why risk a job or a career for a joke? It bothers me. They must have made the switch after Keven's tour left Main Cave and did it quickly and efficiently. More than one person."

"Bob, could this be all one mystery? What does Bill Soonscen look like?" I say.

"Well, he's shorter than me—not as big—dark hair, beard. Wait. What are you saying?"

"With your description of Bill, we can guess where Bill was hanging around this morning."

"Not another pun." Bob then considers my argument.

"He was in the cave. But Bill wouldn't risk a trick like this. Not in front of a tour. Someone is playing a serious game. We can't solve either mystery here. Let's go get some fried chicken, and you can have some Kentucky wine. We may see it in a new light when we get above ground," says Bob.

"Bob, are you making a pun about shedding light on the mystery?"

"A pun? From me?" He laughs.

* * *

We cross the Rotunda, pass through the turnstile, and climb the stairs. We walk through the white nose decontamination pans. Water drips from trees after the thundershower. The humid air smells rich. Passing beyond the bank of cool, exhaled cave air, my glasses fog up and obscure my vision. Until the lenses warm up, I walk in the blurry world of the near-sighted.

Eighteen
Update with Denise

I huff and puff as we enter the visitor center through the side door. Bob, who walks the hill several times every week, is not breathing hard at all. He leads us to Denise's office, where he knocks on the frame of the open door.

"Oh! Bob. How did your trip go?"

"Excellent, thank you. An excellent group. Have you heard from Bill?" asks Bob.

"No. It's a little odd," says Denise. "I sent Sarah—from this morning—by Bill's place. She didn't see his truck, and he didn't answer the door. But someone left a phone slip for me saying he called while I ate lunch."

"Did he leave voice mail?" I ask.

"No. Nothing more than a written message saying he's sick, which Bill never is. Why do you ask?" says Denise. "Oh, and how did your tours and rambles go?"

"Great, A lot of fun. Thank you. And I saw my favorite guides in action." Denise smiles. Bob looks at me and then back at Denise. "Plus, an actor from Atlanta I know was on Keven's tour, and he delivered Hamlet's speech when the spot didn't work, and the audio failed. He was fantastic!"

"Keven told me about Mr. Ammerman. We're getting the superintendent to write him a letter commemorating the event. Bob, I owe you for making you miss that." She eyed Bob with a frown and then a smile.

"Yes, you do, Denise. Big time!" Bob smiles back.

"My tour went off without a hitch, but Walt should report what he saw. Someone tampered with the Edwin Booth figure, and it may involve Bill," says Bob, motioning me to describe my observations.

I brief Denise about the figure I saw on Keven's trip, and how it wasn't the wax figure standing on Stage Rock now.

"After my Historic, Walt and I checked back at Stage Rock, and Walt saw the real Booth figure, not the one he saw on Keven's tour. Walt asked me what Bill looks like," says Bob.

"His description of the first figure describes Bill," says Denise.

"Could Bill have been playing a joke on someone?" I ask.

"Bill enjoys a joke, but nothing like this. No. He takes guiding seriously," says Denise.

"Denise is correct. Deadly serious."

"Why would anyone bother making up another figure?" I ask. "I side-tracked up Pensacola and saw Daran and Courtney. They said Bill stopped by at quitting time last night."

"Did they say if he walked out with them?" asks Denise, checking the duty roster on a clipboard.

"He left them at the Pensacola gate headed for the Trap and the Misery. They came out behind Giant's Coffin," I say.

"Bill pulled the end-of-the-day sweep and lock up last night," says Denise. "He would have gone out through Scotchman's Trap, Fat Man's Misery, Great Relief, River Hall, and on up through Mammoth Dome."

"Daran mentioned a sweep. You do a sweep after guided tours?" I ask. When they made the Historic self-guided in the seventies, the last guide, a GS-5 or higher, made the round, bumping the other guides and dawdling visitors along after locking the Iron Gate behind them. Somehow, I worked the next-to-last position most of the time, and I walked out with the last guide.

"With our need for increased security, we instituted a last sweep of the Historic. For some reason, kids like to hide and get behind the trailer more on the Historic than on the other tours. We've gated all the side passages to keep the curious from wandering. They wind up falling in with the next tour— except for the last Historic. A thirteen-year-old found the call box in River Hall and called the ranger desk at eight-fifteen one night. Bill ran the sweep last night," says Denise.

"Does the guide on the sweep report to anyone when they're done? Did anyone see him after he came out of the cave?" I ask.

"Yes. They call the ranger desk after locking up for the night. I'll check with them later. No sense getting things all stirred up for no good reason."

"With the new lighting control system, can you tell when he turned the lights off last night?" asks Bob.

"We certainly can," says Denise, already moving out of her tiny office and down the hall where she stops at a control panel in the larger work room. We follow, crowding in around her. She logs onto a computer and brings up a map of the cave. She highlights the sections of the cave from Great Relief Hall to Mammoth Dome. A table with red and blue highlighting appears on the screen. "Great thinking, Bob. The lights from River Hall through Mammoth Dome stayed on all night. The lights were turned off from the mouth of Pensacola all the way to the Rotunda."

"What about the elevator?" asks Bob.

Denise manipulates the mouse and brings up another table. "The last tour left it at the top. The sweep double checks it and leaves it down for the first Historic the next morning."

"There's a light switch at the end of Great Relief Hall and one after River Hall. So, Bill must have made it to River Hall. If Bill continued the sweep into Sparks Avenue, he would have turned off the lights for River Hall," says Bob.

* * *

Denise turns, "Either Bill didn't go past River Hall, or if he did, he turned nothing off, which still means something bad happened."

Bob says, "For the moment, let's deal with what we know. Bill enjoys a good time, but he takes guiding, the cave, and its welfare seriously. Bill ran into trouble on his sweep last night, and he never made it past River Hall. He didn't show up for work this morning. Someone left a message saying he's sick, but he's not at home. And most unsettling of all, the figure Walt saw makes me fear it was no figure but Bill himself." says Bob. "Do we know anything else?"

"Yes. Bill met Daran and Courtney around six or six-thirty last night and completed the sweep through Great Relief Hall. And, Denise, PharmARAMA staff disappeared this morning—except Daran and Courtney," I say.

Bob nods, "Let's begin there with Bill on Stage Rock. Let's assume the worst case, and anything less will be better."

"Prepare for the worst and hope for the best. I like it," says Denise.

"To be clear, are we are thinking someone diverted Bill from his sweep of the Historic, and this morning they hung him unconscious up there on Stage Rock?" says Bob. Denise frowns in disbelief.

"They could have tied him up there last night. Then this morning they could have taken him down and hid him," I say.

"And then put the real Booth back on Stage Rock?" says Denise. "After Keven's tour?"

"How did Bill get to Booth's Amphitheater from River Hall?" asks Bob.

"Do you think they left through Fat Man's Misery and not through Mammoth Dome?" asks Denise.

"No," I say in the middle of my revelation. They turn on me with expectant expressions. "No, not through the dome. They climbed through the Corkscrew to Main Cave and then over to Booth's Amphitheater."

"Why the Corkscrew?" asks Denise. "And how?"

"Well, it's a lot shorter, for one thing," I say. "In distance, if not in time and effort. It sounds like whoever's running this body switching didn't want anyone, like Courtney or Daran, to see them."

"But what made you think of the Corkscrew?" asks Denise.

"Bob mentioned they've installed some temporary ladders in there for a study or something," I say. Denise eyes Bob. "In

River Hall, something disturbed the clay on the trail leading up to Vanderbilt Hall. I saw marks in the dirt—looking at the trail, you know. I did not realize their significance until now. Maybe they're signs of a struggle or a body being dragged."

"You think someone made Bill climb up the Corkscrew, then tied him up on the support in place of the wax figure of Booth?" says Denise.

"It looks like someone either forced him or carried him. If Bill didn't walk up there under his own power, someone lugged him all the way from River Hall up to Stage Rock. From what I saw this morning, he didn't get up there on his own." I say.

"So, whoever did this must have put Bill up there before Keven's nine o'clock Historic," says Bob.

"They must have put the wax Edwin Booth back up before you came through, Bob. Would they have had time?" I say.

"It would be tight, but if they had one of those jitneys, they could have got in and out ahead of us easily," says Bob.

"Keven reported the burned-out spotlight," says Denise. "I'll find out what's been going on around Stage Rock and at the Corkscrew. If someone's messed around with the Booth figure, the trail around the support should show signs of it.

"You're worried, Bob, and I appreciate how you and Walt feel. But leave things with me for the time being. No reason I should fire up management until we understand a little more about what's going on. The closer we keep this, the better. There's a simple explanation for all of this. Your theory suggests something too bizarre. I'm sending someone down the hill. Where are you two headed? You have the five-fifteen Frozen Niagara, remember?"

"And you have the Domes and Dripstone tour. Lunch at the hotel and then out Green River Bluff trail," says Bob. "Who will you send?"

"I'll pull John off the information desk. He's back from his Frozen Niagara. John already knows Bill hasn't shown up, and frankly, I'd rather have John working on this. If we need real help, he's the one. If anything pops up, I'll call you." She pulls a cell phone from a holster on her belt. "Let me double-check your cell number, Bob."

She says nothing about my ID or key, and I don't bring it up.

Nineteen
Wine at Mammoth Cave

It's a little after two o'clock when we enter the lobby of the hotel, but the dining room is still serving. Bob gets us a table while I go wash my hands. As I approach the table, Bob goes and does likewise. Always wash your hands after coming out of a cave—but never fail to wash your hands before eating. A woman in the blue and white uniform of the dining room approaches.

"Hidey. You must be Walt. Bob said you would be right out. I'm Maybell. Do you want a glass of wine?"

"Yes, Ma'am. Did Bob suggest one?"

"He said you were the wine connoisseur, and he would be happy with your choice. The back of the menu describes the local wines if you're interested. Myself, I don't drink spirits of the devil." I nod and study the wine list, and apparently Maybell has nothing else pressing. She waits.

"Bring us the Dripping Springs Norton. Thank you, Maybell."

Bob returns ahead of Maybell's bringing our wine.

"Did you order the wine?" asks Bob.

"Yes. I got the Dripping Springs. The Norton?"

"That should be an excellent choice. It's a rich, full-bodied, dry red wine," reads Bob from the back of the menu.

Few diners remain at this hour. Maybell returns in a short time with our wine and takes our orders. We both have the skillet-fried chicken, mashed potatoes, pinto beans, and cornbread.

"There must be several former concessions folks spinning in their graves with all this going on—wine with our meal, top-notch accommodations. Do they stay busy?" I ask. I steer the conversation away from Bill. The restaurant has too many ears even at low occupancy.

"They seem so," says Bob. "The parking lot looks full whenever I go by, but since I'm not working exactly every day, I don't have a regular sense of it. I'm sure they have a lot of corporate guests in addition."

Maybell returns with a basket in hand. "Here's some biscuits and butter and preserves. The folks at Berea College hand-wove that basket from grape vines. You could take it home to your wife," says Maybell. A price tag hangs from the side.

Photographs of Mammoth Cave cover the walls, and they hold my attention. Black and white. A few in color. Ray Scott took the black-and-white pictures, all classic scenes of Mammoth Cave. Classics because he took great pictures, and they appeared on postcards, posters, calendars, brochures, and other concessions' literature for decades.

"Scott did not take the large color photograph. But he took the others. You met him, didn't you?" I say.

"Yes, several of times. I didn't know him at all well. He stopped cave photography before I started working here. His pictures have withstood the test of time."

"Yes, indeed," I say. "I remember talking with his brother in his photography shop in Cave City. He talked a lot about Edgar Cayce."

"You remember John Yakel?"

"Yes. Does he read Cayce, too? You two taught at the same high school. We've met Pam and him at least once when they were here in Kentucky. He's a guide now?"

"Right. No, he's never mentioned being a fan of Cayce. They moved down here and built a house right next door. The one on the corner. He likes cave guiding."

"It's an outstanding job all right. I am jealous, but what can I do?"

"You still have a few years until you can retire?"

"More than a few," I say. But jealousy remains. "Good for John and Pam."

"They have fit right in."

"So, you think John is a good pick for Denise?"

"Yeah, he's the one."

"This chicken tastes good," I say. And it does. The beans and mashed potatoes taste fresh and well cooked. The cornbread, excellent for a restaurant. The wine exceeds its description. We finish the meal talking about Edgar Cayce and his readings and about some older guides Bob saw at the last guides' reunion.

After some discussion, Bob accepts my argument of his providing the entertainment, and my buying lunch. I pay the check, and we cross the bridge to the visitor center for an update from Denise.

"This whole sponsorship thing, the entire park—such major changes. It's surreal," I say.

"I'm sure you're overwhelmed by all this in one day. But then, my view remains unaffected by a warning from the spirit of Mammoth Cave." More chuckles.

* * *

In the lobby, we scan the Eastern National sales area for books and maps. Bob introduces the manager of the bookstore who runs a much larger operation than when it shared the corner of the old visitor center with the Miss Green River II ticket sales. We discuss cave books and what cave visitors buy.

Bob goes to check with Denise, while I browse for new books. I pick up a photo-reprint of Helen Randolph's *Mammoth Cave and the Cave Region of Kentucky*. I remember a copy of the book in a blue cloth slipcover in excellent condition, printed in 1922, in the University of Kentucky geology library. I own the *Rambles* reprint and the revised, hardback edition, with Dr. Call, of the Reverend Horace C. Hovey's *Mammoth Cave of Kentucky*. But finding Randolph's book offers more of a challenge. I'll settle for this reproduction.

I pick up a copy of *Grand, Gloomy and Peculiar* by Roger Brucker, a giant of exploration and research in the Mammoth Cave System. Another book with a black jacket entitled *Ultima Thule* grabs my attention. Davis McCombs, a former guide, has published a book of poetry about Mammoth Cave. On the back cover, *Jacket illustration adapted from photograph © Robert Cetera: lard oil lantern.* The illustration shows a ghost-like, green lard-oil lantern used on the cave tours of long ago.

"John isn't back yet," says Bob. He approaches on silent feet. I jump.

"Oh."

"Sorry, has the spirit of Edwin Booth followed you above ground?"

"More like whatever brushed the back of my neck at Mummy Ledge."

"I never felt anything anywhere in the cave, but I know others have reported it. There and at other locations."

"Do you know this guy?" I hold up the poetry book.

"Yeah. He worked here for a while. Interesting poems. I like them. Won the *Yale Series of Younger Poets* prize. He's teaching at a small liberal arts college. I forget where."

"It's your picture," I say.

"Yes, but it's their modification. The green ghostly part. We do not know when Denise will hear anything. Let's see if we can find a baby owl." I pay for the three books, and we turn to leave the bookstore and the visitor center.

"Are you talking about the owl Bill saw along Green River Bluff?" asks the store manager.

"Yes, have you seen it?" I ask.

"I walked out there on my lunch break. No sign of it. I hope you have better luck."

"Thanks," I say. "We'll let you know if we see it."

Twenty
Green River Bluff Trail and a Splash

Bob steers the SUV around the visitor center parking lot and up toward the pavilion and the start of the trail.

"I hate leaving Denise with this," says Bob. "But it seems like we can be the most help if we make ourselves scarce. You do feel like checking out Bill's baby owl, don't you? No dream about the surface?"

"I'm up for it. No worries," I say. "I've walked none of the surface trails in years."

"You have done nothing up here in over ten years," Bob says. "We may be wasting our time looking for an owl in the middle of the afternoon. Especially if the store manager has been out there at lunchtime. And not a lot of time either with a five-fifteen Frozen Niagara."

* * *

Bob drives past the resource building at the back of the picnic grounds. The building looks like always, sandstone masonry with Park Service brown wood trim. Zona worked out of this building over several summers with the Youth Conservation Corps, a group for teenagers volunteering in the parks.

"Is YCC still active?" I say.

"No. PharmARAMA replaced it with Microbe Camp, a sort of Future Microbiologists of America kind of thing. They have a lab and a classroom. It runs all summer. They fill reservations way in advance," says Bob.

"What about Trog?" I ask. Trog stands for troglodyte or cave dweller.

"Trog is still popular," says Bob. It's for eight to twelve-year-olds. They wear hard hats and electric headlights—sort of a kiddy wild cave tour. Barbara and I helped Bob photograph two Trog Tours. One in White's Cave and the other, in Gothic Avenue back past Stage Rock.

Bob parks the SUV and opens the back. He hands me the tripod and grabs the bag. "Hope you don't mind this."

"No. Not at all," I say. "This is great."

"Did you bring a camera?" asks Bob.

"No. I'm not in the digital age, and I'm not doing much with film anymore. I'm fine."

"Bill said he saw it about a quarter of a mile along the trail, and he saw the owl in a fallen oak tree downhill from the trail. It sat in the limbs of the dead tree late in the afternoon. Must be the day before yesterday."

"Is Bill a guide or a ranger?" I ask.

"Guide. He worked with the resource protection rangers but didn't stay long. He enjoys guiding more. When I first worked here," Bob says, "The guides knew the cave and surface trails. The rangers gave out tickets and enforced the rules on the surface. No speeding, no poaching, and the usual National Park rules."

"Several years back, the superintendent blurred the lines between guides and rangers involving the rangers more in the cave. And they refer to guides as rangers working in interpretation. Technically, that's always been the case. Now there's a mixing of guides and rangers on tours. You noticed the woman trailing Keven's tour and Darryl on mine?"

"Randi?"

"She wore a law enforcement badge, not the standard ranger badge. Law enforcement rangers now trail tours large enough for a second person. Visitor experience falls in second place after security. These law enforcement rangers may absorb information about the cave, but they focus on law enforcement and security."

"So, it's like a Nevada Barr book?" I ask.

"No, not much," he says. Mammoth Cave, compared with most other national parks, is unusual. Few parks, except the ones with caves, have guides or an interpretive staff this large. The employees trying to build a career consider a ranger position offers more opportunity for a job in another park. And that's important with the Park Service requiring transfers for promotion. The park employs more law enforcement and resource protection rangers now than when you worked here. Some of them transferred from the guide staff.

"They've added caving rangers besides the armed trailers. When the caving rangers go in, they dress out in black tactical gear with helmets, headlights, ropes, climbing gear, backpacks. They practice rescues, rappelling, and bomb threats."

"Did they get the idea from climbing rangers in the mountaineering parks?" I ask.

"I think they intended it as a rescue squad, but the group grew more SWAT-like. Personally, I don't want to work in law enforcement, but it seems a lot of the younger guides do. Bill thought resource protection meant being in the cave more. He doesn't seem all that cop-like at heart, but he has seen more action than a standard rifleman. I know that," says Bob. He pulls out his cell phone and checks for signal strength in case Denise calls. "You and I tuned in on our security agency work in the military, right?"

"Sometimes connecting with another veteran—one with our shared experience—doesn't take much conversation." We keep walking.

"Well, I get the same sense with Bill, but we've never talked about it enough to connect," says Bob. "He asked me where the Army sent me. When I told him where in Japan, he smiled knowingly, as they say. He says nothing about his own background, but I have an idea."

"Security Agency?" I say.

"Could be. But it might be straight military intelligence out of G2."

"And now he's a cave guide?"

* * *

We walk along the Green River Bluff trail under oak and hickory trees. Sunlight breaks through the forest canopy and sparkles off the crystal faces of mica in the outcrops of the sandstone ridge cap, the Big Clifty Sandstone. The caprock protects the cave like a roof. Without the sandstone, Mammoth Cave would be shorter, less continuous, less mammoth.

The trail winds around the outcrop among the boulders broken loose from the bedrock. Lichen and moss decorate the faces of rocks laying still long enough.

"One guide when I worked here had a surface tour. He warned everyone about staying on the trail and watching for copperheads. When a visitor complained about not seeing any snakes, the guide pointed out one copperhead after another. The visitor then complained the tour wasn't safe," says Bob. "He actually enjoyed leading surface trips more than cave tours."

Many trees topped by the ice and strong winds two winters ago stand bare and twisted with stubs of limbs. Mere reminders of once magnificent trees. Woodpeckers have pocked the smooth, barkless surfaces with exploratory holes. Chunks of wood fall from a nearby tree. A pileated woodpecker half-way up the trunk pile drives its beak into the decaying wood. I point to him when Bob comes up behind me.

I whisper, "Pileated." Bob sets down his camera bag and does not rattle the dry leaves, and I unfold the tripod and set it on the trail between us. He pulls the 11.1-megapixel digital SLR camera from his bag and mounts it on the professional tripod. With speed accrued from much use, he mounts a 300-millimeter f/2.8 lens and focuses on the big woodpecker, still disassembling the dead oak. Bob squeezes off three shots and looks up.

"Great shot. The lighting is perfect, and we can fill a good part of the frame. Later, we will digitally enlarge and edit." The pileated shifts its position for a fresh attack on the tree. Bob shifts the tripod a little closer. The woodpecker cooperates, and Bob re-focuses, grabbing three more shots.

"In the side pocket of my bag, you'll see a small yellow notebook. Would you mind making some notes for me?"

"No problem." I find the notebook and a black ballpoint pen, with some small-lettered inscription starting with a *U*. On the next clean page, I note the date and subject. "OK, I'm ready." Bob calls out photograph numbers and exposure settings.

With the mystic powers of woodpeckers, the big bird senses another tree and launches into flight with its characteristic *Woody-the-Woodpecker* call.

"If you'll take the tripod, leave it extended, I'll leave the lens on the camera, and we can set up faster."

"Sure thing. You have professional gear. No need for slide processing in Bowling Green."

"The quality over film amazes me," says Bob. "Have you seen any of my digital cave pictures?"

"No. We haven't come up here since you started using digital. Good, huh?"

"Excellent. I'll show you some when we get home."

* * *

Less than two hundred yards along the trail, we find an oak tree fallen over with its crown lying down the hill. The big root base beside the trail extends fifteen feet in the air. The reddish-orange soil clinging to the roots along with small cobbles of sandstone contrasts with the green leaves, blue sky, and gray rock. A Virginia creeper vine, at least three inches in diameter hangs in mid-air where the tree once stood. Runners of the vine extending to neighboring trees keep it suspended.

"This must be the tree," says Bob.

"No kidding. What a tree."

We stand still. Bob scans the fallen tree, and I scan trees still upright. No baby owl.

"Let's walk on down the trail and see what we find," says Bob.

We move with what passes for stealth in older folks, our eyes scanning back and forth along the trail and in the trees. We cross the contact between the Big Clifty Sandstone and the

Girkin Formation, the first limestone below the caprock. Professor Palmer writes in his book that Broadway and Gothic Avenues occur in the lowest part of the Girkin, the Paoli Member. The dark gray color, the more rounded features, and the characteristic curved fracture of the limestone marks the change from sandstone. No glints from mica or quartz. Junipers grow along the outcrop. Still no baby owl.

The trail takes a slight turn westward, and we look down from the northernmost nose of Mammoth Cave Ridge to the Green River in its valley several hundred feet below. The stream in Floating Mill Hollow disgorges from the right. Across the hollow lies Flint Ridge. A gnarled juniper eighteen inches in diameter at the base clings in precarious balance to the limestone cliff.

The juniper anchors itself with roots growing into cracks in the rock. The tree holds on and by enduring, over time, its roots break the rock apart. Over the aeons, the boulder will break free and begin its life of rolling and tumbling—on the geologic time scale—down the slope to the river. Will the tree remain or go with the rock?

I gaze at Flint Ridge across the hollow. An FRC cave map showed line traces of cave passages superimposed on the topographic map. One lone passage runs out under the nose of the ridge across from where we stand. It's called the Northwest Passage, and it turns north along the cliff. Having read about the long passages that FRC pushed out to the edges of the ridge in their search for a connection to Mammoth Cave, I think the Northwest Passage must be a dry, dusty belly crawl a long, long way from any entrance.

For now, the juniper holds fast to limestone rock with its spread of roots. In a shaft of light from the late afternoon sun, it defines picturesque. Bob drafts me as a model for scale. Twisted junipers, particularly in this afternoon light, present great photographic subjects on their own. No need for me in the shot. I'm not even wearing red. But it's a rare location where he can get the tree, with good lighting, and the Green

River valley in the background in one photograph. The shots take about thirty minutes. Still no baby owl.

"I think we're done," says Bob. "If we see the baby owl going by, we'll pass it up. I've got a cave tour."

"You sound like you're up for it."

"I am. I feel ready for my second cave tour of the day."

Crows call from the trees on the sandstone cliff across the river, their caws raucous. Somewhere up the slope, a woodpecker drums with loud authority on a dead limb. Down the cliff, the loud crash of falling rock, and then something large moving through dry leaves. Before we turn back, a tremendous splash in the stream in Floating Mill Hollow. The crows across the river launch into the air with loud cawing.

"What the hell was that?" says Bob.

"I don't know. I jumped about a foot. Didn't sound much like a deer. Nothing more than the natural process of erosion?"

"Maybe. I jumped, too," says Bob. "Thinking about Bill's disappearance and wondering if it's got anything in common with Floyd Collins's post-mortem excursion."

"May be a little too much, don't you think?" Silence.

The plaintive chatter of a gray squirrel in a hickory tree breaks the quiet of the ridge-top, hardwood forest. We regain the sandstone cap leaving the limestone behind. The top of the ridge lies almost flat, with windrows of leaves and fallen limbs accenting the subtle undulations in the surface.

We store the gear in the back of the SUV, and Bob checks his cell phone before cranking the engine. I roll the window down, relishing the atmosphere of the woods and the rocks. I laugh.

"That might be your pileated, Bob. See how appreciative he was." A large bird has adorned Bob's windshield on the driver's side. He mutters a syllable or two of frustration and completes the drive around the picnic area and parks in the employee lot of the visitor center.

"What will you do?" asks Bob.

"Mind if I tag along on your tour?"

"No. Great idea. I'll enjoy having you along. Like in the good old days." He smiles.

"You get ready, and I'll meet you at the buses."

"Don't you need a ticket or a pass?" asks Bob.

I finger my ID, "I got a badge and a key. I'm all set."

Twenty-One
Frozen Niagara

I pick a bench near the bus-loading area and punch in Barbara's number on my cell phone. It rings three times, and she answers.

"Hello, Cave Man."

"Hey. How are you?"

"We're on our way back, but still on I-65. Where are you?"

"I'm at the visitor center. Denise drafted Bob for a couple of tours. One of their regulars didn't show up, and she already had a tour."

"Did you get into the cave at all?" asks Barbara.

"Oh, yeah. I got in the cave. You'll never guess who was on Keven's tour. I'll tell you. John Ammerman!"

"What was he doing there? Did you talk to him?"

"The tech gear at Booth's Amphitheater malfunctioned, and John performed Hamlet's soliloquy from Stage Rock. It was amazing."

"Was Kathleen with him?"

"No, she's in rehearsals. He's in Kentucky delivering a series of workshops and remembered us telling him about Booth in Mammoth Cave, so he came to see for himself. He said it was thrilling to stand where he knew Edwin Booth had stood and to deliver the same lines as Booth. I followed Keven up to Giant's Coffin, then wandered back to Mummy Ledge on my own. I caught up with Bob's tour at River Hall. You remember Mummy Ledge, don't you?"

"They found a gourd bowl *in situ* while I watched."

"Right you are. So, I've been underground most of the day."

"Poor baby," she says.

"Yeah, sad, but I miss you. I'm going with Bob on the Frozen Niagara tour, and then we will head straight to you."

"I miss you, too. Be careful."

"You, too. Tell Zona and Mary hello for me."

A few minutes before five-fifteen, Bob shows up. He hands me a bus pass. No free rides except for the guide and the trailer. He organizes the thirty visitors waiting for the tour and reviews the metal scanning process as Keven did this morning. Darryl shows up. Acknowledges me with a nod. He helps the visitors with scanning and boarding the bus.

The bus ride brings back more memories. Bob chats with the folks in the bus's front. Where are they from? First time here at Mammoth Cave? How long are you in the area? The bus driver doesn't mind me at all, all business, focused on driving. He doesn't know who I am or what I'm doing except I must be some nosey, government official.

Out front of the Frozen Niagara entrance, we disembark. The bus driver waits because we won't be long, and he's making his last trip of the day. Bob addresses the visitors, explains about Darryl being the trailer, and officially welcomes the visitors to Mammoth Cave and Frozen Niagara.

A fifty-foot-long, concrete extension blends in with the limestone. I realize it's the airlock. Bob mentioned an airlock for the Industrial entrance, which must be around the ridge from here. The cave inside the entrance showed the need for an airlock back in the seventies.

"This tour operates a little backward," says Bob. "What we ask of you is follow me straight on back to Flat Ceiling. Please don't stop for photographs on the way in. You will have plenty of time for photography on your way out. Remember. No flash photography at any time in or out. As strange as this idea will sound to you, believe me, you will enjoy the trip more if we can get in quickly and then stroll out. Thank you for understanding. Any questions?"

"Will we see lots of bats in the cave?" asks a nine-year-old.

"Good question. This part of the cave never housed much of a bat population because this is a man-made entrance, and they had no way to get in the cave before they blasted this opening. You're unlikely see a bat. All the rocks, animals, plants, and the bats are protected in this national park. Please do not touch a bat or any other creature in the cave. Or the formations. Just handrails. OK? Let's get started. Darryl will collect your tickets at the door."

I linger at the rear and flash Darryl my ID badge.

"You're good, Walt."

Inside the cave from the airlock, I notice how the new lighting enhances the views of the passage. When I guided here, algae grew on a lot of formations. Moss grew on the ceiling at the entrance. No moss, no algae now. A pack rat used a fluorescent light fixture in the wall on the left for its nest. In 1976, the rat displayed a flash cube. The new LED fixtures illuminate the formations in subtle light.

Familiar formations line the right side of the trail as we walk in. The Great Wall of China—a rimstone dam—runs along a now-dry pool. Several other formations I don't remember the names for appear fresh. And then, the Temple, which featured in many photographs, including a large poster once as recognizably Mammoth Cave as the view of the Teton Range from Jackson Lake Lodge in Wyoming.

A large stalagmite, conical in cross section and about eight feet across at the base, occupies most of the space on the right side of the trail. From there, we pass by Rainbow Dome and pause at the overlook for Crystal Lake. Visitors form a short line as they gaze at the clear water below. Two white, underwater lights show off the small lake. No evidence of PharmARAMA's intrusion here. The surface of the water lies perfectly placid, still crystal clear.

We swing into the Onyx Colonnade where we bend under a low ceiling. A wire-mesh screen protects a dense group of formations from oily hands and pushy arms.

* * *

The history of Frozen Niagara with its man-made entrance differs from that of the rest of Mammoth Cave accessed by the natural entrance. It lay undiscovered until 1925, when George

Morrison's New Entrance guides found their way through a giant jumble of house-sized boulders named the Big Break. With that breakthrough, they discovered a lot of cave formations, including the namesake of the tour, Frozen Niagara.

Morrison fell in love with the cave and, because of lax security, conducted secret surveys in the cave, and proved this end of Mammoth Cave ran out from under the property of the Mammoth Cave Estate. With his survey and the corresponding surface map in hand, he bought or leased property next to the estate covering enough cave that allowed the blasting of the New Entrance to Mammoth Cave. With his own entrance, he set up a ticket office, started offering tours, and eventually opened a hotel. Morrison had the advantage of being first on the road leading to Mammoth Cave.

The Estate claimed they owned the cave and all the displayable cave connected to their entrance. However, the state court ruled whoever owned the surface property owned the cave below it—entrance or not. In 1925, after the Frozen Niagara discovery, Morrison blasted in a second entrance. With this arrangement, he could offer more tour options. He could run a tour from the New Entrance back to the Mammoth Cave Estate property line and back out through Frozen Niagara. Hailing from New York, Morrison named landmarks in the New Entrance/Frozen Niagara section with New York place names, including Grand Central Station, the Hippodrome, and—the headliner—Frozen Niagara.

From the overlook at Crystal Lake, I walk on, urged politely by Darryl. An enormous piece of flow stone on the right side of the passage bears the name for the tour, a waterfall captured in stone. Chains block the optional forty-nine steps down to the Drapery Room under the stone waterfall and the top of the mandatory forty-nine steps back up. Visitors amble past the head of the steps, but Darryl gently urges, and they cooperate and keep moving.

Over a small rise in the trail, we arrive at the top of twelve steel steps. Darryl stays at the light switch at the head of the steps. The last few visitors descend and walk up the opposite hill to Flat Ceiling, where Bob will give a brief talk before heading them back out.

"I'm walking back to the KEA formations," I say. Some decorative flow stone named after the Kentucky Education Association.

"You got the badge. Have at it. You have your flashlight, but remember, Bob will do a blackout in a couple of minutes."

"Right. Thanks for reminding me. I'm not going far." I will stroll around and find whatever PharmARAMA research or damage I can. I ease down the steps and wait until the last visitor walks out of sight up the hill at Flat Ceiling.

Within a hundred yards, a bright yellow, plastic sawhorse blocks the trail, and a big sign announces in red letters.

RESEARCH AREA!
NO ADMITTANCE!
For more information, visit our website at
www.PharmARAMA.com/MACA/Research/Bacterial.

So, the sponsor has erected this sign and nothing else. No cameras, trip wires, or other sensors. I could go around the barrier, but I won't. Being on Bob's tour, I don't have a lot of time. As I come back to the trail, the lights go out. I ease along the path based on memory and pause before I crest the little hill.

"How many of you can see your hand in front of your face?" says Bob. "If you can see it, please hold it right there and raise your other hand." A ripple of laughter runs through the group. A dim light flares up on the hill. Bob strikes a match. "Amazing what you can see when your pupils open wide, isn't it?" The match dies. I scoot a few feet farther up the hill where I'll be close when the group turns back.

"OK, Darryl, give us some light."

I move along ahead of the group. At the bottom of the hill, I step aside and wait for Bob. He chats with members of the tour and waves at me. I fall in behind.

"No, sir. Over time, water dissolved all these passages. Except for the trail, the handrails, and the lights, everything else is natural. No blasting except at the entrance," says Bob to a grizzled visitor walking along with him. Miners visiting the cave have long raised these questions. They look for the profiles of holes drilled for explosive charges. One fellow guide in 1976 explained this to one of his visitors on the self-guided Historic. He convinced the fellow who then said, "We're just little turds on this Earth, aren't we?" The guide agreed with him. I smile and keep up.

* * *

At the airlock, Bob says, "Well, you have seen a lot of cave. Three tours in one day. How did you like it? Were you ever overwhelmed?"

"Great. I enjoyed it a lot. Not that it wouldn't have been better with you along, but given that, it was good. It was a lot to take in, but other than a moment at Mummy Ledge, no. How do you feel?"

"Not bad at all. I guess I'm still a cave guide after all."

"Good news," I say.

Outside, Bob boards the bus last. He stands in front behind the driver and talks with the visitors in the front rows. I stare out the window and enjoy the ride back.

Twenty-Two
Recap at Bob's House

Bob stops the SUV at the concessions service station to clean the windshield. I get out and stroll up the rise that screens the amphitheater from the station and the road. I reflect on slideshows presented by cave guides of the past, including Bob's, then turn and walk back to the truck. Bob emerges from the campground store with two bottles of water.

"I think paying for water is bad enough, but now it's too complicated with flavors and additives. I hope I got the right stuff," and he hands me a bottle of vitamin-fortified, grape-flavored water. But it's cold and wet.

"The river's down. No point in going somewhere else, like Echo River Spring," I say.

"Haven't seen it in years, but it would be quiet now. I'm about adventured out. Ready for home?"

"Let's go," I say. Before we get into the truck, Bob's phone rings.

"Wait a minute, Denise. Let me put you on speaker. Walt should hear your report." Bob pushes a button on his cell phone and signals me inside. From the driver's seat, he says, "Denise?"

"I'm here."

"Go ahead," says Bob, and he rests the phone on the console.

"I told John the whole thing. He confirmed something—or someone—scratched up the dirt around Edwin Booth." Something? I wonder. "Someone had marked up the top of the Corkscrew area. He scanned the trail all the way to Mammoth Dome. He saw the marks you described, Walt, leading into Vanderbilt Hall. Lots of activity at the base of the Corkscrew. He saw nothing else on his way out of the cave, but his trip raised as many questions as it provided answers."

"Once John got back up the hill, I had him leave a note at Bill's trailer. Bill has to call me when he comes in, whatever the time. John won't feed the rumor mill, not like some others. If Bill doesn't check in by eight in the morning, I'll report it. Oh. No one called in an end of sweep report last night. I'm going for coffee and then get back to my paperwork. Call me if you hear anything."

"You do the same," says Bob. "Thanks for getting me on board today. It cleared up some things."

"No problem. Have you seen Walt?" she asks.

"He's right here." says Bob.

"Bob, please ask him to not run off with the ID and the key. You won't let him, will you?" says Denise.

* * *

Bob pulls out of the service area. Given the gravity of the day, I resist commenting about how we are content to return to camp having contributed to our knowledge of the *Wild Kingdom*. The trip out of the park and back through Cave City takes no more than a few minutes. We pull in at seven thirty. Zona and Barbara arrived ahead of us.

Barbara comes out of the house when we exit the SUV. I walk over and give her a hug and kiss.

"Hello. How did you like Bowling Green?"

"You need to see some of those shops," says Barbara. "Used books, postcards, and hand tools. I found something I've been looking for, remember? Something for packets of sweetener. See?" She holds out a small blue tin with a brass butterfly affixed to the top.

"Looks great. Did you find something good for lunch?" Zona joins us outside.

"Bob, we ate at the Green for Lunch place downtown, and they have fantastic food!"

"Great. Glad you enjoyed it. Barbara, did Zona wear you out?" asks Bob.

"She came close. I had a lot of fun, but I didn't see John Ammerman as Edwin Booth. I mean, really!" Barbara says, looking at me.

"He was amazing, as always, but still. The whole PharmARAMA thing is a lot to take in. Not as bad as the dream, but I did not see the cave I thought I knew." I look at Bob, and say, "We have some bad news too. But where's Mary?"

"We dropped her off over at her house. She'll be here in a few minutes with her green beans. Walt, you did two cave tours today?"

"Let's go inside," says Bob. He opens the door, and we file through to the den. Jesse meets Zona in the kitchen.

Once we're seated, Bob says, "Bill Soonscen didn't show up for work this morning. No one's seen him since last night when he swept the Historic."

"Oh, Bob! How dreadful," says Zona. "What happened? If you guided two tours, what did Walt do?"

"No one knows what happened to Bill. Part one, Denise sent a guide by Bill's place, but no luck there. When we stopped by her office for our passes, she drafted me for the eleven o'clock Historic and the five o'clock Frozen." Bob points to my badge. "She gave Walt a photo ID and a cave key. He tagged along with Keven up to Giant's Coffin, wandered out to Mummy Ledge, and linked back with me in River Hall. Around lunchtime, Denise got a phone message slip saying Bill was sick. The person who took the call didn't recognize the voice.

"Part two comes from our cave trip—or trips. When Walt followed Keven's tour this morning, the trailer could not turn on the spotlight, but Walt noticed the figure on Stage Rock didn't favor the Edwin Booth in his mind. And he noticed all this despite his excitement over seeing the live performance on Stage Rock. You remember that show we saw, 'Booth, Brother Booth'?"

"Yes, I do. You saw his performance? Fantastic!"

I translate for Barbara, "I saw a beard on the wax figure. He slouched, no uplifted hand, not like the actor in the play at all."

"Edwin Booth is in the cave?" asks Barbara.

"A wax figure up on Stage Rock. At the entrance to Gothic. I made little of it at the time except to wonder why it didn't match my mental image of Booth. John Ammerman commented on it as well. He said it looked more like Caliban than a role for Booth."

Bob says, "By the time I got my tour to Booth's Amphitheater, it looked like the regular wax figure of Booth. Well lighted. Someone had fixed the spot. No beard, no slouch. Right hand raised in the posture you'd expect from the pre-eminent late nineteenth century Shakespearean actor, as if portraying the Dane in his famous soliloquy. Walt, tell your story."

"When Keven's tour continued behind Giant's Coffin, I walked by myself out to Wright's Rotunda, the Cataracts, and on to Mummy Ledge. No hotel at Wright's Rotunda. A real relief."

"A relief for Walt, but I wanted to see it." says Bob.

"When I stopped at the Cataracts, I thought I heard someone calling for help. It was faint. I turned my flashlight off, and it seemed to be stronger. I turned on my light and saw Orville from Maintenance standing in the trail. He said he hears that call all the time. And he talked about *haints* back at Blue Spring Branch and Mummy Ledge. We had a really enlightening chat."

"You haven't said anything about this before," says Bob. "You say his name is Orville? I don't think I've met him, but I might not if he works the Lantern tour route."

"Did he have an explanation of the call for help?" says Zona.

"He thinks it's an acoustical trick caused by the falling water and the shape of the passage. When a tour is there, the acoustics change, and there's no call."

"At Mummy Ledge, during one of my little blackouts, a slight breeze raised the hairs on the back of my neck and arms. But it died away. While I had the flashlight off, I thought I heard a dog running toward Violet City. Have you heard of a dog in the cave?"

"A dog?" says Bob. "No one has ever mentioned a dog. Did Orville say anything about it?"

"No, he didn't."

"Walt, do you think the cave talked to you on this trip? You heard a voice call for help and felt a breeze on your neck. Do you think that's what it was? The spirit of Mammoth Cave?" says Zona.

"I'm not sure. Not while I was there in the dark alone. Maybe so. Upon reflection, so to speak. On the way back, I managed to not run all the way to Giant's Coffin. From there I turned into the lower passages and crossed Bottomless Pit. By the time I got to Pensacola Avenue, I had calmed down. So, I followed Keven's suggestion and wandered up the passage to see Daran. Barbara, you remember Daran, Keven's son?"

"Sure. He's gone on photography trips with us. Does he guide now?"

"No," says Bob. "He works for the sponsor."

"PharmARAMA?" asks Barbara.

"I'll fill you in, in a minute," I say. "Daran said Bill conducted the sweep through the Historic and stopped by their research area at quitting time yesterday. Bill headed toward Scotchman's Trap and Fat Man's Misery, and Daran and Courtney came out by Giant's Coffin."

"Who is Courtney?" asks Barbara.

"Courtney works with Daran in Pensacola. Walt, I don't know if you understand, Courtney and Bill are secretly dating," says Bob. "If folks still *date*."

"She turned paler after we talked about Bill not showing up. But she looked pale when I first met her."

"Why secretly?" asks Barbara.

"PharmARAMA's policy prohibits fraternization with other staff or with Park Service folks," says Bob.

"Thanks for reminding me. Zona, I invited Courtney for supper. Hope you're OK with her coming," I say.

"That's fine, Walt. We have plenty of food."

"After leaving Daran, I stooped through the Misery into Great Relief Hall. On the steps down into River Hall, I looked back, and out popped Bob ahead of his tour. Can't beat the timing, can you?"

"Then, Walt followed us up through Mammoth Dome. Did you ride the elevator?" says Bob.

"I went up the tower with Darryl," I say as Barbara asks two questions.

"What elevator and who's Darryl?"

"They have installed this huge, bright-yellow, mine elevator alongside the tower in Mammoth Dome. Hideous. Darryl trailed Bob's tour." I tell her about the trailing rangers they have now in place of lowly GS-4 Park Aides like I had been.

"We went out with the tour," says Bob. "Walt told me about the problem with Booth's figure and persuaded me to turn around and go back to Stage Rock."

"And what did you find?" asks Zona.

"The figure Walt saw had gone away, but the one from my Historic—the regular Edwin Booth wax figure—stood there in bright light. We turned around, exited the cave, and climbed the hill to report. Denise sent John down on a reconnaissance of Stage Rock and the top of the Corkscrew," says Bob.

"Why would anyone go up the Corkscrew?" asks Zona.

"Someone, or something, scuffed up the trail at the base of the Corkscrew and in Vanderbilt Hall. John said someone had scuffed up the cave dirt at the top of the Corkscrew. He saw recent scuffs, maybe drag marks. Although I'm not sure how he could tell."

"Well, you two spent an unexpectedly adventurous day," says Zona. "Bob, I'm sorry you missed the performance. After our discussion this morning, how do you feel about guiding?"

"I'm surprised to feel as well as I do. We also took the camera out Green River Bluff trail and got some shots of a pileated woodpecker. No owl, though," says Bob.

"What owl?" asks Barbara.

"A couple of days ago, Bill told me about seeing a young owl, and we checked out the trail after lunch before my Frozen Niagara tour."

"What trouble is Bill in?" says Zona as she gets up and goes to the kitchen. Barbara follows.

"We don't know," Bob says. "The weird thing is, from Walt's description, it sounds like he saw Bill, not the wax figure of Booth. No one turned off the lights after River Hall last night. Either Bill skipped turning out the lights—very unlikely—or he never left the cave. Neither sounds good. Denise will call when she knows more. She implied we might be gossipy if we got around other guides. She's afraid we will let something slip out before she's ready."

"And don't forget the jitney tracks at Mummy Ledge," I say. "I saw no white domes or PVC pipes after Wright's Rotunda. PharmARAMA must not have any research out there. Why would someone take a cart back past Mummy Ledge?"

Bob says, "Yes. All true. The sponsor's staff stayed pleasantly out from underfoot today. No white coats ruining the scene. They usually run all over the place during my talks. Walt, I'm glad you figured out about the technicians being thin on the ground."

While Zona digests the story about Bill, I give Barbara my short version of the sponsor's research activities, the elevator at Mammoth Dome, and the wine with fried chicken lunch.

"Well, we can do nothing until we hear from Denise, let's get dinner started," says Zona. "Bob and Walt will grill steaks for the guys. And Barb, for you, Mary, Myrna, and me, I've fixed some nice kabobs with fresh vegetables and a little meat trimmed off the steaks. How about a glass of white Zinfandel?"

"Sounds good," says Barbara.

* * *

Bob hands me a crystal tumbler containing an amber liquid, and we go out to the deck. "It's a different single malt. Maybe an anodyne against anymore nightmares."

"Cheers." We sip and admire the Scotch. Before we work on the grill at all, Bob's cell phone rings, and he answers it.

Bob sticks his head inside and tells Zona, "Courtney called. She's coming over right away for a chat." I follow Bob back inside.

"OK, when she gets here, I'll send her out to you guys on the deck."

Mary comes in from the garage bearing a white ceramic bowl of green beans and a large plastic container. When she puts the bowls down, I give her a hug, say hello, and follow Bob back out to the deck.

As we sip Scotch and admire the sunset, I work on the grill. Courtney comes through the door carrying a glass of wine. She's changed her white PharmARAMA coveralls for jeans and a red Western Kentucky University—Go Hilltoppers—sweatshirt. She doesn't smile and looks out through the dull, haunted eyes I saw earlier. She's been crying.

Twenty-Three
Courtney Comes for a Chat

"Hi, Courtney. How are you?"

"Thanks for letting me come over early."

"No problem. You remember Walt from this morning. Do you mind if he's here while we talk?"

"Hi. I guess it's OK."

"Good," says Bob. "Why don't we sit over here, and Walt can finish getting the grill ready. What shall we talk about?"

Courtney sits in one of the handmade rockers, then pauses. She stares at her glass of wine, still full. "You're aware Bill and I are seeing each other, aren't you?"

"I suspected." Bob sits in another rocker and sips his Scotch. I address the grill with a wire brush. "Bill had me coach him on lines from 'Twelfth Night.' And, you're a huge Shakespeare fan. I put two and two together."

"So that's how he did it," Courtney says with a smile. "Well, you know the policy. And Wolfgang—I'm sorry W.G.— is extremely strict. If he found out about Bill and me, he's capable of anything. He's vicious." She shudders.

"I understand about the non-fraternization rules, but why would you think he might go overboard?" asks Bob.

"W.G. began asking me out right after I started working here. He follows his own set of rules for himself."

"I see."

"So, this morning I came in ahead of my usual time and walked up the hill at Booth's Amphitheatre?"

"Yes."

"This will sound silly, but I always quote Shakespeare when I pass Edwin Booth—his wax figure, anyway."

"That's interesting, but not silly. Any particular lines?" Bob's expression shows he's not the least bit surprised.

"I like the song Balthasar sings in 'Much Ado.'" She laughs.

"And one of Helena's speeches in 'Midsummer.'"

"Terrific," says Bob.

I turn from the grill and ask "So, you recite lines every morning going past Edwin Booth?"

Courtney looks at me and says, "On Monday morning, Bill stood there on Stage Rock in front of Booth. He delivered Feste's speech about journey's end in lovers' meeting. From 'Twelfth Night?'" She fidgets and her feet bounce up and down on the deck.

"It was great! Since we don't get the same days off, we can't schedule much time together. In a small community like ours, you must work hard staying under Wolfgang's radar." She lowers her hand to show how low his radar goes.

"What happened this morning?" asks Bob.

"I walked along like normal, all set with lines of Viola's, in her dialogue with Olivia?" Bob nods, and Courtney continues. "Right in front of Stage Rock, I saw Bill's face on Booth. For a split second I knew it was Bill, but he didn't speak. He didn't move at all. So, I thought someone changed the makeup on Booth to favor Bill.

"Once I knew our secret was out, I knew who. But that image made it much bigger than our secret getting out. It threatened me. I got frightened and ran all the way past Giant's Coffin. Bill hasn't contacted me all day. And Walt told us he didn't show up for work. And now I'm even more frightened. I'm worried about more than my job, you know?"

"Walt saw that figure on Keven's tour. The spotlight had burned out. Although, he did not recognize Bill, having never seen him. He described a figure that did not match the regular Edwin Booth, but resembled Bill."

"The spotlight was on when I came along," says Courtney. "It shone right on what I'm afraid was Bill his own self."

"The light must have burned out before we got there," I say. "Or someone pulled the breaker."

"It was Bill, wasn't it, Bob?" asks Courtney. "I'm worried out of my mind."

"It seems he was up there. I didn't see him on the eleven o'clock Historic, nor when we doubled back after the tour. Booth—the wax one—stood on Stage Rock lit up from head to toe."

"Bill can't be dead, can he?"

"We can't be sure. We don't know where he is, much less what condition he's in. Denise started looking for him, and we're leaving the follow-through to her. She sent someone by his trailer. His truck never showed up in the visitor center parking lot. He'll turn up, I'm sure."

"Does she need help looking for him? Can't we form a search party?" says Courtney.

"Denise is doing everything short of calling in the calvary. If Bill's not back tomorrow morning, it will be all hands-on-deck," says Bob. To mix metaphors.

"I can appreciate Denise's concerns, but we need to find him sooner than later."

I finish cleaning the grill and turn on the four burners of the big grill. They light with a series of pops.

"From Booth's Amphitheater, where would you move— uh, an unconscious person?" I say.

"Courtney, is there any reason why a PharmARAMA employee should go to Violet City?" says Bob.

"The end of the Lantern tour, isn't it? No, there's no research back there. The cave beyond Wright's Rotunda is off limits for all personnel. Even though I'm not sure where that is." Her eyes widen.

"I know where he is," says Bob, jumping up, flashing a smile, eyes twinkling.

"Where?" asks Courtney jumping up from the rocker sending her glass of wine flying over the rail into Zona's koi pond. It doesn't break.

"Walt, remember you saw those jitney tracks in the cave?"

"Sure. I saw them all along the way in Main Cave. They continued on past Mummy Ledge."

"Where is the farthest point from Stage Rock that they could drive a jitney and be close to an entrance?" says Bob. We shrug. "Violet City. That's where Bill is. I hope we aren't too late. I'm calling Denise. Walt, dinner may be a little late." I turn off the grill, finish my Scotch, and follow Courtney and Bob into the house. Bob punches in numbers on his cell phone.

"Denise, this is Bob."

"No luck? Well, I have an idea. Can you meet us at the Violet City entrance?"

"You're still at the park? Good. Listen, don't use your radio, and don't call anyone else. It's seven-thirty now, can you meet us there at eight o'clock? We'll bring John and Keven. And maybe Daran."

"See you then."

Bob says, "They moved Bill out near the Violet City Entrance with the jitney. Then stashed him somewhere near the entrance where they can retrieve him after dark. Zona, we're headed to the park. Call John. Ask him to meet us at Violet City. We're keeping this quiet until we have more information. If Bill is alive, and if we can find him, he will shock whoever did this when he shows up for work tomorrow."

At that moment, Keven and Myrna come in through the door from the garage.

After greetings drag on past fifteen seconds, Bob says, "Excuse me. Hate to butt in and all. Keven, we're headed into the park to check on Bill, and we need you with us. We'll be back when we can."

"Bill? Bill Soonscen?" asks Keven.

"Right. I'll explain on the way. You got your flashlight, right?"

"Sure, in the car. I'll grab it."

"Good, let's go," says Bob.

"What about me?" chirps Courtney.

"Come on. If we find Bill, you can comfort each other." Bob says. "We are on a photography trip, if anyone asks." We don't have a single camera. I give Barbara a quick hug and a promise I'll call when I can.

Keven joins us with his three-cell flashlight, and the four of us pile into our red station wagon. We're headed out of the driveway when a silver and flame two-seater screeches to a stop in the road.

"There's Daran," says Keven.

"He should go with us," says Bob.

Courtney says, "Oh, yes. Get Daran." She seems pleased someone she knows will be along.

Keven gets out and tells Daran to park his car and come with us. While waiting for Daran, I open the back of the car and pull up the rear-facing, back seat. Once we're headed for Cave City, Bob briefs Keven and Daran on the day's events and tells them about the jitney tracks and why he thinks Bill might be at Violet City.

"Bob, who do you think did this?" Keven asks.

"I know Wolfgang did it," says Courtney.

"He seems a good bet, but do you think he's that crazy?" asks Bob.

Everyone falls silent.

"I've always known he was a nut," says Daran.

"We've speculated on how Bill got from River Hall back to Booth's Amphitheater. We wondered if Bill climbed the ladders or if someone carried him up those ladders. Could Wolfgang carry Bill up through the Corkscrew," I ask Daran.

"The Corkscrew? What—Uh, sure. He could. He's a former Olympic decathlon bronze medallist. Climbing the Corkscrew carrying a body sounds like more work than I've ever heard of Wolfgang doing. His minions do it all. Truth is, if he wants someone to do something, he *persuades* them. Everyone knows he carries a pistol in his pocket. Another rule he doesn't follow, the one about no firearms in the cave."

"I guess it doesn't matter much how Bill got to Stage Rock." I feel uncomfortable. I expected Daran's information would mean Bill climbed the ladders, if at gunpoint. Now we face a worse possibility.

"Bob, have you been on those ladders in the Corkscrew?" asks Keven. "I sure wouldn't enjoy carrying a person up through that. A tough climb."

"No. I haven't. They're scary?" says Bob.

Courtney relieves the tension somewhat, "I don't think Wolfgang would have risked a gunshot. There are too many lab types around, plus security. Even *he* couldn't shrug off a gunshot. I have heard no gossip about Bill or W.G. from the other technicians. I believe Bill may be down, but he is not out." Since this occurred after hours, it appears Wolfgang made sure no one would bog him down with PharmARAMA stuff. Why should I add to Courtney's anxiety?

"Bob, I know a great hiding place for something—or someone—at the end of the Lantern tour," says Keven. "Do you remember the little dead end on the left before Ultima Thule?"

"Where they keep the backup lanterns?" asks Bob.

"Right. It's a great place for hiding stuff," says Keven. I wonder what Keven hid there in the past—and why.

Once we cross I-65 and pass through the development, I drive as fast as I can. The curving road limits how fast I can push the loaded station wagon. In seventeen minutes, we pull around the circular drive separating Violet City from the Carmichael Entrance to the Grand Avenue tour.

"There's Denise's pickup," say Bob and Keven together. "And here's John coming in behind. He was quick."

Twenty-Four
Ultima Thule

Denise carries her flashlight in her left hand and an extra-large, fanny pack with a red cross on the green nylon fabric in the other. She's been thinking ahead.

"Bob, I was pulling up your number when you called. What's going on? John—oh, Bob must have called you.

"Right, and here I am. Hey, Walt. Heard you were coming." We shake hands.

"So, what are we doing?" says John.

"I think they hid Bill near Ultima Thule."

"What makes you think so?" says Denise.

As we approach the entrance, Bob explains the evening's discussions, how the jitney tracks in Wright's Rotunda and at Mummy Ledge, and Courtney's confirming Wright's Rotunda and the area beyond are off limits to the Sponsor.

"Well, she's right about that area of the cave being off limits," says Denise. "Are you Courtney?"

"Hi. Courtney Elliott. Nice to meet you. I've heard a lot about you."

Denise looks puzzled—who told Courtney about her?

"John, meet Courtney. Courtney works with Daran up Pensacola Avenue," says Keven.

With introductions over, we move ahead. Everyone except Courtney carries a flashlight, and we approach the brown, cast-in-place, concrete tube extending from the old entrance.

"Another airlock?" I ask.

"Yeah. Over at Carmichael, the contractor ran the airlock inside down the stairs. Here they put it outside for obvious reasons. It works well," says Denise. "

As Bob points the beam of his flashlight onto the lock while Keven uses his key, he says. "I think we should minimize conversation and light until we see what's inside."

Keven unlocks the outer door, we file in, and he closes the door behind us. Bob leads us through the section of concrete tunnel and opens the unlocked inner door.

"Not good," says Denise in a whisper.

This end of the Lantern tour has no lights. Bob's flashlight shielded by his hand illuminates little. Once Keven closes the door, Bob switches his light off. More total darkness. This time, it's not a demonstration. No light leaks around the door.

We stand still. The members of our little band breathe hard. Someone has infected sinuses. We can hear water dripping from the stalactites. Extreme post-nasal drip?

We hear nothing unusual. After what seems like five minutes, Bob switches on his flashlight. It dazzles. He points it down the wet concrete steps. The stainless-steel handrails gleam. No sign of Bill.

We follow behind the spot of light, taking great care on the wet steps along the left wall. At the end of the steps, we follow the trail. On the right, the cave floor slopes away.

"I guess they couldn't drive the jitney through Ultima Thule. Too low. To come this far, they would have to walk," whispers Bob. Where the trail turns uphill before Ultima Thule, Bob stops. He scans ahead with his flashlight. Nothing unusual. "To paraphrase an old guy with a pointy hat, I think we might try some more light." I half expect him to blow onto a crystal and hold it aloft on his staff.

Bob coordinates us, and every other person turns on their flashlight. Spots of light kaleidoscope all over the passage while we walk along the trail beside the pit. To our relief, we see nothing in Bishop's Pit.

"I sure hope you're right, Keven," says Courtney.

"Roger that," says Daran.

We proceed up the rise to the low ceiling of Ultima Thule. The other side of this hill once marked the end of the cave— the extreme limit—until nineteen oh eight. Max Kaemper, the German engineer mapping the cave, and Edward Bishop, the Black cave guide assisting Kaemper, found a way through

Ultima Thule. The Park Service blasted the entrance in 1931. Edward Bishop may have been Stephen Bishop's great nephew.

Once we cross through Ultima Thule, we turn on our flashlights. I see the jitney tracks approach this point where they end. It looks like they turned around. Bob fans us out for the search. Keven and Daran head for the side cut. I follow.

"Oh, Bill! Where are you?" says Courtney. No reply.

"We got something," yells Keven. Behind a small slab of breakdown near the end of the short passage, Keven and Daran have spotted a canvas tarp. Everyone clusters at the mouth of the passage. Daran lifts the tarp. Nothing. We sigh. Courtney's face looks like a mask. Her hopes must have been high, and now they crash with such disappointment.

"Looks like we missed him." says Daran. "Do you think they've already come for him?"

"I don't think so. Too many employees and visitors still moving about." says Keven. He kneels next to the tarp. "Broken zip ties. Looks more like he escaped."

Denise crouches down by a dark stain. "Could be blood," she says.

"Oh, please don't let him be dead," whispers Courtney. Her face keeps the fixed expression.

"But which way did he go?" asks Daran.

"Let's bag the zip ties and fold up the tarp," says Bob. After Keven and Daran fold the tarp, I move in closer for a look around. Down on hands and knees, I shine my flashlight parallel to the ground accentuating the uneven surface.

"Wait, Walt. Go back a little," says Keven. I scan back. "See those letters? *C E*."

"Bill wrote my initials in the cave floor where anyone could see them?" Courtney seems more bewildered than pleased that Bill thought of her while in distress.

"Here. These marks show where they dragged him in here. None coming out," says Bob.

Nothing else shows up in my light.

"John, why don't you, Denise and I go back and give the pit a more careful review. Keven, take the rest on toward Mummy Ledge. Let's regroup at the steps when you get back," says Bob.

We wander down the hill with Keven and Courtney behind us. Almost on tiptoe. Our spots of light look like a disco.

"Daran, why don't we look on the left side, and Walt, you and Courtney look right?"

With the new organization, the lights bounce around less, and the search proceeds. We see nothing but jitney tracks. Two sets.

"Walt, stop. Swing your light back some," says Courtney. Where had I been looking? Well, we found something anyway.

"What did you see?" I ask.

"There, something shiny."

I kneel on the path and see a narrow brass strip with two pins sticking up. "Look. A jitney tire ran over the strip," I say.

"Pick it up," says Keven.

"It's Bill's nameplate," I say and hand it to Courtney.

"He came this way, didn't he?" Courtney no longer seems hunted. Her face shows more spark. Now, she is the hunter.

"He passed this way, but did he drop his name plate on his way up Ultima Thule or on his way back into the cave?" says Daran.

"The pins don't have backs," Keven says. "If they stowed him in the back of the jitney, he could have dropped it on the way to the dump site. If he left it on his way back into the cave, the jitney tire couldn't have run over it because Wolfgang would have left before Bill escaped.

"And if he left his name plate to show he had headed back into the cave, why didn't he put the retaining backs on the pins?"

"I think he pulled it off with his teeth while still tied up and dropped it as a sign he was here. While in the back of the jitney," says Daran.

"You must be right," I say. "Do we keep going or report back?"

We return to the group at the base of the steps. Bob and John shake their heads. No body. Courtney shows them Bill's name plate. They agree Bill dropped the name plate and did not place it.

"So what? He's not in the cave anymore?" asks Bob. No one answers. "I knew he would be here."

"He escaped. He must be a hard man to keep down," I say. "If he didn't go back into the cave, he must have gone out, right?"

Bob leads us up the steps toward the airlock. We study the wet steps and the formations. The stalactites along the right wall shine with water seeping over their surfaces. Bob holds us in the airlock while he makes a quick check in case Anderson or henchmen lurk outside. All clear. We file through the airlock disheartened.

"Well, we're done, aren't we?" says Denise.

"*C E, C E.* Courtney thinks he wouldn't advertise her name. He scratched those in the dirt for a reason. What else could the initials mean?" says Bob.

"Chicken 'n' eggs. Curry eggplant. Clay elephant. Close encounter. Oh, we don't want to go there," says Keven.

Above the din of frustrated and tired people, Daran says, "Well, there is Carmichael Entrance," Silence hangs in the air for a moment before Courtney throws her arms around Daran.

"Oh, Daran. That must be it." She looks around at the rest of us. "Right? Bill has to be there?" Daran looks uncomfortable.

The disjointed voices making wild guesses a moment ago now speak in one voice, "Yes!"

Twenty-Five
Down Seven Steps

"Daran! Excellent!" says Bob, pumping Daran's hand. "Well done."

"What? You think he's gone over to Carmichael?" says Denise.

"It's right over there. Let's find out," says Keven. We follow Keven around the circular driveway to the Carmichael Entrance. Again, Bob holds his flashlight while Keven unlocks and opens the door revealing a shock of bright light.

"We got him," says Keven and moves down the first of the steps. We all crowd in behind. Bill sits on the steps hunching over his knees.

"Don't move him," says Denise. She jumps in with the first aid kit. "They could have drugged or injured him—or both." She checks Bill's pulse. "OK, and now this." Denise mumbles to herself as she digs out a small flashlight and lifts Bill's left eyelid. Bill shifts his head sideways out of the light.

"Good. He's responding. Pupils are needle points." Denise holds him in place with both hands on his shoulders. "Stay put, Bill. This is Denise. Do you recognize me?"

"No. Where am I?"

"It's Denise." Bill looks at her. Still unfocused. "Bill, stay still, OK? Do you understand?"

He winces when he nods his head.

"Your head hurts. I need to check it, OK? Turn to the right."

When Bill turns his head, I see blood in his hair and a small dark stain on his uniform collar. Denise shines her light on the left side of the back of his head.

"I think we've found the wound. It looks like someone hit you on the back of the head. Do you remember being hit? You can turn back now."

"No. Can I sit up straight?"

"You know this drill better than me, what with all your military experience. Stay put." She goes through the whole routine of checking breathing, heart rate, bones, etc. "Do you hurt anywhere but your head?"

"No, only my head."

"Rapid pulse, clammy. Shock. Probably a concussion. Your eyes aren't synching. Sit up. Easy now. Getting over here from Ultima Thule must have required enormous effort."

"You've been over there?"

"Yes, we saw the broken zip ties, the blood, and the initials. Were you telling Courtney your last thoughts were of her?" says Bob.

"Who's talking?"

"Bob Cetera, Bill. We're sure glad we found you. We also found your nameplate."

"If Anderson got there first, he would think of Courtney. If a guide got there, it might make them think of Carmichael. Looks like it did."

First aid protocol or not, Bill sits up and looks around.

"Wow, what a gang. Who all's here?"

"Oh, Bill. Are you all right?" asks Courtney parting the group on her way to Bill. She sits beside him.

"Courtney? What are you doing here?" He grabs her hand.

"Careful, now," says Denise. "Keven, you and Daran help him up."

"I came with Bob and Daran," says Courtney.

"Whoa," says Bill. Keven and Daran ease him back to a sitting position. "Thanks, Daran, Keven. Where'd you guys come from?"

Denise hands Bill a bottle of water. He smiles and drinks the whole thing down before she can say anything about small sips. He immediately throws it all up.

"Yep. Shock. Concussion. Should have been more careful with the water," says Denise. She checks his pulse again. "Not surprising. He's been in the cave well over twenty-four hours and no food or drink. Dehydrated. Cold as the tomb. He needs an IV to re-hydrate him. I'm taking him to the ER."

"No, I'm OK. Sorry. I'm thirsty." Denise hands him another bottle.

"Take a sip or two. First, wet your mouth and lips. Daran, the first aid case down at the bottom of the steps—oxygen tank and mask—we need them. Quick."

Daran takes off down the stairs and through the bottom door of the airlock.

"Bob, can you go out and call for an ambulance?"

"Sure thing." Bob moves up the stairs.

"Bob, No." The sudden tone of command in Bill's voice stops Bob.

"Bill, you're in awful shape. Stage two shock." Denise takes a foil blanket out of her first aid kit and wraps it around his back and shoulders. "Hold this."

"No, I'll be all right. I need a minute." We stand there. Bob turns around. Then we hear Daran climbing the steps. He pops through the airlock door with a green cylinder, tubing, and a mask. He has run up about a hundred-sixty steps. He's breathing a little heavily, but not bad. Ah, youth.

"Here, Bill. We'll put you on a little supplemental oxygen, and your head should clear a bit." He lets her put the mask on him without resistance.

Denise applies some antibiotic ointment and a field dressing.

Eventually, Bill's head clears, and he seems steadier. "We need to get you out of the cave, so you can warm up, re-hydrate, and eat. Soon," says Denise.

Bill looks around. "You looked for me at Ultima Thule?" He looks at Bob.

"Yeah. Walt provided the clues. Courtney and Daran saw you in Pensacola last night."

"Who's Walt?" Bill's mind has returned to the present.

"Hey, Bill. Former cave guide and friends with Bob and Keven and all."

"Walt. Nice to meet you. Thanks."

"How do you feel?" asks Denise.

"Much better."

"Do you think you can make it up a few steps?"

"Sure." Then looking at Courtney, he says, "The course of true love never ran smooth." During Denise's ministrations and all the questions and introductions, Courtney kept her silent, still vigil while holding Bill's hand. She erupts into short bursts of laughter, and her eyes grow luminous with more than tears.

"He's delirious," says Denise.

"No, he's not," says Bob. "Look at this guy. Knock him out, tie him up, wake him up in the cave, and he can recite Shakespeare. But he's lain in the cave too long."

Keven and Daran get on either side and get him standing. Then they turn him around facing up the steps.

Courtney follows behind with a hand on Bill's back. He walks up the steps and out into the dark night. Then, he climbs the ten steps to the road.

The waxing gibbous moon poking above the edge of the trees shines on us walking along the driveway.

Bill stops on the loop road and takes a deep breath. "I love the cave, but this air smells so sweet." He looks around at all of us where we stand by the cars. "Thank all of you. Keven, Daran, Bob, Denise. But how did you get here?"

"Don't worry about that. How did you get to Ultima Thule?" says Denise. "We understand how you got over to Carmichael."

"Anderson, and I suspect, his accomplice. He must not have worried about anyone looking for me but you," addressing Courtney. "And he thought he frightened and controlled you. Looks like he underestimated you once again. Did you bring in the cavalry?"

"In due course, he underestimated me. And he frightened me, but it didn't have the effect he thought it would. Once I knew you were missing, I talked with Bob. He organized the cavalry," says Courtney.

Bill looks around and stops on me. "And you? Bob said you found some clues. What did you see?"

"First, impressive performance on Stage Rock this morning. But you look better now. Second, the jitney tracks all the way back to Mummy Ledge and beyond. And the scuffed-up trail in Vanderbilt Hall. Bob put it all together."

"If Bob and Walt hadn't gone in the cave this morning, you'd still be here waiting for Anderson or the first Grand Avenue tour tomorrow," says Denise. "If the minimum number of visitors had bought tickets."

"When I opened my eyes, I sure didn't expect you would shine your light in them. I expected Anderson and his little pistol. You guys are a damn site more pleasant. Thank you." He shakes Denise's hand with an exaggerated motion.

"We're taking you to Bowling Green and the ER. Thank all of you. I'm sure the chief ranger will need statements from everyone in the morning. Courtney, why don't you ride with us?" says Denise, having figured out Courtney's and Bill's relationship extended beyond the professional.

"No, we can't! What time is it? What day is it?" asks Bill, looking at once more alert and, for the first time, alarmed.

"That son of a bitch took my watch!"

"It's nine forty-seven," says Daran. "Saturday."

"No time for Bowling Green right now. They're taking it out of the Industrial Entrance at oh three hundred tomorrow. I can still catch them."

Twenty-Six
Bill Soonscen Unmasked

"Catch who?" asks Denise.

"Taking what?" asks Keven.

Courtney says, "Did Wolfgang do this to you? Because of me?"

"Catch who, doing what?" says Bob.

To Courtney, Bill says, "Yes, Anderson got me, but it's about a lot more than what's between you and me. A lot more. I'll explain it all later. Let me tell you the short version—"

"Hold up. Even for the short version, sit down. If you won't go to the hospital, at least sit on the tailgate, and put some ice on your head," says Denise.

John lets down the tailgate. And, in spite of himself, Bill seems relieved when he sits. Courtney takes the ice pack from Denise and sits next to Bill holding the bag to his head.

Bill picks up where he left off. "When I heard Anderson following me, I decided to confront him and find out what he was up to. He pulled his little pistol on me, but his gun was a diversion. The real threat came from the rear. A sting in my neck. My little plan contained a near-fatal flaw. He co-opted Hilda Floren. She gave me an injection.

"I woke up when they took me down off Stage Rock. He must have hit me over the head then. I passed out for a minute or two and played 'possum for the rest of it." Bill paused.

"Hilda Floren, Anderson's assistant research director. I must be getting soft. I never expected he would trust anyone, especially a woman. She shot me up with something. I never saw her. Right now, I got to organize this thing. I overheard a lot of their conversation. PharmARAMA made a major discovery."

"Define major," says Bob.

"PharmARAMA, well Floren and Anderson—but I can't tell you folks about it. It's too much. I'm better on my own."

"Bill, if it's happening at three o'clock in the morning, tomorrow morning, we're not sure you will be in any shape for helping, much less running it on your own. Whatever it is, you better tell us or the rangers—someone—what's going on," says John.

"John's right, Bill. You could slip into deeper shock any minute," says Denise.

"OK," says Bill. "You're right. It's like this. They discovered a programming bacterium in the cave. To be more accurate, a proteobacterium."

"What's a programming bacterium?" asks a chorus of voices.

"First, it's an ancient organism. And when I say old, I mean very, very old—very old."

"Do you mean like pre-Pleistocene?" asks Daran.

"I mean Paleozoic." Bill gets my attention talking geological time.

"The bacteria survived in a dormant state in the residual sea water in the pores of the limestone?" I say.

"Exactly. And in the cave, the bacterium lay protected for a long time in constant temperature, perfect salinity, mostly free from other organisms, free from ultraviolet light, and almost free from other forms of radiation, like cosmic rays. However, as we all know, not from neutrinos.

"Anderson and Floren believe this bacterium acts as the perfect vehicle for transferring DNA strands from one organism to another. From what I overheard, in its current state, if it infected a mammal, it would replace the gene for hemoglobin with one for chlorophyll. Those compounds are similar from the organic chemistry point of view," says Bill.

"It's one of nature's gene-splicers. It will revolutionize genetic modification, cloning, and—not insignificantly— reduce the cost to a fraction of what it is now. If the bacterium does what they say, and they sell it to the wrong people, things will get big and scary real fast. If you become infected with this bug you will, over a short time, exchange your nice pink glow for a greenish pallor."

"And we all know how hard it is to be green," says Daran. Am I the only one who thinks Daran is funny?

"How infectious?" Keven asks.

"It's from the Paleozoic. Mississippian-age limestone. Over these many years, no record exists of anyone being infected. No one that we know of. But who can say? Who's volunteering for a trial?"

I glance around. No hands go up. Daran shrugs.

"Anderson will take the culture out of the cave in the morning before anyone else finds out. Even at PharmARAMA." Bill pauses. "And by stealing it right out from under PharmARAMA, they can sell it for a lot of money. To anyone!

"A friend from the Army's infectious disease research unit at Fort Dietrich is dropping in tonight. His team should be here any minute. He may have intel on the connection. I've worked on this idea for a while, but if Anderson hadn't given me an opportunity to eavesdrop, we wouldn't know his schedule for tonight."

"But, Bill," says Keven, "If you didn't overhear his schedule until today, how could your buddy from Fort Dietrich know about tonight—tomorrow morning?"

"I've watched Anderson closely. Even so, I don't have any actual evidence. I called in Zack and his team for some recon. Take some samples, some pictures. Simple in-and-out. You could hardly have timed your rescue any better. Close, but great! If you hadn't sprung me, I'd have missed the rendezvous with Zack."

"Bob and Walt figured it all out. Keven guessed where they might have hidden you there at Ultima Thule," says Denise. "But your condition demands a rendezvous with no one but a doctor."

"No. Thanks, guys. Thank you all," says Bill. He looks all around for something. "I had stowed my cell phone in my pack. Did you find it?"

"Nothing but two zip ties under your tarp," says Keven.

"Can I borrow a cell phone?"

Daran passes him a slim black rectangle.

"Thanks." The blue glow of the screen lights Bill's face. He punches in a number and shifts the phone to his right hand. He takes Courtney's hand in his left.

"Zack?" Bill tells Zack about the changes in his status.

As we listen in on Bill's end of the conversation, we learn something unexpected has happened. Bill takes the phone from his ear and ends the call.

"Zack's team got diverted. When I told him about these latest developments, he re-diverted back to us. He will get authorization on the way. They're six hours out, including the drive from Glasgow airport. He had planned on landing in Bowling Green, but because of the tight timing, he's going into Glasgow. A C-130 Hercules ought to interest the folks out there. With Anderson taking the culture out at oh three hundred hours, Zack won't get here in time."

Denise says, "We need Mary Ann in on this operation."

Bill in a serious tone says, "Denise, I appreciate the position I'm putting you in by asking this, but I must do this. Alone. I shouldn't be telling you this much. If you report up the chain of command, they may pass it along to someone else, and we have no way of insuring someone won't tip off PharmARAMA and Anderson. He's slippery. I'm asking you, please forget all of this. I have to catch them in the act." Bill looks at Courtney, "I meant to tell you later, but I guess it should come out now."

"What?" says Courtney. "What should come out now?"

"I'm part of USAMRIID on detachment with the Park Service." At the expressions on our faces, Bill continues. "U.S. Army Medical Research Institute for Infectious Diseases." Bob looks at me, and I nod back.

"But you've worked here for over two years!" says Denise.

"I came in right behind the sponsor and Anderson. I love guiding," Bill says and looks at Courtney. "In lots of important ways."

Denise says, "OK. I'm hanging way out on a limb for this little expedition, but we'll do it your way for now. You should rehydrate, eat, and rest."

"Well, let's all go to my house. Zona's preparing supper, anyway. Your lying unconscious on the cave floor for however long can't be good for you. You can clean up, eat, and organize your mission from there." Bob looks at Denise for concurrence.

"Your house and dinner sound good." Denise says in a deliberate manner, "Wolfgang must answer for a lot. Alone in a dark spot would be a good start." Don't mess with Denise's schedule.

Everyone pauses in surprise when they hear Denise use Anderson's nickname combined with her tone of voice. She breaks the tension we have felt since before entering the cave. Denise will be the one facing the music, including Anderson's buddies at Homeland Security, if things go wrong tonight.

"It won't hurt for Zona to look at your head either."

"OK. Let's go to Bob's house. Do you have more water?"

Twenty-Seven
Getting Organized and Reconstituted

We split up among our Taurus, John's pickup, and Denise's pickup. Bill goes with Denise to discuss the likely end of her Park Service career. Courtney, as expected, goes with Bill. They seem confused over who is helping whom into the truck.

We cross Mammoth Cave Parkway once again headed for Cave City by the quick route. Denise follows.

On the way, Bob calls Zona and tells her we have Bill and more folks coming for supper. He tells her someone hit Bill over the head, but he insists he can't stop for a doctor yet. Zona can put her nursing skills to practice and prepare for his head injury.

"He's bloody, but seems unbowed," says Bob into the phone. "I don't think Bill eats meat." He pauses, "And since he's spent the day unconscious on the cave floor, he'll need something for a boost. Denise thinks he's shocky and concussed." Bob listens again and then says, "I know. Denise told him the same thing, but he insists he'll be OK. Yeah. Dehydrated." He listens some more. "Good. We'll be there in fifteen minutes. Oh. And Zona, there's a lot more to come. Dinner will be a planning session."

Bob punches off the phone and turns to me, "Zona says your wife brought tomato-basil soup from some French restaurant?"

"She did," I say. "It's a thick tomato soup. Bill should like it."

* * *

We pile out well enough for old guys in a hurry. Old, except for Daran. Bill emerges slowly out of Denise's pickup. No question who is helping whom this time.

"A little stiff?" asks Bob.

"More than a little," says Bill who hobbles some, then loosens up, but still walks with obvious discomfort. As I enter the kitchen, I follow right behind Bill and hear his stomach growling at the same time the aroma of the food hits me.

"I told them in the truck the worst things wrong with me were hunger and dirt. Hi, Zona."

"Well, hello, Bill. You do look a sight. And, it might be a tad more than hunger and being dirty. While Mary, Barb, and Myrna took care of the food, I got things ready to patch your head and get you cleaned up. Are you steady enough for a shower? OK then. If you'll come with me, we'll take care of your problems." Zona hands Bill a bottle of green Gatorade and leads him toward the master bathroom.

Mary announces, "We put extra towels in the hall bath, call me if you need more. We're eating buffet style. We have steak, baked potatoes, vegetables, three kinds of bread, plenty of salad and a variety of dressings, a little leftover lasagna, and my special green beans, in the main course."

"We're saving the soup for Bill." says Barbara. "And for dessert, we have brownies from Mary plus Myrna ran out for Gatorade for Bill and ice cream. Chocolate, Neapolitan, and butter pecan. Hello, John. Where's Pam?"

"Hi, Barbara. She's at practice but she'll be here before too long. I called her on the way," says John, speaking of his wife, who teaches music.

By the time we get our hands washed and go through the buffet, Zona returns.

She says, "His eyes look mostly OK. I expect only a mild concussion. We'll see if he keeps the Gatorade down. Then he can try some soup. If nothing stays down, he's going to the ER. No more questions. We'll tend the gash on his head, but it isn't bleeding right now. Denise, you did a good job cleaning and bandaging. I'll look at it again after his shower."

Courtney says, "What a relief! Thank you, Zona."

"Well, don't thank me yet. He's in the shower right now. I put a robe in there for him when he gets out. Bob, he can wear one of your shirts, and his socks and things are in the washer. We can brush the dirt out of his pants, but I don't think we have time for more than brushing if he wants to wear his uniform."

"Thanks, Zona. He'll want to wear the uniform," says Courtney.

"Where's his hat?" asks Zona.

"We didn't see a hat anywhere. Wolfgang must have claimed it as a souvenir," says Bob.

We spread out, eating at the breakfast table, in the den, and in the dining room. All of which are parts of a large open space.

"OK, with Zona here, we'll start the background briefing," says Bob. He recounts our tours of the cave, the substitution of an unconscious Bill for Edwin Booth, the jitney tracks, and how we discovered Anderson had dumped Bill near Ultima Thule. How Bill escaped and made it over to the Carmichael Entrance. He briefs them about Bill's mission for the Army while guiding at the cave. He ends by saying Bill plans on catching Anderson in the cave tonight with the bacteria.

"It seems like Bill plans on doing this alone," says Bob. "We discussed how we could help on the way over. We decided we should lend a hand. Let's start with the biology. Daran and Walt, you understand hazardous stuff better than the rest of us. Do you think you can put what Bill said in layman's terms?"

Daran and I glance at each other.

Daran says, "How about we do the science later. The bottom line is Hilda and Wolfgang have found and kept secret the cave's version of cloning ancient creatures—not dinosaurs, but a primeval, gene-splicing bacterium capable of replacing hemoglobin in blood with chlorophyll."

"Oh, no," says Zona.

"Genuinely, scary bacteria," says Daran. "Bill guessed something about the discovery and learned the rest in the last twenty-four hours."

Bob says, "Bill came out of the U.S. Army Medical Research Institute for Infectious Diseases—USAMRIID, as he calls it. At Fort Dietrich in Maryland. He took this job at the park undercover monitoring PharmARAMA. Daran, you're experienced in working with biological hazards, right?"

"I'm on the biological incident response team," says Daran.

"And, Walt, don't you have hazardous waste training?"

"Yes, but I've never used it except in training."

"If we can pull this off," says Keven. "Wolfgang's attack on Bill will result in our catching him red-handed and stopping this illegal operation before it gets any further."

A chorus of female voices asks, "We? If this bacterium is so important, where is the Army?" Their expressions show a decided shift. "Where are the rangers? Where is the CDC?"

"Bill arranged for backup, but only for reconnaissance, not action of this nature," Keven says. "Events sped up on the PharmARAMA end, but Bill's Army buddies got diverted. Until he overheard Wolfgang's timetable while he feigned unconsciousness, Bill didn't know about the rush. The team from Fort Dietrich is on the way, but Bill figures they won't be here for another five or six hours."

John says, "He can't—we aren't—in a position to wait for the Army's arrival. By the time the Army gets here, Wolfgang will have made the transfer."

"Barbara, you know your policy of prepare for the worst and hope for the best?" I say. "We need that approach now."

Denise, hearing her own sentiment repeated, looks up. She fills in what Bill told them in the truck. "He was in the back of the jitney while Wolfgang and Hilda discussed the logistics for stealing the culture. It happens tonight—in the morning. Three o'clock. They attacked Bill when they did because they thought he threatened their schedule. If they had left him alone, they could be free—and rich. And the world would be a more dangerous place.

"Anyway. Hilda and Wolfgang plan to use one of PharmARAMA's refrigerated trucks to load the samples and take off. Bill plans on stopping them," says Denise. "At the Industrial Entrance."

"He can't be much help. He's running on adrenalin now, but he will crash fairly soon," says Zona.

"I agree with you, Zona," says Denise. "However, Bill's thinking is that he will do this himself, and he regrets he told us about it. We should persuade him we can help. But what can we do? Can we be as effective as an elite Army team?"

Keven says, "Of course we can. Bill runs the operation. He directs it even if he can't actively take part all that much. However, we have some ideas how we can help. It requires a lot from you, Denise, and we should run it by, or over, you before we present it to Bill. From there, we're in his hands. If this bug presents the danger he says, he should understand we're in danger anyway because we crossed Wolfgang by rescuing Bill. Not even considering the minor matter of biological warfare."

"But can we fight a mad scientist?" says Myrna. "What can we do?"

"And at what risk?" asks Mary.

"Well, we plan our operation to minimize the risk. Everything from a run-in with security to exposure to the bacteria," says John. He looks at Keven.

Courtney comes in, and we look to her with concern.

"He sounds more like himself and said he'll be out shortly. He insisted I come report. The Gatorade stayed down, he's starving, and he used all the hot water."

Mary and Zona pick up dirty plates and go to the kitchen with Courtney.

Bob says, "Once we clear the tables, Walt, let's rearrange the furniture enough to put everyone closer together. We want everyone's input on this."

Courtney fixes a plate for herself and discusses the soup for Bill with Mary.

Zona says, "Walt, can you and Daran move the kitchen table into the dining room the way we do for theater group meetings? Everyone can't sit at the table, but if we stagger the chairs and bar stools, we can squeeze in everyone around and nearby."

"Hello, everyone," Pam comes into the kitchen from the garage.

"Hello, Pam," says the group in unison.

"I'm Pam's husband," says John explaining to Courtney. "Honey, I don't think you've met Courtney. You remember Denise and Daran, don't you?" says John.

"I do. Hi, Daran. And Denise, you, too. It's nice to meet you, Courtney."

"It's nice to meet you, too. The author of all chaos will be out in a minute."

"Let me get you a plate," Mary says.

"We ate after practice. Coffee please, creamer and sweetener."

Daran and I shift the dining table and carry in the kitchen table. Others squeeze the chairs around the tables. Barbara and Myrna dish out ice cream and brownies. Jessie, the big, black shaggy dog, who lay sleeping under the kitchen table, doesn't like the disruption and lumbers out of the room.

As we sit down, Barbara says, "I think better with notes. Let me grab a tablet from our room." She returns with a yellow legal pad and pen in hand. Daran looks disappointed. He must have been expecting an electronic tablet.

The mood grows serious as we settle down to work. While we focus on the risks ahead, couples and families sit together. Barbara and I take the backside of the table. She sits at the table to make notes. I shift a chair slightly behind on her left where I can see what she writes. The others follow suit. Pam sits next to Barbara and John takes up a position behind her. Myrna sits at the end of the table with Keven and their son Daran behind on either side. The sisters, Mary and Zona, take the seats opposite Barbara and Pam. Bob pulls a chair up between and slightly behind his wife and sister-in-law. Courtney takes a chair at the other end of the table from

Myrna. From there, she can see when Bill comes in from his shower.

Bob summarizes what we discussed on the drive back. We eat our desserts, talk about the required tasks, and discuss who among us may be best qualified for each job. The process flows along a wandering, but productive trajectory.

"We've worked out all we can without more information from Bill, assuming he hasn't drowned," says Bob.

A throat clears, and everyone looks up from the table.

Twenty-Eight
Cave Guide Spec Ops

Courtney reacts with brief confusion then shoves her chair back. She leaps to her feet and throws her arms around a clean-shaven, powerful man who—even weak with shock—stands inches taller than the one who left for a shower. The graying hair disappeared along with the beard. His eyes sparkle with intelligence.

I whisper to Barbara, "He didn't look this good when he came out of the cave. Clark Kent has taken off his glasses."

Bill smiles all around. "Sorry about eavesdropping. I intended to execute this project alone, but if the *Guide Force* has developed its own spec-ops branch, well then..." Bill shakes his head and continues, "It violates procedures, but my head is still fuzzy, and it sounds like you have a plan. Let's do it. Who all's on this cave tour?"

"Cave guides," says Keven. "Teams of two."

"We're ready to give your mission a shot," says Bob.

Zona interrupts, saying, "Bill, do nothing until we examine your head. Come on back to the bathroom." Mary and Myrna start on the dishes. Barbara draws an organization chart on her pad of paper. Zona and Bill return after several minutes.

"His head looks okay, but he should see a doctor. For now, I applied antibiotic ointment and three steri-strips," says Zona. "Since he kept the Gatorade down, he can try some soup."

"Did I smell baked potatoes? I'll have one of those if I may." says Bill.

"Zona, can Bill have a potato?" asks Mary. "Bill, you have a meeting. We'll bring it to you. What do you eat on your potato?"

"If you keep the soup down, Bill, then you can have a little potato. You need to take it easy."

"Thank you. Whatever you have for the potato—onion, cheese, anything except meat. Normally, margarine on potatoes, but butter will be OK." He sits in the chair vacated by Courtney. She slips a stool slightly behind Bill, her hand on his shoulder.

The group at the table focuses on Bill. Zona hands him a mug of soup and puts the bread in front of him. As he reaches for a piece of bread, he says, "I'm ready. What are my orders?" He starts in on the soup.

Barbara passes Bob her chart and task list.

"Our brainstorming has brought us this far," says Bob. "We hope we can flesh it out, but we'll start by outlining the three primary tasks. First—and the one we hope we won't need—containing, or at least minimizing, the biological threat. Second, keeping any PharmARAMA staff out of the way. Third, and most important, stopping Wolfgang. Dividing into teams seems the best way. Walt and Daran have trained on hazmat procedures. We have them set for the first task. If it becomes necessary." If, and not when, I hope.

Mary puts down a plate with a baked potato mounded with cheese and onion. Zona sets the butter dish in front of him, and they both return to their places at the table. Chairs shift a bit giving Bill more elbow room.

I ask, "Daran, what about the personal protective equipment, PPE?"

"There's a hazmat locker right outside the loading dock at the Industrial Entrance. We can get everything we need there.

Everyone voices their opinions about bacterial infections and turning green.

"We get our gear from the locker," says Daran. "Then we can move back to watch the entrance. We won't be able to set up a decon station without giving the show away. If Wolfgang shows up early, Walt and I can cut the battery cable on the truck. We'll suit up and stand by ready to help if things go wrong in the lab or on the loading dock. Like a spill."

Bob looks back at the chart. "The second task deals with security in the cave. Bill, we're looking to you for direction on this. But we will handle whatever happens with a cave guide's charm—and reluctantly if needed—a three-cell flashlight.

Every cave guide's trusty friend." No one seems to hesitate at the idea of Bob or John coshing someone. I don't see it happening.

Bill holds up his free hand acknowledging a full mouth, and he takes a minute to swallow. He puts his spoon down and drinks some water.

"Denise, what about security schedules around the industrial entrance? How many folks work the midnight shift?"

"They have one rover in and around their research area, but I do not know about schedules," says Denise. "No rangers or anything from our side. The sponsor provides security for the research area and the nearby cave passages."

Bill shows that he's moving back to going out on his own, but Daran catches the drift.

"Bill, we've all agreed to work on the buddy system."

"Right," says John.

"All right, you win. It's the buddy system," Bill says with grim acceptance. Then he outlines his ideas. More discussion follows.

"John and I will go in the Frozen Niagara entrance," says Bob. "We'll deal with any security guards we find between the entrance and the steps at Thanksgiving Hall. We'll be in uniform, and the security guards will recognize John, even if they don't me. We'll meet with Denise and Keven and continue out through the Industrial Entrance."

Bill, looking satisfied, asks John, "Can you distract him or her while I grab them?" John looks at Bob.

"No, Bill. You're going to stand in reserve. If you're on the playing field at all. You're still none to steady," says Keven.

"John and Bob will clear security."

"But…"

Before Bill can object, Courtney stands up, puts her hands on her hips, and focuses a severe frown on him. The frightened young woman who came over this afternoon has changed, no longer frightened.

"Bill, we will take care of it. You can stand by outside with Walt and Daran," says John.

"OK. I'm on board," says Bill and raises his hands. "Really, I am." Courtney eases back into her chair.

"Whoa! Time out," says Daran. "If Walt and I go in the Industrial Entrance in suits and respirators, can Bob and John come out through that same potential hot zone dressed only in their Park Service uniforms?"

"Great question, Daran," says Bill. "What will they need when they go through the lab?"

"They have to suit up," I say. "No other way to do it."

"Where and when will we suit up?" asks John.

"We can hardly go through the cave posing as innocent cave guides and truss up a security officer while wearing moon suits," says Bob.

"No, we can't," says John.

"What if Walt or I take the gear into the Industrial Entrance and leave it for you outside the containment barrier?" asks Daran.

Bob says, "And we dress out right there?"

Daran says, "Sure you do. I'll go over donning the PPE with you when you drop us off. It's not complicated."

"Sounds like we can handle it," says John.

"But you won't be able to wear your hats in the moon suits," I say.

"Then it's ball caps," says Bob.

"Good. I'm glad we ironed out another problem," says Bill. "Has anyone seen my hat?" We shake our heads.

"What about Keven and Denise?" asks Bill.

"Their route takes them in New Entrance and out Frozen Niagara. They won't have to come out through the Industrial entrance. On the clean side of the plastic barrier, they won't contact anything from the lab," says Daran.

"I'm not sure about wearing a moon suit," says Bob. "And a respirator less so."

"It's a lightweight suit. No mask. The powered-air-purifying respirator, the PAPR, blows filtered air into the suit and keeps it inflated. It's a low-impact kind of thing," says Daran.

"Your key problem will be to avoid snagging the suit on a rock," I say like I know anything about wearing protective clothing in a cave.

"I like the sound of this better," says John. Bob shrugs and looks at Zona. She does not appear happy. She has no reason to be happy. No one has reason to be happy. Except Courtney.

"We're getting serious," says Zona.

"It's a short walk in Frozen Niagara—the easy tour. Only steps are down into Thanksgiving Hall. Walt, you need to take my camera. We need to record this if we can," says Bob. No way I'm carrying his expensive camera while wearing a moon suit. In the cave.

"I'm not armed, but if we swing by my place on the way to the cave, I can pick something up."

"I don't think you'll be needing a firearm. The security guards in the cave don't carry, right Denise? And if we play this right, Wolfgang won't have an opportunity to use his," says John.

Feeling hesitant, I say, "This sounds crazy I know, but I can't help it. Some of you already know about my nightmare. It contained too many of the actual changes in the cave, and it's more than a little spooky. Based on that thin connection, Denise and Keven, you need to search for monitoring devices near the light switches. Look at the lighting control switches, maybe at Big Break or further along. In my nightmare, a big red box monitored cave traffic through there. What I've seen of this operation, you should have no trouble finding it. If this bit from the dream proves accurate, deactivate any alarms you see."

Denise looks skeptical. Keven points at me showing that he too feels Mammoth Cave itself can communicate with those of us in tune with it.

"We'll keep our eyes peeled. We shouldn't ignore any warnings from your crazy dream or from any other source," says Keven.

* * *

We discuss details of the scheme with Bill. He adds his input, and we shape our final plan.

"OK. John and I will deal with anyone in the section we cover," Bob says and summarizes the plan for anyone not paying attention.

"And we're doing all this on flashlights, not the tour lights, right?" says Keven.

"This all sounds good," says Bill.

Courtney and Barbara say, "And, where do we fit in?"

Bill turns to Courtney. "I'm going to ask you to be the comm link with Zack if things fall apart, since we may be out of cell phone range. Also, we need a second line of defense. If they get past us, you'll have to deal with things from a safe location. If something goes wrong, it may contaminate Frozen Niagara and New Entrance. If you don't get contaminated, you can react and report. If I can borrow your cell phone, I'll start entering the numbers you'll need."

Courtney goes to retrieve her phone from her purse, and Bill turns to Daran. "May I borrow your phone a while longer?"

Daran grins, saying, "I guess I can trust you with it."

Twenty-Nine
Move Out

Barbara turns to Zona, "The plan includes the possibility of disabling their truck, we should get some tools."

Mary, Zona, Myrna, Pam, and Barbara head for the garage. I'm looking over Barbara's notes when Zona returns with a toolbox. She puts it down with a pair of diagonal cutters on top. Mary brings in a coil of rope, a coil of clothesline wire, and a small plastic bag. Myrna comes back with a whistle, an air horn, and two rolls of duct tape. Pam carries a big pipe wrench and a hacksaw. Barbara returns last. She carries an unusual collection of a ratchet limb pruner, her chisel-point rock hammer, a pry bar, and a towel from our stash of miscellaneous material we keep in the car.

Barbara adds her collection to the pile. "These pruners are dirty. They live in the car for use at the Chattahoochee River. I forgot them once, but never again." I smile.

Courtney looks up from her conversation with Bill. Her eyes moisten, but her face glows. Bill looks over at the odd assortment on the table and wrinkles his brow.

"It's a stone soup tool kit for your project. We don't have any guns, but Barbara brought up the possibility of disabling the truck with the pruners, and we collected some other things you might use," says Zona.

"I apologize, Zona. I thought Bob included too many civilians in this op. I stand corrected. Great!" He picks up the plastic bag Mary brought, "Zip-ties. We call them flex-cuffs. These'll come in handy," and hands them to John.

Courtney, looking at the pile, reaches in her purse and pulls out a small canister of pepper spray. Instead of laying it on the pile, she hands it to Bob.

"I bought this to use on Wolfgang—if necessary. If you get a chance, will you deliver it for me?" Bob takes it and puts it in his pocket.

"Zona, let's make some coffee," says Mary, stifling a yawn. "It's getting late. How much do you want?

"Make at least five pots. We have thermoses to hold four and we need one for those of us waiting in reserve here at headquarters."

Bill addresses the entire group, "I accept your part in this with gratitude, but also with caution. We are dealing with dangerous criminals. Don't think of them as merely rogue scientists. They are exponentially worse."

"And, you have the head to prove it," says Bob.

"Oh, my head and more. He thought he killed me when he hit me, and I must have disappointed him when I kept breathing. While I pretended to be unconscious, he promised to do the job right once he had time. He's a methodical man, but his having to deal with me put him off schedule. If you hadn't rescued me, I might well have gained a shocking, but lasting acquaintance with the Green River."

Bob and I nod at each other. I assume he, like me, remembers the big splash in the river we heard this afternoon. I'm glad it didn't mean someone threw Bill in the river, but what fell in? Who threw what in the river?

"Based on the fright Courtney got from seeing you on Stage Rock this morning, you may have been a part of his plan all along. Or he improvised on the go. He could have stashed you in any of a number of places before dragging you on stage," says Bob.

"Courtney, Daran, tell me about the inside of those refrigerated trucks PharmARAMA uses. Are they all the same? With the single back door like an ice cream truck? And what's inside? I assume there's room for at least one person to stand," says Bill.

"I've seen nothing but the single door jobs," says Daran.

Courtney says. "Inside the exterior door, there is a short vestibule and a roll-up door. The chamber behind the roll-up holds four refrigerated wells for the transport canisters. They secure the inner and outer doors with a hasp and padlock on each."

"Can you describe the loading process? I've never seen it. The transport people appear to be professional—effective."

"Oh, they have a procedure for loading. You bet. They started training some of us, but then he stopped it. But here's the procedure. It's supposed to be a team of two. Always. Accountability and routine. That is the rule," says Daran, looking at Courtney. She nods.

"They bring the canisters to the loading dock on a cart. Team member number one uses the key to unlock the truck. Number one climbs in the truck, unlocks the inner door, and tests the restraining straps at each canister well. Team member number two secures the cart at the loading dock— PharmARAMA-speak for hold on to the cart. Don't let it roll off the loading dock. Number two hands each canister to number one. Number one straps in each canister before the next one goes in.

"Once they fill the four compartments, number one rolls down the inner door and secures it. Number one leaves the truck, and number two goes in to check the lock on the inner door," says Daran. "Together they lock the outer door and double check it."

"Is it a dead lift from the handoff to the well?" asks Bill.

"No. There's a shelf inside the roll-up door. You can rest the canister before putting it in the well."

"Do they ever transport one or two canisters, or must it always contain four?"

"Always four. Each well must have a canister. They may be empty, but there must be four canisters to balance. I don't know if it requires four, or Wolfgang's OCD needs all four to be in place. He's creepy about the little things especially."

"Creepy," says Courtney, an eerie tone in her voice.

Bill looks at the time on the cell phone he's holding "It's twelve forty-six. I want to have the cave secure and all of us in place within the next hour. Let's move. If I can have my clothes." Bill looks at Zona.

"They're all dry and mostly clean. You can change in the bathroom," says Zona.

"Of course, they are." Bill disappears into the hall bath between the two guest rooms.

* * *

"Thanks, Bob. The shirt is a little big, but it'll do," says Bill, once more in the kitchen in Park Service uniform.

"Is the cap mine, too?"

"I guess so. Do you have my nameplate?"

"Here it is, but we couldn't find the pins." says Courtney.

"Those I have. They fell inside my shirt." Bill takes the name plate and adds it to the shirt. "I think I'm all set."

* * *

We all stand. Those of us preparing to leave, study the collection on the table. John snags a roll of duct tape and clothesline to go with the zip-ties. Keven pockets the whistle, reaches in the toolbox, and pulls out a pair of lineman's pliers and takes the other roll of duct tape. Bill picks up the air horn.

Bob takes the towel and says, "You have to know where your towel is at all times." I take the ratchet cutters and rock hammer.

Bill says, "OK, last-minute restroom break, and then we move." He stands by the door.

Daran grabs the toolbox and pry bar, and says, "We may think of a use for more of this before we get to the cave."

"How many vehicles do you think we need for the seven of us?" asks Bob.

"If we want to use the Taurus again, we can squeeze everyone in," I say.

"Let's take the SUV," says Bob. "Less squeezing."

As we follow, Zona intercepts Bill saying, "We in the rear guard have divided our labor. Courtney gave me all the phone numbers and instructions. My sister Mary, Myrna, Pam, and I are staying here to man the phones and execute Plan B if it becomes necessary. Barbara and Courtney have decided they should take up an intermediate position. They're going to take Barbara's car and use it to block the access road. Then wait in Courtney's car at the Sand Cave parking lot."

Bill protests when Barbara, having taken advantage of the restroom break, comes into the room and says, "Bill, Courtney flatly refuses to be any farther from the action. And, let me assure you, I helped Walt with a hazardous waste training class in North Carolina, and I'm not exposing myself to decontamination unless it's absolutely necessary.

"Once Wolfgang goes in the cave, you call Courtney. I'll park my red car, which he won't recognize, across the access road, and Courtney will pick me up. Then we'll go back and wait at the Sand Cave parking lot. Zona should be able to alert us when Zack heads our way. Then, we can move the car out of his way. Until we hear from one of you, Zack, or Zona, we'll stay put. We can block the drive and provide an intermediate protective measure, which you have to admit sounds good." Bill pauses and, with obvious reluctance, accepts her reasoning.

"Zona, when you talk to Zack, refer to me as Solo. That's my code name. No one uses actual names in that unit."

"What? Solo?" says Courtney.

"I began with Sierra, but it didn't feel right. Solo. They assign names at random. They have nothing to do with identity. I got tagged with *S*, and a woman in the unit got tagged with Juliet. It could have been a man. All random stuff. It's an Army unit, but they don't use rank designations. Speaking of Zack, let me call and brief him on what's happening here. He's going to freak when he hears I brought civilians in on this." We may be in deeper than mere involvement, but maybe I'm nit-picking.

Bill makes the call and leaves a message. In the message, he gives Zack the number where he can reach Zona for a status report when he lands.

While Bill talks on the phone, Denise talks to Zona about making certain she has Mary Ann on the list of contacts, as necessary. The rest of us move out to the cars. Barbara puts a large box in the back seat of our Taurus. Myrna and Pam bring a large ice chest.

Barbara and Courtney will both need cars for their part of the mission which allows some of us to ride to the parking lot with our significant others. Bill will ride with Courtney and I with Barbara.

When Bill and Courtney pull out of the driveway, Bob turns to me with a smile, "Must be love."

I smile. "If we wait a few minutes after you leave, we'll look less like a convoy?"

* * *

Solemnity and tension thicken the air. The resolution, palpable. Denise, Keven, John, and Daran ride in the SUV with Bob. Barbara and I follow a few minutes later. On the way, we talk about my walk with Bob looking for the owl and getting the pictures of the pileated woodpecker. Neither of us seems to want to talk about what the next few hours will bring.

Thirty
Deployment

Barbara turns the Taurus into the Sand Cave parking lot beside Bob's SUV, but I stay with her. Barbara and I are saying goodbye when Courtney rolls up in her school-bus-yellow mini-SUV. Anderson would recognize that vehicle at once. There can't be many that color. Bill and I get in the SUV, and Bob pulls out of the parking lot. I look back and see Barbara get in the car with Courtney.

The plan is, Bob will drive us all to the Industrial Entrance where Daran will review the moon suits with Bob, John, and me. Bill, Daran, and I will stay at the Industrial entrance. Then, Bob will drop Keven and Denise at New Entrance before going to Frozen Niagara where he and John will go into the cave.

In the SUV, we run over our responsibilities once again. A short period of silence follows. I wonder about Barbara back at the Sand Cave parking lot with Courtney and remember a family story in which an older relative boarded a bus of excited young men leaving for service in World War II. Cousin Byron, whom they drafted when thirty-five years old, married, with two kids, did not share their high spirits. The mood in the truck seems an echo of Cousin Byron's. We're going, but we're not thrilled about it.

* * *

Bob pulls out of the little parking lot and soon stops at the road to the Industrial Entrance. He exhorts us to be careful.

"Bob, you and John need to familiarize yourselves with your PPE," says Daran.

"I'm glad someone remembers the plan," says John. Bob turns up the access road.

The parking lot and loading dock lights show us we've timed it well, as far as it goes. We've been lucky.

As the rest of us get out, Bill moves with care. He's stiff and sore. It's obvious. Besides everything else, the trip up the Corkscrew must have bruised him all over. Keven gets behind the wheel of the SUV in case they require a fast escape. He and Denise wait.

* * *

Bill takes up a position where he can watch the access road. Daran hurries to the hazmat locker and snaps the combination lock open in quick order. John, Bob, and I gather round him while he opens the two doors on screaming hinges. Three of us jump at the noise and start looking around for Anderson, fearing they have caught us before we even begin, much less execute, our plan. Bill vanished from sight. Apparently, he's not in such awful shape that he won't be able to react when necessary.

Once our hearts start up again, Bill reappears and gives us the all-clear. Daran pulls out four moon suits—white, fully encapsulating, lightweight suits with hoods—gloves, and rubber boots. Powered, air-purifying respirators with pink and black filters for fine particulates and acid gases. After he eases the doors closed and replaces the lock, he shows us how to don the ensemble.

"What do you think?" asks Daran.

"OK, I guess. I don't know about all this," says Bob.

"I've got it," says John. "We'll be fine. Thanks, Daran."

Reluctant, but mostly satisfied, Bob and John turn for the SUV.

"Hurry," says Daran. "We don't know when they'll get here. Could be early."

They load up, and Keven steers the truck back down the access road. We hear the SUV turn left and head for the New Entrance.

* * *

Daran collects the gear for Bob and John.

"Don't you have a garbage bag or something? It's too loose and bulky, plus it's a lot to carry," I say.

Daran opens the locker again and rummages for two black garbage bags. We deposit a set of gear in each bag.

"Since I know the setup inside, I'll take their gear in. I can hide back behind the supply cabinets next to the zipper door in the barrier. Wolfgang and Hilda won't see me," says Daran. "You can signal me after John and Bob lock them in the truck."

"Sounds like a plan. Let's move over in the bushes and get our gear on. Then, you can go inside."

"Give me a minute. I'll watch the road from the other side," says Bill.

Bill has crossed half of the parking lot, when we hear a truck turn off the Mammoth Cave Road. We see headlights coming in our direction. Daran is halfway in his moon suit, and I'm not even started. We scramble into the bushes. I glance over my shoulder. Bill disappears.

We see a white pickup with NPS logo on the side and blue lights in a rack across the top. It stops and backs into the loading dock. Rangers. The engine runs, and the headlights remain on. We can't tell who's in the cab. What are they doing here? They could be making a routine check. The rangers on night duty probably use this place for breaks. I raise my head. Bill pokes his head up to scan the scene, and he looks in my direction. He shrugs his shoulders. I drop back.

The pickup door opens. After a minute, a rattling sound from the loading dock indicates someone checking doors. The noise stops, and we hear a long sigh. I ease up. The ranger is demonstrably male. He urinates off the end of the dock. Our end of the dock. I duck back into the brush.

After a few minutes, the pickup door slams, and the tires squelch in a tight turn on the concrete apron. The truck stops at the start of the access road. The door opens. Boots crunch on the gravel driveway. What now? I sink quietly and deeply into the forest floor. I want to look up, but I lie still as a rotting log. Across the parking lot, a whitetail buck snorts. Even with my head down and covered, the flash of a strobe flares in my vision.

"Got you, you big, beautiful son of a bitch." The deer bounds into the undergrowth.

"Whoopee!" The truck door slams, and the vehicle rolls on toward the Cave City Road. My shirt's wringing wet with sweat.

After the truck turns back toward the park, I ease up and brush leaves and sticks from my hair and clothes.

"Well, that was entertaining," says Daran. "Help me get ready to go in."

We move further into the trees to find places where we can suit up. We test the PAPRs, and they work. I hope they've kept the batteries fully charged. I help Daran get the hood over his head and then zip him up. Inside his hood, no light shines in his eyes for the movie audience to see his face. He grabs the two bags and waddles toward the loading dock.

"Hey, isn't the door locked?" I say.

"Yes, it's a cypher lock on the personnel door. The roll-up door doesn't open from outside. The code is one nine two one. Same all over. Some security, huh?"

"Great."

Daran waddles over to the steps to the loading dock. At the door, he keys in the code. The door buzzes, and he pulls it open. The door closes behind him.

I am about to settle in when I spot Daran's flashlight laying on the ground where he suited up. He will need it because the laboratory lights will have to be off when Anderson goes in. I retrieve his flashlight and head to the loading dock.

Daran shuffles out the door and down the steps.

"Thanks. I hope I have everything," he says.

"You're doing good. Be careful."

"Got it."

Daran goes back inside. My previous hiding place seems exposed. Further into the woods feels like better cover.

With this equipment, I can't wait until Wolfgang shows up to put it on. Leaving the suit open and the hood down until the last minute makes it more bearable. I hope, but with no expectation, that the suit won't be too hot. Sweat rolls down my back. The cave will be cooler, and I could have left Daran out here to sweat.

Bill pops out of the undergrowth on the far side of the parking lot. No truck noises. If we have timed this well, Bob and John will have secured the cave and moved out through the Industrial Entrance before the refrigerated truck arrives. If Bob and John get delayed, Bill and I will disable the truck and improvise after that. I can't run with any speed in this getup, and Bill can't keep finding bursts of energy all night.

* * *

I wait for what seems hours, but it's no more than twenty minutes. What is Barbara doing? I guess she's talking to Courtney. The bit of moonlight filtering through the trees from its position in the western sky renders a beautiful picture. A flash of movement behind me makes my heart pound. Before I can react more, I recognize an owl. Such a silent display of power amazes me. I want to share this with Barbara. More waiting. More sweating.

Thirty-One
Unexpected Arrivals

A diesel engine clatters when the driver downshifts to turn off the Cave City Road onto the Industrial Entrance access road. Again, Bill pops up like a meerkat. The headlights pierce the darkness ahead of the truck. It rumbles in first gear along the road. Still no Bob or John. Bill and I will have to handle it.

Then John steps out of the loading-dock door and looks around. His moon suit glows in the lights of the dock. He goes with careful deliberation down the steps and into the woods near me. After a few seconds, Bob comes out the door, crosses the dock, and pauses at the edge.

"Move!" I yell. Bob glances over his shoulder, and I spot right away what he sees. He left the door open. He glances at the headlights bouncing up the road but moves with surprising speed back through the door. He's inside. He did not catch his suit in the door. Good going, Bob.

What now? Well, at least Bob can go hide with Daran. John looks back at the loading dock and moves toward it.

"Duck!" I yell.

He disappears into the undergrowth.

The truck turns and backs up, bouncing off the rubber dock bumpers. Then it eases back to touch the dock. The headlights go off, and the engine dies. Again, we wait. Impatient but still. Bill and John will have to handle Wolfgang and Hilda. We are in position. Zip up my suit, switch on the PAPR, and I'm ready.

A white panel van with a PharmARAMA logo rolls into the parking lot. We missed this second vehicle on its way up the driveway. What's this now? Our detailed plan did not account for a second truck. The van turns and backs up to the loading dock next to the refrigerated truck. I don't understand, but I settle into a position to watch through the bushes.

A man in white coveralls emerges from the refrigerated truck and goes onto the loading dock. A second man gets out of the panel van and goes to the door at the rear. He unloads bundles of white material—lab coats? The man on the dock opens the personnel door and then the roll-up door. A four-wheel cart squeaks out of the roll-up door pushed by the man from the refrigerated truck. He loads the white bundles onto the cart and pulls it back inside. He closes both doors, comes down the steps, and climbs in the panel van. The van sits there.

Bill pokes his head out of the bushes. He's going to wear himself out. The van sits there. After what seems like another hour, orange sparks spin through the air from the driver's side of the van. The engine starts, headlights come on, and the van squeals out of the parking lot. The refrigerated truck stays in place with no one in the cab. Quiet except for the ticking of the cooling engine.

"Bob, all clear," I say. He can't hear me, and I can't run over there in this moon suit and risk exposure should someone else drive up. Bill scuttles out of the underbrush and trots up the steps to the personnel door. He knocks loudly. The banging reverberates through the woods. Anyone in the vicinity heard it.

Bill must have decided to not risk further noise. He retreats to his position on the other side of the parking lot.

No response from Bob.

"He must be deeper in the cave," says John. "I would be. The passage from the lab area leads back to a fork. That's where I would go."

We wait. It's 0255 hours.

Another set of headlights comes bouncing up the driveway from the Cave City Road. A beige station wagon of European extraction turns and backs up to the loading dock next to the refrigerated truck. Its diesel engine dies, and the lights go off.

Show time!

Thirty-Two
Wolfgang and Hilda

A tall, athletic man emerges from the passenger side. He stalks around the front of the Volvo. A blond woman gets out of the driver's side and joins him. Based on my seeing her on Keven's tour, she is Hilda Floren. The man must be W.G. Anderson. He speaks in a low voice, but the tone rings clear, and the woman receives the vicious tirade. No reaction. She's suffered this abuse before. He walks straight towards me, but stops less than halfway, bends down, and picks something off the ground.

"Look at this, Hilda." A higher octave and louder. "A damned cigarette butt! Can you believe? It must have been those imbeciles who delivered the truck. Oh, you won't recognize those two after I get through with them."

"W.G., don't you think we should load the truck?"

"Hilda, it is the *little things*. You must take care of the *little things. Every little thing*." He says the last phrase with significant pauses between the words.

"Yes, W.G. Training can achieve only a minimum of correction. It must be instilled during childhood. Let us be happy they are not leaving beer cans all over the place."

"Happy, Hilda? No, not happy. Content? No, not content. They need rigorous behavior modification, but can we do such modifications? *Nein, es ist verboten!*"

This guy sounds more than a little afflicted with dissociative personality disorder, plus whatever else he has going on. Come on. Load the stuff in the truck.

"W.G., let's focus on the bacteria, and then after we deliver it, we can discuss this modification you want. OK?"

Anderson brings himself erect. Head held high, he holds the offending cigarette butt at arm's length, walks to the trash can at the loading dock steps, and deposits the butt in the can. Executing an about face, he marches to the rear of the truck, unlocks the door, and secures it open with a black strap. He steps into the truck sputtering. Loud, angry tones roll across the parking lot. Hilda runs up the steps and unlocks the personnel door. We've been standing all quiet for nothing. With this guy's arrogant and loud voice, we could have been singing and yelling. From all the way inside the truck, he booms and blasts.

Anderson emerges from the truck onto the dock, goes quiet, and peers around. OK, not yelling, but noisy, nonetheless. Satisfied they can proceed undisturbed, Anderson pushes past the woman and strides into the cave ahead of her. No signal from Bill or John. I switch on the PAPR and zip up my suit.

Bill slips in the passenger door of the truck. Silver flashes in his hand when he leaves, easing the door to. He removes the padlock from the hasp and climbs inside the back of the truck. From the way he moves now, he's still stiff if no longer shocky. Exiting the truck, Bill disappears into the undergrowth on the far side of the truck.

We wait. John's suit glows like neon in the moonlight. I assume my suit glows, too, and shift even deeper into the trees. Cars stop out on the road, and then one car leaves. Barbara and Courtney are blocking the road. If Floren and Anderson get past the rest of us, they will have to drive around or through our Taurus to escape with the cultures. After seeing Anderson's mood, we may need to rent a car to go home.

The seconds tick by. After a long wait, the overhead door slides up with squeaks and rattles. Anderson walks through the opening onto the loading dock. Floren follows pushing the squeaking cart. Anderson takes the cart from her and points to the truck. No words. She climbs into the back, and he hands her the first canister.

The loading takes something like twenty years, but at last he passes her the fourth cannister. She says something from inside the truck to which he replies with another burst of profanity. She must have lost something. He calls her a vile name and insists he left it in the door.

Ah hah! When Bill ducked into the back of the truck, he took the padlock used to secure the inner door.

"I am surrounded by damned incompetents." Anderson steps into the truck.

Bill jumps from the woods. John, even in his moon suit, leaps into action. Bob waddles out the personnel door and down the steps. Bill unstraps the outer door of the truck and slams it shut at the same time John and Bob reach it. They brace the door with their backs. It bounces once and slams back with a thud. Bill closes the hasp and snaps the lock in place. John and Bob step away from the truck and bend at the waist with hands propped on knees like a recovering sprinter. They're running on adrenalin. Bill moves to the loading dock and slumps on the steps.

The truck rocks with Anderson and Floren banging the sides. He rages at high volume. Loud, but incoherent. Incensed that someone interfered with his plan. Questioned his authority. We may not need to signal for any additional help. Their noise will alert low-flying aircraft. I understand how he bluffed and bullied his way into his position of power. Even trapped in a truck, caught red-handed, he's the one in charge. Still.

* * *

I waddle over to the truck, ready to check on conditions inside the cave. Bill sits on the steps. He doesn't look well.

"Bill, we have him." says Bob.

"Great, you guys did great," says Bill.

"Bob, I'm going on in. Did either of you see anything suspicious?" I ask, having to yell over the confinement of the suit, the noise of the PAPR, and the racket from PharmARAMA's senior staff.

"I saw nothing, but we rushed to get out. Hard to do much in these suits. We have things in hand here. John, did you spot anything?"

"No, nothing. Be careful, Walt."

"Bob, where did you go when you got trapped inside?" I ask.

"The passage forks this side of the plastic wall," says Bob. "Daran waited there. When they turned the lights out, we sneaked back into the lab area. We scanned with our flashlights, but I did not know what to look for. And I needed to get out here to help John."

"Bill, do you feel like setting up the decon and running these two guys through?" I say. "Then you can decon us when we come out."

"Good idea, Walt. Yeah, I can decon these guys. Be careful inside," says Bill, showing more energy now that he has a task.

"What about our two culprits?" I ask.

"Since they were removing the cultures at this hour of the night, I assume Anderson and Floren planned to be at work tomorrow as if nothing happened. Because they would not risk their own wellbeing, they probably have left things undisturbed in the labs. And the cultures must be secure inside the truck. You go on in and check with Daran," says Bill.

"The combination for the equipment locker is nineteen twenty-one," I say.

I climb the steps to the loading dock. Bill will call Zona and Courtney. Zona will give him an update on Zack's arrival status. I hope. He will tell Courtney and Barbara to move the Taurus from where it blocks the road. After his calls, he will set up the decon.

When I reach the top of the stairs, Bill calls out, "Walt, catch." He tosses me the air horn. In accordance with the plan, we will give three blasts through the plastic barrier. The horn will signal Denise and Keven to leave their position and walk out of the cave through the Frozen Niagara entrance. Keven took one of Bob's spare keys, and he'll drive the SUV around here to the loading dock.

I plod into the airlock. Daran waits at the edge of the shadows. He punches the button to lower the roll-up door, and

I pull the personnel door closed. I'm relieved to be in the cave with its thirty degrees cooler temperature.

Daran leads the way. I'm here to back him up as part of the buddy system. Daran's experience with PharmARAMA should allow him to identify anything out of place. Although I'm not sure if he's worked in this area or only at Pensacola Avenue.

Daran turns on lights with switches on the wall. We move through the airlock tunnel to the workspace in the cave. From behind the face shield of my moon suit, the cave seems surreal. I waddle along with care to prevent snagging the inflated suit on projecting equipment and racks. Everything looks normal to me, but then, what do I know?

The extreme contrast of stainless-steel lab tables, glassware, and cabinets against the brown and gray limestone increases my anxiety. If you saw a photograph of this, you would swear someone photo-shopped a lab into Mammoth Cave. PharmARAMA forced this lab into it. Daran studies the area with care. The lab contains some sophisticated analytical equipment, centrifuges, incubators, and a table with four microscopes. Serious business.

We leave the work area and walk between large coolers and a freezer. Past that, we walk through supply storage and down the passage past the fork where Bob and Daran hid. Daran gives the thumbs-up.

"This all looks normal to me."

I return his thumbs up, and we head over to the plastic barrier. The door zipped up and sealed with the plastic wall intact. I give the horn three long blasts. If it weren't for the suits, it would deafen us. I don't doubt that Keven and Denise heard it.

On the way out between an instrument cabinet and a lab bench, I snag my inflated suit on the end of a piece of Unistrut—sort of steel tinker toys for laboratories and research spaces. A plastic rack of about 400 tiny test tubes slides to the floor. My suit deflates.

"Daran! Look." I grab his shoulder and point to an eighteen-inch rip in the side seam under my right arm.

"Uh-oh." He grabs a roll of tape off a table and does a quick mending job. The suit re-inflates, and the seal looks good.

"You're bleeding beneath the rip," says Daran. "How bad does it hurt?"

"I can't feel a thing. Must be a scratch. What about the rack on the floor?" I point to the rack of test tubes sitting right side up.

"Ah, damn. Let's see." He kneels beside the rack and spends a minute or two inspecting all the tubes but touches nothing.

"It seems OK. There's no liquid on the floor. Let's leave it here for someone else to deal with." When he stands, he looks at me and says, "Must be nice to be graceful." He laughs.

"I'll take that as a compliment. Are the tubes full or empty?" I ask.

"Oh, they're all full. Lucky for us, it landed right side up."

"Yeah. I hope nothing else is running loose in here. Let's go ahead on out." Something trickles down my side.

* * *

Out the door, Daran signals for me to wait by the personnel door. He goes to the steps and yells at Bob, now out of his moon suit, with wet hair and in his sweaty uniform.

"No air testing, you understand, but the lab space looks normal. There's no sign they spilled anything. Nothing broken stands out. We checked the passage back to the barrier. Nothing to report there. Walt ripped his suit, and I did a quick patch. He scratched himself. A rack of sample tubes for an autoloader fell off the table. I didn't see anything broken, but we left them on the floor. We'll need decontamination. Walt for the full deal. He's a patient now." Bob gives me a thumbs up. Bill continues deconning John. I wait by the door.

Decontamination protocol dictates I stay in the moon suit because of the rip. Daran because of the dropped sample tubes, and both of us for what we don't know. It's not much fun, and I'm sweating like crazy. Then headlights. Barbara pulls the Taurus into the parking lot and leaves room for other vehicles.

She gets out and says, "I'm here to help. It's one of Walt's Air Force expressions. He can explain. Courtney is talking to Zona, but you can't keep her away. The Army will have to adapt."

Barbara comes towards me.

"I'm glad to see you." I wave her back and move closer to the roll-up door. She smiles and waves.

"Barbara, Walt ripped his suit inside. Daran patched it up, but he has to go through decon," says Bob.

"Is he hurt?"

"Well, Daran said he got scratched, and he's possibly contaminated. They didn't see any spills or broken containers, but we will be careful," says Bob.

"Right. I understand. How will he get decontaminated?" asks Barbara.

"Bill is finishing up John's decon over there. If Zack's troops don't get here soon, Bill should be able to handle him," says Bob. John climbs out of his suit and removes his gloves. Everything except the PAPR goes into a trash can with a black liner bag. Bill moves over to the loading dock and hoists himself up on the edge.

"Thank you, I hope they show up soon." Barbara looks at me with a sad expression, then waves at me. I wave back and motion toward Bill sitting on the dock. The day seems to wear on him. Barbara goes over to check.

"How are you?" she asks.

"Oh, I'm OK. My second wind kept me going there for a bit, but I'm out of wind right now. As soon as I can go somewhere for a cup of coffee, I'll be fine." says Bill.

"The time you lay in the cave unconscious didn't count for sleep, did it?" Barbara says. She pats him on the shoulder and says, "I'll be right back." She walks to the car. Bill turns and looks at me with a question on his face.

"There's coffee in the car," I yell, trying to project beyond the moon suit.

At the car, Barbara stops for a moment to answer her phone. She speaks for a couple of moments, then pulls out the box from the backseat. John joins her.

"Get the ice chest out of the back, please." John carries the chest and Barbara the box, with her bright yellow 'sit upon' and two folded items on top, to where Bill sits. She gets Bill to, what else, sit on the bright yellow square of oilcloth and wraps a beach towel around his shoulders.

Barbara's mother, Alice, managed a swimming pool for years. She made Barbara a believer in the usefulness of having towels available long before she read Doug Adams' *Hitchhiker's Guide to the Galaxy*. In no time, Barbara lays out the plastic tablecloth that protects the bed of the station wagon, and John sets the ice chest beside it. She pulls out four Stanley, stainless-steel thermoses, paper coffee cups, a plastic bag of sugar cubes, a second bag with little blue and yellow packets of sweetener from the box, and a bottle of creamer.

"Thank you, John. We have bottles of water," she says, pulling out a jar of milk.

"How do you like your coffee, Bill?"

Bill grins. "Damn! You guys plan and support one of the smoothest operations I've seen, and you cater it, too." Then with focus, "Normally black, but I think milk and sugar are indicated."

"Courtney's talking with Denise and Keven," says Barbara, phone in hand. "Do they pull in here, or do they park along the road and walk in?" She hands Bill his cup of coffee and then offers him a plastic container with brownies.

Bill calls Courtney and says, "Zack's late. He and his troops can walk in if there isn't room."

"Bob, a cup of coffee?" asks Barbara.

"That would be great. Yes. Thank you." "John, coffee for you?" asks Barbara. "We brought brownies, too. And wet wipes."

"Thanks, Barbara. Both please," says John.

Bill, his cup of coffee in hand, brightens when Courtney pulls in a few minutes later. He hops off the loading dock, but he stays by the edge bracing with his right arm. In a shocking display, he kisses her with urgency—and with passion. The eastern sky lightens.

From the elevation of the loading dock, I can see headlights turn off the Cave City Road onto the driveway. One set of lights.

Thirty-Three
Outside Security Patrol

An unmarked white panel van squeals into the parking lot blocking Barbara's and Courtney's cars. Two men in blue, security uniforms jump out.

"OK, folks, what in the hell is going on here?" asks the burly officer from the passenger side. The thin man from the driver's side holds his left hand over his sidearm.

"Hi, I'm Bob Cetera. I'm a supervising cave guide with the Park Service. Bill and John, over there, also work with the Park Service. What can we do for you?"

"This is private property, and you're trespassing in a restricted area. No picnicking. Didn't you see the signs?"

"Oh, well. For one thing," says Bob. "We're in a national park, and we are National Park Service employees as you can see from our uniforms. Second, we're out here on a National Park Service project, and we do not need you." A cacophony of yells and swearing comes from the two locked in the truck.

"What's that noise? Is someone in there?" asks the driver.

"Yes, but they're OK. We're waiting on some backup. We caught some thieves."

"OK," says the driver and pulls his sidearm. "Hands up. Line up facing the loading dock. Everyone." Bob, John, and Barbara ease back and line up along the dock, hands in the air but facing the officer with the gun. Bill and Courtney don't move. While they line up, the burly security officer notices Daran and me on the loading dock. Even in our bright white moon suits, they had missed us.

"What the hell?" says the burly guy.

"I'm Daran Neff and we're with PharmARAMA. Could you put your weapon away, please? We carry no firearms."

"Why are you suited up?" asks the driver. "Get down here, now."

"We're waiting for decontamination after going inside. We have to stay up here."

"Decontamination for what? What happened?"

"Some bacteria may be loose inside the cave. We're taking precautions," says Daran.

The two security officers back up a couple of steps.

"Hey, don't we need to call this in?" asks the thin officer.

Before the burly man can answer, another set of headlights announces a vehicle entering the parking area followed by more vehicles. We are done for now.

Thirty-Four
In the Nick of Time

Bob's silver SUV flies in ahead of five black SUVs all with bristling antennae. Before the last vehicle stops, three soldiers with M4 rifles jump out of the first, and three more from each additional vehicle join them. Two of the troops hold pump shotguns.

"Drop your weapon and go face down on the concrete. Now!" The voice commands the respect the security officers only hoped to project. The driver lowers his weapon to the concrete, and they both assume the prone position. They don't understand what's happening, but they can figure odds. Their odds have declined rapidly. More yelling and blaspheming from the refrigerated truck.

Keven and Denise remain in the SUV.

"Where's Solo?" asks the soldier in front of the phalanx.

"Are you Zack?" asks Bob. "I'm Bob. Solo's over there by the loading dock."

"Solo, are we good?"

"Roger that, Zack. I've been on the side-line. Bob's running everything," says Bill.

"Are you injured? Medic!"

"No. Anderson and his sidekick doped me up, left me in the cave overnight, and bashed me in the head. I'm dehydrated and concussed. So, I'm good."

Zack laughs. "Good to hear." A soldier with an enormous pack runs up to Zack. "Whiskey, go check out Solo over there. You might not recognize him. He's out of uniform." The soldier double-times to Bill and unlimbers the pack.

"Tango, deal with our two security officers here. Hard frisk. No radios. No belts, no laces, no nothing. Secure them in separate vehicles."

"Roger that."

As two soldiers jerk the thin driver up, he says, "We're security officers for PharmARAMA. We caught these…these trespassers. We need to report them."

"Had they called this in?" asks Zack.

"We don't think so," says Bob. "They were talking about it when Denise and Keven pulled in ahead of you guys."

"When we got here, you two held a weapon on my associate and his friends. You will report to no one. Understand?"

They hang their heads and go with the soldiers to the rear vehicles.

"Now, Bob. You must be Zona's husband?"

"I am."

"Good to meet you. Are the two guys in the white suits friendlies, or what?"

"Friendly. Well, the one on the right can be grouchy at times. Daran, on the left, works for PharmARAMA, and the grouchy one, Walt, guided tours here at the park back in the seventies. They checked the work area in the cave. Walt got a rip in his suit and knocked a tray of sample containers onto the floor. Daran says he saw nothing spilled, but they are waiting on decontamination to be safe." Daran and I wave. Zack stares.

"Secure the perimeter. Set up a decon station."

"Bill deconned John and me using the setup over there," Bob points.

"We'll use ours, and then we know they're clean. Set up for patient decon. Ready an entry and backup team. Level A. Move. Bob, what about the silver truck? More friendlies?"

"Yes. That's Keven. He's Daran's father and a guide at the cave. Denise is the shift supervisor and is the senior Park Service person in on all this," says Bob.

"Where are they coming from?"

"They came out another cave entrance after making sure no PharmARAMA employees were wandering the tour routes to get in the way," says Bob. "They did not go into the lab and exited the cave before Walt and Daran came through the lab space. They shouldn't have encountered any contamination."

"OK. They can join us here," says Zack and waves to Denise and Keven. They jump out and trot over to the loading dock.

Zack surveys the scene, speaks into his headset, waits a minute, and goes over to Bill on the loading dock. Whiskey hands Courtney an IV bag to hold aloft and stitches up Bill's head wound. Bill stays quiet.

Zack surveys the thermoses, the ice chest, and the container of brownies. "So, Solo, you're catering your ops now?"

"Guide Force Special Ops always caters their ops," says Bill—Solo. His grin turns to a grimace when the next suture goes in.

"Zack, how do you like your coffee?" asks Barbara. She moves to a thermos and picks up a paper cup.

"Black, ma'am. Thank you. And you are?"

"I'm Barbara, Walt's wife," pointing at me on the dock. "Nice to meet you." She hands him a cup of coffee and offers him a brownie.

"Damn. Sorry, ma'am. Are you folks available for other operations?" asks Zack. "Is Guide Force Special Ops a real thing?"

Thirty-Five
Decon and Wrap-Up

"Zack, may I call in my supervisor?" asks Denise.

Zack looks at Bill, who isn't paying attention, then at Bob.

"Denise works for Mary Ann, who will be better able to liaise with whoever you need in the Park Service. If anyone."

Zack says, "So you folks aren't even rangers?"

"Well, we are rangers, but in the Interpretation Division," says Bob.

"Interpretation?"

"Cave guides. Naturalists."

"Sure. Yes, please call Mary Ann," says Zack.

Denise pulls her cell phone out and hits a speed dial number. She says, "Mary Ann, this is Denise. It's four forty-two, and I need you to come to the Industrial Entrance ASAP. It's not exactly an emergency, but you need to be here. I don't have time for a detailed explanation. I have to take care of things here. Don't use your radio and come at once."

It looks like Mary Ann accepts the urgency of the situation and agrees to come because Denise punches off saying nothing more than, "See you in about an hour."

* * *

I'm in my moon suit, sweating. Daran looks to be doing the same. Sweat has plastered his hair and beard to his head and face.

The prisoners in the truck bang again and again. Zack looks to Bob, who grins.

Zack walks to the truck and says, "This is the United States Army, and I suggest you shut the hell up. If not, I'll turn Solo and Tango loose on your ass. Trust me, you do not want that."

We can't help but glance in Bill's direction. His smile is weak. A big guy who I take to be Tango smiles ear to ear.

The noise in the truck subsides. Denise walks over to Bill who introduces her to Zack and a Black soldier called X-ray. Zack is large, but X-ray looks like he would tilt the scales north of two seventy-five. While Denise checks on Bill and Whiskey, Zack and Bob walk away from the truck toward the other end of the loading dock. X-ray follows.

"Zack, the cave is secure, but we haven't checked the surrounding area," says Bob. "Walt and Daran didn't see any evidence of a spill, but I expect you'll want to treat it like a hot zone.

"W. G. Anderson and Dr. Hilda Floren are in the truck. He's the director of operations for PharmARAMA, and you may hear him referred to by the less-than-affectionate nickname Wolfgang. He usually carries a small pistol. She's his assistant director of research. We don't believe they contaminated the inside of the truck."

"Obviously, those two think they're safe," says Zack. "If they release something now, it's contained in the truck with them."

"I don't think Anderson would ever endanger himself, even in revenge. Since they used a refrigerated truck, I give them credit for knowing it could be more active out here where it's warm. Unless they have something else in the other canisters, they pose little threat," says Bill, joining the group. "However, we don't know for certain they have it all."

Zack speaks into his headset again, "When we extract the prisoners from the truck, we'll do it in containment. Full, aggressive decon." He turns to Bob, and smirks. "They'll enjoy a good decon."

Bob says, "Daran can lead the entry team and show them what's what. There's a tunnel inside, that's the airlock. Inside the cave on your left, a laboratory, incubators, scopes, and storage areas. Be alert to a sharp point on a rack that ripped Walt's suit. They have partitioned off the research area from the tourist trails with a plastic barrier wall and a zippered airlock. The section outside the barrier includes collection domes and monitoring equipment. They took four stainless steel, insulated canisters from the cave and put them in the storage racks in the truck."

* * *

"Hello, X-ray."

"Solo, it's good to see you in one piece. Your soft civilian life seems to have some excitement."

"Cave guides have plenty of excitement, and," Bill turns to Courtney and takes her hand, "I don't seem to be *solo* anymore."

* * *

Zack says, "Daran will take my initial entry team in to make certain nothing has gone undetected. They can collect air samples and surface swabs." He points to Daran. Daran waves back. Sweat pools inside my rubber boots.

Zack speaks to a woman, "Juliet, take over the hot zone and decon. The guy on the left in the lightweight suit will accompany the entry team. He knows the area. Go ahead and decon Walt, the other suit."

"Denise, don't forget Bob and John's security officer, bound up with cable ties and duct tape or the litter we left in the trail," says Keven.

"I'll take someone with me to retrieve him from the Frozen Niagara Entrance after the entry team gets back, and we get the all-clear." says Denise. "Since he's far enough away to not be in danger from contamination, he'll have to wait. Maintenance can pick up the box we left in the trail."

Daran enters the cave with two soldiers in full Level A protection, green, multi-layer-plastic, chemical resistant suits with self-contained breathing apparatus inside the suit.

Courtney says, "Zack, good going on the stitches and all, but it's high time a doctor looked at Bill's head."

Zack says, "I've said the same thing for years." Bill smiles, but Courtney's expression makes Zack look again. He glances at Courtney and Bill's held hands. A fleeting expression of surprise crosses his face. His eyes jump to Bill's face and then to Courtney's. "I'm sorry, ma'am. I've known this guy to be in far worse shape and still carry his buddy out." The bantering tone reassures us.

The look in Zack's eyes makes the identity of the buddy clear. Zack says, "Immediately after he briefs me, a driver and escort will take him to Bowling Green and on to Nashville, if necessary." When the expression on Courtney's face doesn't ease, he jumps in with, "Would you escort Solo? In the meantime, we've done what we can with what we have here. Solo's not getting his first field suture by any means."

Somewhat mollified, Courtney turns to Bill, "Tell Zack what he needs to know, and let's get on the road." Tilting her head toward Zack, she says, "He can call you on Daran's phone if you want more information."

Zack blinks, "Right you are. Do you have any idea about the buyer or his meeting place?" Zack looks at Courtney, "Or hers."

Bill shakes his head and grimaces from the effect.

"OK. It seems you've left me with plenty of help. Once Juliet says you're clear, you can go see what the civilian docs can do for you. Whiskey says Zona took good care of your head, but the stitches will help you heal faster." Courtney's face softens. She holds the IV bag.

Zack holds up his hand and says, "Wait one." He listens to someone over the headset. He says into the lip microphone, "Hotel." The man appearing at Zack's side wears his fatigues like a three-piece suit.

Zack motions toward Courtney and Bill, "Drive these two to the hospital in Bowling Green. The lady will direct you."

At the truck, Bill turns and says, "I'm not hurt, and I'll be back tomorrow."

Bob says, "Zona expects everyone who can make it to be at our house for brunch around eleven."

"We'll be there," says Bill. Courtney doesn't look convinced. The truck moves, then stops. Hotel jogs up to Zack and hands him some keys and a lock. "The keys go to the woman's car. The yellow one. She wants Denise to drive it to Bob's for her. This key fits the ignition of the refrigerated truck. The lock secures the cage inside the truck. Solo says he gave Bob the key for the lock on the outer door." The driver jogs back to his vehicle, and the black SUV moves off. Once the truck departs, another moves forward to replace it.

"Something about Hotel tells me the insurance bureaucrats at the hospital haven't got a chance," says Bob. Barbara laughs.

* * *

Bob's, John's, and Keven's phones ring at the same time. Bob listens for a moment and hands the phone to Zack saying, "Zona needs to talk to you." Keven and John move away to take their calls.

After pausing a few seconds, Zack speaks into his headset microphone, "Bravo, Mike, prepare your squads to depart." Six troops assemble, and the engines of two vehicles start.

Zack returns the phone to his ear and says, "I will call you en route." He gives Bob the phone. "Did you copy what Zona told me?"

"We did," says Keven. John nods.

"Keven, will you brief X-ray and Bob?" He turns to X-ray, "I'm turning this area over to you. Secure the prisoners, process the hot zone, and assist Bob and his crew as they direct. I'm going back to the Glasgow airport. Zona's team found our buyer."

"Zona has a team?" Bob says. "But I have a crew?"

X-ray fakes a salute, and Zack fakes an acknowledgement, and jogs to the lead vehicle, "Thank you all. I promise to report when I know anything." And they leave.

Bob holds out his hand to the soldier, "X-ray, I'm Bob Cetera, Zona's husband." X-ray shakes Bob's hand.

"How do you do, sir. What are your instructions, sir?"

Bob looks uncomfortable at the *sir*, but grins and turns to the rest of us who shake our heads. Since none of us gives him any instructions, X-ray turns to Keven for his briefing.

Keven explains how Mary had been shopping in the 24-hour grocery in Glasgow for tomorrow's mass brunch. She ran into a friend from the theater, Catherine, who was buying a hundred pounds of ice.

"Catherine works nights at the Glasgow airport. An Asian herbal expert PharmARAMA must have courted, called ahead to the airport from his plane. He wanted four big ice chests with twenty-five pounds of ice each waiting for them when they landed.

"When Mary remembered all the discussion about PharmARAMA's refrigerated truck, Mary called Zona. Not sure who was where, Pam, Myrna and Zona called John, Bob, and me at the same time, thinking one of us could tell Zack," says Keven.

X-ray smiles and shakes his head. "One question, sir. Are you all civilians?"

"Mammoth Cave guides," says Keven. "You know Bill became a Park Service employee. Denise, John, Bob, and I also work for the Park Service. Walt, former Park Service. Daran, my son, grew up spending summers at the cave. He and Courtney work for PharmARAMA."

One of the decon squad waves me over to a plastic swimming pool set up with pump sprayers and long-handled brushes. They soap my suit down and rinse it after I step into the next pool. Then the suit comes off with the PAPR, and they bag the suit. I keep the inner set of gloves.

Barbara hovers as near as she can.

"Your clothes, sir."

"Right." It's only Barbara and a few busy soldiers. Only a couple of them are female. The decon soap solution feels cool. The rinse water, cold. No brushing of the skin. For which, I am thankful.

"Medic! Sir, you scratched your side where the suit tore." He hands me blue disposable towels, and I dry off, shivering. When I'm dry, Whiskey looks at the scratch.

"Didn't you feel the scratch, sir?"

"No. Did it break the skin?" I say.

"Yes, sir. From the blood on your clothes, you bled a good bit. This may sting, sir." He applies what must be some industrial—or military grade—disinfectant and scrubs at the scratch with a sponge.

"You got that right," I say. "It did sting. Thank you."

"Sir, there's no debris in the wound. But I'll put in a couple of field sutures, then we'll put on a dressing. We'll grab a couple of blood samples and some nasal swabs. Here, put these on." He hands me blue polypropylene scrub pants and a clean pair of white rubber boots.

"And you'll keep the clothes?"

"Roger that, sir. We'll bag your personal effects for you to take once they come out of the ultra-violet decon unit."

"Thank you, Whiskey." He extracts two vials of blood, applies a band-aid, and then swabs deep in each nostril.

"We're here to help, sir." So, the Army knows that expression too.

He sprays the wound with what must be Novocain and within a few minutes puts in three stitches and applies a bandage.

"You're quick. Thanks."

"No problem, sir. The battlefield doesn't give us much time. You're good to go, sir." He hands me a scrub top.

* * *

Barbara joins me with a hug on my good side. We walk over to X-ray, Bob, and Keven. John takes up a position out of the soldiers' way, but where he can monitor the back of the truck.

"I saw what they did. How badly are you hurt?" says Barbara.

"Not bad. I didn't even know about it."

"I'm glad Whiskey took care of you. He put in stitches, didn't he?"

"Yeah, but he sprayed it with some deadening stuff first. Not sure he extended the same courtesy to Bill," I say.

"Stitches sounds like more than a scratch to me. Do you want coffee or water?"

* * *

"X-ray, we have nothing else to do here," says Bob. "Mary Ann Robins will be here in a minute. She and Denise can handle anything you may need. What can we do, except get out of your way?"

"I got nothing," says John. Keven shrugs.

I ask, tilting my head in the truck's direction, "Did anyone tell you Anderson carries a small firearm?"

"Roger that, sir."

X-ray speaks into his headset, "Juliet, can you clear these folks and let them go home?"

She appears and takes nasal swabs from the others. While we wait for our test results, we work out the logistics of leaving. What are they swabbing for? Flu? Strep throat? Are they going through the motions to impress us civilians?

Barbara says, "Shall I leave the coffee and brownies for your squad? Can someone return the thermoses and ice chest to Bob and Zona's?"

X-ray blinks twice then says, "Roger that. Much appreciated, ma'am."

Bob says, "Daran led the entry team and will have to go through decon. Denise will need to help Mary Ann get oriented and then retrieve the security officer. Denise and Daran can drive Courtney's car back to my house to pick up their own vehicles." Bob turns back to X-ray, "Do you have my number?"

"If it's Zona's, I have it."

"Good, you can reach me, Walt, and Barbara at the same number. You can reach everyone else through me, and they will be at my house for brunch tomorrow at eleven. We expect to see you then." Bob gives him their street address. More like an afterthought, Bob says, "Mary Ann, the visitor services chief you are expecting, drives either a blue mini-van or a gray Kia."

Barbara says she will follow in our car, while I ride with Bob, John, and Keven to hear about their part of the adventure.

Whiskey shows up with my personal effects and a warning. "Sir, follow up with your physician sometime next week. If you complete this form, we will e-mail you the blood test results unless conditions warrant a more expeditious approach."

I fill out the form and hand it back.

"Whiskey, I appreciate all this."

"Sir."

Thirty-Six
Cleared to Go Home

When our test results pop up, Juliet tells X-ray she has cleared us to leave. We load up our assorted tools, and Bob pulls out with the three of us. Courtney's car stays behind for Denise and Daran. Barbara follows in the Taurus. When we get to the Old Mammoth Cave Road, Mary Ann's minivan turns onto the Industrial Entrance road. She stops. She and Bob zoom down windows.

Mary Ann says, "I need to hurry, but want to make sure you're OK." Her eyes look a little wild, but from my position in the passenger seat, it's a little hard to be sure.

"The Army took Bill to Bowling Green, but he claims he's not hurt much," says Bob. "Daran led a hot-zone entry team into the cave. Denise waits for you at the loading dock. We are exhausted and headed home. See X-ray at the loading dock."

Mary Ann says, "Soldiers? Is X-ray a person?"

"Denise has it all in hand, she can explain."

Mary Ann waves and drives on toward the loading dock.

As we leave the dense forest cover of the park and break into the open fields on the road to Cave City, the orange ball of the sun peeks above the distant tree-lined hill to the east. I am relieved to see this dawn. Some things followed the plan, and we feel good, but everyone looks exhausted. My side throbs a bit. I glance at my hands. Not green yet. In the mirror of the sun visor, bloodshot eyes stare back. But no green.

"You good?" asks Bob.

"Doing good, Bob. I don't think we have contributed to our knowledge of Mammoth Cave. I am not content. How about you?"

"I'm old and out of shape, but maybe not too old." He chuckles. "And not content either."

Bob, John, and then Keven, tell their story in alternating sections.

"The security officer assumed he was escorting us, but he learned different when John trussed him up in a matter of seconds," says Bob.

"We stowed him at the steps zip-tied to a handrail. And duct taped," says John.

"John handled him with care. He left him in a sitting position, gave him the towel to sit on, and left his spare flashlight to keep him out of complete darkness," says Bob.

"He's a good guy. He goes to our church," says Keven.

"How did the PPE work?" I ask.

"We ran into a few problems—zippers mostly—but it didn't get all that complicated, did it, John?"

"No," says John. "Since the cave maintains fifty-four degrees, we didn't get too hot. We noticed a big change when we got outside. Thank you for suggesting Bill set up the decon for us."

"No problem. Keven, did you find any monitoring equipment?"

"Your cave dream got it right, but you had the location a bit off, Walt," says Keven. "We didn't see an alert sensor or alarm at Big Break. Denise saw it at the light switch in the passage before the turn into Flat Ceiling. We tried to disable it, but it didn't give us the requisite red and green wires to cut, or a timer to bypass like in the movies. When it started wailing, we cut every wire, bashed the box with a rock, and threw it out into the middle of the trail. We figured anyone checking on it would see the box and give us a moment to grab them."

Bob says, "We heard that alarm right before Daran's horn blasts. I thought my heart was going to stop. John jumped about a foot. We expected Wolfgang and every bit of PharmARAMA's security staff to show up. When we heard the whistle, we figured you meant for us to proceed according to plan and meet you at Frozen Niagara. Like you, we split up in the hope one of us would make it. When you two showed up without escorts, we were relieved."

"It sounded loud enough I thought Floyd might show up," says Keven. "We couldn't believe it didn't bring the troops down on us. Denise thought she might stall anyone coming to check on the alarm. She blew the whistle as the decoy, and I stuck to the shadows, Flashlight at the ready. We hoped the whistle would tell you we were OK.

"No point to being quiet after that. We enjoyed a tense stroll through the cave, met you at Thanksgiving Hall, waited for the all-clear, and came out through Frozen Niagara. Anderson's secrecy helped us."

I explain to Keven that from where Daran and I were, everything proceeded according to plan except for the ranger patrol, Anderson showing up at the same time Bob's coming out the door, and the security patrol. I did nothing but see nothing needed doing. I describe how weird I felt going through the cave in a moon suit. I included scratching myself and knocking off the rack of sample tubes. Being deconned at the skin level. And the sutures.

"How's the wound?" asks Bob.

"More of a scratch," I say.

"Field sutures make it sound like more than a scratch."

"Nothing a good Scotch won't take care of. Or for that matter, any Scotch."

"I hear you," says Bob. Bob always maintains an array of single malts and blended to supply a medicinal dram.

Thirty-Seven
A Time for Rest

Bob drops John at his house next door extracting promises of Pam's and his coming to brunch later in the morning.

When we arrive back at Bob's, Mary has left, but Myrna comes out of the house to meet Keven, and they walk to their car saying they will be back for brunch. Barbara, who passed us when we stopped at John's, and Zona greet us in the kitchen.

"Well, are you all, all right? Anybody hungry?"

"The execution was smoother than we expected," says Bob. "No one got genuinely hurt, if Walt doesn't sprout a tree or something else green from the gash in his side by sundown." Zona looks alarmed.

"So far, no greenish tinge, and it is only a scratch," I say, looking at my fingernails. "When the Army medic got to Bill, he hung an IV bag and sutured up his head wound. The medic, Whiskey, said your treatment gave Bill enough for most patients. Whiskey thought a suture or four might be a good idea, knowing Bill."

"And Walt's scratch also needed a field suture or two," says Bob.

"Three sutures," says Barbara.

"What? Walt, you need to sit down. How bad does it hurt?" says Zona.

"I'm fine. Nothing to worry about. I didn't even know I broke the skin until Daran saw blood when he patched the rip in the suit. Adrenalin I guess."

"Decontamination? This doesn't sound good at all. You need to sit down."

I sit and respond to Zona's question, "Fatigue has hit us, but you wouldn't miss with a Scotch and a few snacks."

"Walt sounds normal to me. Even though I have done nothing but drive a car and watch Walt get decontaminated, I would enjoy a glass of wine," says Barbara.

"Right you are," says Zona. "I'll get chips and dip. Bob, why don't you fix Walt—and yourself—a Scotch. Barbara, the dip is in the fridge. Wine's in the door. Third shelf."

Bob and I sit and exchange brief comments about the operation while sipping a superb, single malt. Barbara and Zona join us, and I fill them in on the details. Bob fills in the blanks and adds the part about John and him in moon suits. After short good-nights, we go to bed. Barbara's fears that we hold on to too much tension to sleep do not materialize. I assume because I'm soon out.

Thirty-Eight
Skin-Level Decon

Through the bright work lights, Anderson and Floren emerged from the back of the truck. They spied rifle barrels pointed in their direction.

"I am W.G. Anderson, director of operations for PharmARAMA. I demand..."

"Sir, under the waiver of *posse comitatus* for bioterrorism, and regulations promulgated forthwith and thereunder, you are under arrest for conspiracy to support bioterrorism, aiding and abetting bioterrorist operations in the Homeland, and theft of microbiological property from the U.S. Government. Related charges including assault with intent, kidnapping, and dispensing dangerous drugs without authorization may pend from the U.S. government and any state and local authorities having jurisdiction. Ma'am that's a ditto for you. Strip," said Juliet.

"I protest most vehemently!" Floren said.

"Ma'am, you may do this the easy way on your own, or Tango, here, can do it for you while you're in shackles. It's your choice."

Thirty-Nine
Debrief and Brunch

The sound of the shower wakes me. Whenever I wake up away from home, I take a little time to orient myself. I remember a hyper-realistic dream. In a few seconds, my side throbs. Not a dream.

Barbara comes into the room from her shower, and says, "Good morning, did you sleep?"

"I slept, but not long enough. I'm trying to figure out if last night happened or if it's another dream."

"How's your wound?"

"It's only a scratch, but it throbs some."

"I am sorry, but the throbbing should tell you whether you were dreaming, and that it isn't turning into another nightmare," she says. "I wonder if Bob and Zona have heard what happened after we came home."

"You go find out, and I'll shower. Can you bring me some Saran wrap for the bandage?"

The smell of wonderful cooking and coffee brewing perks me right up. Barbara knocks on the door while I'm getting the shower started and sticks her head in.

"Here's the Saran wrap. Someone texted Bob. Bill looks OK. They made a discovery in the cave. Zack caught the bad guys. Details at eleven."

* * *

Bob and Mary sit at the breakfast table—restored to its proper position in the kitchen—drinking coffee. Zona checks something in the oven. Bob answers questions about the part of the evening Zona and Mary missed. I'm relieved to find coffee cake on the counter next to the coffee. With the cooking aroma, my stomach isn't at all agreeable to waiting until everyone gets here for brunch.

"Good morning, Walt. How about a cup of green tea with lemon and a piece of cake?"

"Great, Zona. Thank you." She hands me a mug. I grab a piece of cake and sit in the third chair at the breakfast table.

Barbara comes in the back door announcing, "I have company with me." Pam and John come in right behind her.

"We saw Zona walking Jessie, which told us you must be up over here," says Pam. "You won't believe the wild stories we heard this morning in Cave City. My favorite one says Bill and Wolfgang fought a duel over Courtney in the cave last night."

As the laughter dies, John jumps in, "Well, I like the story where the National Guard came in to break up a North Korean spy ring and you," he points to Bob, "Led the troops into the cave."

Bob stands to greet John and Pam, but before he can get to them, someone knocks at the door to the garage. Barbara goes to open the door. She comes back leading Keven and Myrna.

"Daran reported in at work. He'll be here after he gets through," says Keven. "I'm sure he'll have a full report. He wouldn't tell us much before he checked in at work." The front doorbell rings.

As Bob responds to Keven, Mary goes to the front door. Bill and Courtney follow Mary back into the kitchen. This morning their faces show little of the ordeal. A small cheer greets them. Bill smiles in acknowledgement. Barbara hugs Courtney.

"Hi, Courtney, Bill. How bad are you? We were telling everyone about all the rumors going around town," says Pam.

"Good morning, everyone," says Bill. "Walt, how are you?"

"Only scratched."

"Well, when Whiskey has stitched you up in the field, you understand what health care is all about," says Bill. He smiles. "You're lucky. Well, we'll see how lucky when your blood tests come back."

"Good morning, Bill. All of Cave City knows about your duel with Wolfgang over Courtney," says John.

"I guess our secret got out. Wow." Bill says.

"We stopped at the Many-Mart for milk and bread this morning," says Pam. "The cashier knows me from the pet shelter. She told me Bill fought a duel in the cave. With stitches in your head, you can't deny you were in a fight. And with Wolfgang gone…"

"So, what did they say about you, Bill?" asks Zona. "Is the head the worst of it?" When Bill says he is fine, Zona turns to Courtney for confirmation.

Courtney shakes her head. "Apparently his head rates as only a minor occurrence for him. The doctors showed more interest in the scar tissue from his old injuries than this *minor* bump on the head. After the IV and the field sutures Whiskey gave him, they looked, but couldn't find much to do but hang another IV, take x-rays, and send us home.

"Bill once told me he's accident-prone, which made me wonder how he could be good at…" her voice fades, and she flushes. But she recovers, "How he could be such an excellent guide if he was at all clumsy?" Courtney blushes redder but carries on. "He's supposed to take it easy for a few days, but I've decided if he survived all those scars, he'll get through this, too. He's playing up his condition to keep me from committing additional bodily harm because of all the surprises from the last two days."

Bill says, "I'm fine. Pulled muscles and bruises. Nothing more for my head. Whiskey said he admired your steri-strip work, Zona, but he put in four stitches to be safe. I've got a bit of a headache, but nothing acetaminophen can't handle. During this exchange, Courtney maneuvers Bill into a chair.

Barbara whispers to me, "Looks like Bill and Courtney have gone from secret dating to a settled couple in one long day."

"I think you're right."

Another knock at the garage door, and we answer, "Come in."

Daran walks in with a sullen expression. He waves and goes to sit in the den.

Bob and John follow him in. Keven and I approach Daran from the other side.

"Well, Daran, what happened? You don't look so happy," says Keven.

"They completely wasted our time. All a big CYA operation. We had to add a handwritten paragraph to our confidentiality and non-disclosure agreements. They acted like the lab techs are the criminals, not PharmARAMA's management. Human Resources suspended Courtney and me pending an inquiry from Corporate. Even with Wolfgang gone, they haven't lost his operational style. They are not fully aware of what happened last night except their leader has left."

"Daran, did you say HR suspended me, too?" says Courtney rushing into the den.

"I'm afraid so. And the security officer, too."

"This is awful, Daran," says Bill. "Don't they realize you two helped save their corporate backsides?"

"I don't think so," says Daran and goes quiet.

"John, you better tell Bill the other rumor you heard this morning," Bob says. "Why don't we move in here out of the way of the important cooking going on?"

I help push everyone along, but they sort of clot up around the couch in the den. I raise my good arm in a what-can-you-do? gesture at Bob. He shrugs.

John tells us what he heard about the North Korean spy ring. "While we were talking, a complete stranger joined our conversation. He said, 'Bob, the cave guide who takes pictures in the cave? He showed them in.' This fellow didn't make it clear who Bob helped, the National Guard or the North Koreans." Bill laughs, and Bob joins in.

"Daran, what happened when you led the hot-zone team in?" says Keven.

"Dad, that's the other thing I don't feel like I can talk about unless Zack gives me permission. Sorry."

"What happened?" Keven pursues his question until he sees Zack entering with Denise, who wears her Park Service uniform. Zack wears his headset and holds his fatigue cap in his left hand.

We greet Denise and Zack. His face says he slept a lot less than we did. Eleven o'clock for brunch may have been too early. But they smile.

"Zack, welcome to our house," says Bob. "We were reviewing last night and getting updates from Bill, but Daran says he needs your permission to talk about his part last night."

"That's right, Bob. Daran, good job. I didn't tell him he couldn't talk about it, but he knows instinctively it is a sensitive topic," says Zack.

"Yeah, but..." begins Keven.

"Don't worry," says Zack. "You folks have been read in on this by virtue of having conducted the whole damned operation." He pauses. "Our entry team conducted a thorough search of the whole lab complex and storage area. Daran here, in the back of the big freezer, found a large package wrapped in plastic sheeting and sealed with duct tape. When he didn't recognize it as belonging to the lab, the team members inspected and unwrapped it. It was a body of a man. The skin was green."

I look at my fingernails and then at Barbara. She comes and stands beside me.

"Zack, who was it?" asks Keven.

"No identity yet. The entry team left him in the freezer. We're taking it to Fort Dietrich. The whole freezer and contents to be on the safe side," says Zack. Everyone talks at once except Daran and Zack.

* * *

Zona says, "For anyone who stills has an appetite, help your plate to breakfast casserole while it's hot. Grab a seat wherever you can."

While we fix our plates and find seats, Bob takes Zack aside and motions for Bill to join them. Barbara joins me at the dining room table. Before my first bite, Bob gets John and Pam to join them. Bob must be giving Zack a crash course in the local news transfer system. Zack's face shows alarm that fades to resolution.

"Because that grapevine got us to the airport in time last night, I won't complain about it," says Zack after the little group breaks up. He looks at the food, and addresses Zona, "Are you Zona?"

"I am. And you must be Zack, right?"

"Yes, ma'am. May I continue to call you Zona?" Zona nods. "Hold one, please." He talks into his headset. "I'm sorry to interrupt, but Juliet tells me someone from PharmARAMA has showed up outside. My commander has ordered me to ask if you will let him speak to you."

"Who is he, and where is he?"

"He's an executive with PharmARAMA who does not seem to care about his title, and he brought a little fellow named Ray Valley, who works for their public relations department and cares very much about his title. They're outside on your driveway." The park employees and Daran groan.

"Juliet told them to stay in their car until you say otherwise."

"Well, you folks know Valley. His boss can't be any worse," says Denise.

Bob told me Denise works close to the book, toes the Park Service line. The events of the last day have made her far more candid. In this company at least.

"Bob, what do you think?" says Zona.

"We might learn something about what's going on. It's fine with me."

"OK, they can come in," says Zona.

"I haven't met Mary, Pam, or Myrna," Zack says, looking around the room.

"I'm Zona's sister, Mary."

"Hello, I'm Myrna, Keven's wife."

"And I'm John's wife, Pam."Zack smiles.

"It's nice to meet all of you. And you, Zona. Thank you and the advanced echelon for all you did last night." Then speaking to the room at large, he says, "It's a privilege to meet all of you. What you accomplished last night impressed us. Incredible!" Self-conscious all of a sudden, he jogs out the front door. I continue with the egg and sausage casserole and some wild blackberry jam on toast.

* * *

Zack returns, his jaw tense, and his eyes icy cold. He wears the same guarded look he wore when he first arrived at the Industrial Entrance last night and relieved the security officers of their responsibilities. A pleasant-looking, smiling man and a pasty-faced man with a pinched expression step in behind Zack.

"Everyone, Mr. Martin Roberts is with PharmARAMA, and apparently you know Ray Valley," says Zack indicating the second man with a dismissive jerk of his head. When these two men enter, Jessie moves from under the breakfast table to assume a defensive posture in front of Zona and emits a low growl.

Chapter Forty
PharmARAMA Corporate

"Mr. and Mrs. Cetera, thank you for allowing us to interrupt your brunch—" says Roberts. Ray Valley interrupts slapping papers down in the middle of the table. He stiffens when he sees Daran and snaps.

"You people have trespassed in the cave. You did not have permission from PharmARAMA. You must sign this confidentiality statement, and we will require—"

"Valley, shut up!" Roberts says. "Mr. and Mrs. Cetera, everyone else, I apologize. Mr. Valley has become unnerved by the events of last night. Valley, apologize."

"Apologize? They must sign these non-disclosure forms. I am sorry, sir, but we must impress on these people they are—"

"Not to me, Valley. Apologize to the Ceteras and these other kind folks who did not have to see us. Go sit in the car. Leave me your forms."

Nose in the air and in a clipped manner, Valley mumbles in Bob's direction and stomps out.

"I'm sorry, everyone. I got a phone call early this morning and drove in from my parents' home in Hazard. The office here told me Valley would help. They said he's in public relations and knows the operation here, but he showed he can't even handle simple courtesy. I really don't know what happened to our operation here." Roberts pauses and looks in the direction of the door through which Valley left, "Understandably, what Mr. Valley thinks he knows has overwhelmed him. The thing is, we at PharmARAMA owe you folks a lot, and we have a lot more to worry about than legally covering our assets. Let me take care of those forms."

We pass him the unsigned documents.

"Mrs. Cetera, can you direct me to your trash can, or to your shredder?"

Zona smiles. "I'll take them and call me Zona."

"I'm Marty. You have a wonderful house. My grandmother collected tins." He gestures toward the collection of decorative tins arranged on a shelf near the ceiling in the kitchen. "I appreciate your willingness to listen to me."

We go around the room introducing ourselves.

Bob says, "Well, to be clear, we're employees of the Mammoth Cave National Park. We were not trespassing, as I told your security officers. I told Zack I appreciated his bringing you over. The men and women here pulled your operation out of the ditch. We have several concerns, and I agree, there's a more important issue here than public relations for anyone."

"I'm here for that exact reason." Marty says, "Help me!" Everyone smiles.

"First, Marty, did you have breakfast on your drive over from Eastern Kentucky? If not, would you like something to eat?" Zona asks.

"No, ma'am, I didn't. It smells great. Yes, please, I would love something to eat and a cup of coffee."

"Well, help yourself. Sit next to Mary."

"Thank you. On my way."

Zack watches Marty filling his plate.

"Zack, we expected you for brunch too," says Zona.

Zack says, "You're too kind. My two team members stand by outside monitoring the radio and—"

"Zack, there's plenty for all of you. When Mary went shopping last night, we hadn't counted heads. She bought enough to feed the five thousand. Please help us eat it."

"Thank you, Zona. I'll go tell them the good news."

Before Zack leaves, Marty says, "Zack, I don't mean to imply you are a messenger boy, but, when you go out, would you tell Valley to take the car, go on back to the office, and wait until someone tells him what to do next? If anything? And please deliver the message in a manner he will understand."

"I will deliver your message."

Juliet, who managed the hot zone, comes in behind Zack. He introduces her, "I think some of you have met Juliet." She smiles to the room. She seems to search around the room for someone in particular. She stops when she sees Zona.

"Thank you, Mrs. Cetera."

"You are most welcome, Juliet."

Juliet helps herself and leaves with her plate and a cup of coffee. A young man replaces her.

"Foxtrot, say hello to our hosts," says Zack.

"Hello and thank you, Mrs. Cetera." He fills a plate and mug and goes back outside.

While the team members fill their plates under the helpful supervision of Mary, Zona takes Zack aside for a quick consultation. Zack follows Foxtrot out. Zona says, "Once Juliet and Foxtrot finish their breakfasts, they're going to sleep in shifts in the second guest room." There's a murmur of approval.

After Zack makes all the arrangements, he settles in with his plate in a rocker in the den.

"Zack, you saw the results, but you did not see this group of cave guides—and their families—analyze the problem and work out the solution," says Bill. "They understand the area, the local population, and, most important, the cave." He looks around the room taking in all of us.

Bob says, "If you are willing, Zack, we want you to help us figure out what to do to keep a lid on what Wolfgang was doing besides his official duties."

"Wolfgang?" asks Marty.

"Anderson, W.G. Valley pales in comparison with Wolfgang," says Bob.

"Good grief."

Forty-One
The Buyer

"Since hearing the stories John and Pam told us," says Bob. "I've been thinking about how we might handle this situation. Let's write a script with enough truth in it to cover the key points but throws the rumor mongers off track."

Marty, taking a big gulp of coffee, says, "Well, two questions. First, could you give me at least an idea of what happened last night? My information came from Valley, and I no longer suspect, but know, he's risen past his level of competence. And second, I'm from Hazard, Kentucky, and would one of you please explain to me, what desecration my company has perpetrated in The Great Mammoth Cave of Kentucky?" He uses a guide's inflection on his last words.

Everyone laughs.

Juliet comes in, and Zona shows her to the second guest room.

Keven picks up on Marty's remark, "I hate to tell you this, but you should discuss all of your activities—good and bad—with your people."

"Then I have no hope of a sensible response," says Marty with a shake of his head and a groan. "But I can research the project profile, too. They kept this project in a silo, completely isolated from the rest of the company. It's no excuse, but I haven't followed it at all. Sorry."

Bill gives Marty a brief rundown of the night, starting with Anderson's attacking him in the cave and ending with Zack's trip to the Glasgow airport. He leaves out Daran's most recent news about the green body in the freezer.

When he finishes, Denise says, "Courtney and Daran work for PharmARAMA. Although, as of this morning, your HR department suspended them pending a corporate review. Among the three of us, we can bring you up to speed. How far can we stray from the truth and still tell a convincing tale?"

"You guys work for PharmARAMA?" he says with a hopeful edge, nodding to each of them in turn. "What a relief. I wondered if my company assigned anyone with any sense at all. Why were you suspended?"

"I went in this morning, had to change my confidentiality agreement, and was told because of my involvement last night, they suspended me. And Courtney, too," says Daran.

"Well, I'm high up in the corporate ladder, and I think someone overstepped their authority. We'll take care of that. Don't you worry. Please tell me Anderson and Valley are the exception and not the rule."

"Don't forget Dr. Floren," says Daran. "Most members of the technical staff are good. I respect the scientists and technicians. They care about the science. They want to respect the cave environment, but they have no power."

"I see. And the management staff operate more like Valley?"

"Well. Wolfgang ran the show. Wait until you meet the marketing staff before you judge Valley to severely. The employees seem to fall into two groups, those with local connections and Wolfgang's true believers. Valley was a fervent disciple. You can draw your own conclusions."

"I'll get some sleep and take lots of aspirin before forming any hard conclusions." Marty enters notes in his electronic tablet.

"Zack, did you catch anyone at the airport?" asks Daran.

"We," he takes us all in with a gesture, "And I do mean *we*, stopped them. My squad deconned your management staff, and I called Homeland Security. They have jurisdiction. I could have gotten in a pi—" He censors himself. "A contest with them, but I decided to hand your management folks and the buyer over to Homeland. First, I don't have a Korean interpreter with me. Second, I'm sure Anderson included no one else in on this—other than Floren.

"The buyer's Chinese passport said Hoa. He claimed to be an entrepreneur buying herbal medicines and connected to someone high in the Chinese government. Even though he uses a Chinese passport and claims to sell to the highest bidder, he works for North Korea. But as an agent or as a vendor, we're not sure. I sat in on the interrogation long enough to be confident he's a lone ranger. No pun intended. Then I left him with Homeland Security.

"Your corporate counsel agreed to the deal I made, in part, because they already look bad for failing to clear Anderson with sufficient thoroughness." says Zack. "This deal means no one from Homeland Security should bother any of you," he says, addressing himself to Bob and Zona. "If they do, give them my card." He passes out business cards. "Finally, this could be a diplomatic horror show. Let Homeland Security live in their own paperwork hell." The card reads, "For help, call Zack!" and lists a number with an area code I'm not familiar with.

"If I'm right, and Hoa, or whatever his name is, works alone, and is not an agent for North Korea, we're relieved. At the same time, we're worried. Good news, we know about the bacteria and have contained the threat. And it appears Hoa doesn't have a line of bad guys expecting to receive what Anderson was selling.

"We have to block all information about the bacteria right here and hope no additional interest develops. Scary, because, having North Korea as a client, Hoa may have raised some expectations in Pyong Yang. From there, they could sell it for big money to bad actors around the world. I am grateful to you folks for taking it out of play."

"Where are the bugs?" Daran says.

"X-Ray took custody of all samples in the truck and everything in the lab. Including the freezer. Along with the contents of Anderson's office. Homeland gets those three, but we keep all the material and documents. X-Ray asked me to tell you he enjoyed meeting all of you, and he regrets missing brunch. He sends his thanks for the provisions you left last night. We put your ice chest and containers in the garage. All deconned and empty. X-ray took the rest of the team home to Fort Dietrich. It's easier to deploy from there if we get another assignment. He and the team convey their thanks with genuine feeling to Mary for the brownies." Big smile from Mary.

"Anderson and Floren went with Homeland Security for further conversations."

"Zack, what about you three?" says Keven.

"We'll catch a hop out of Fort Campbell tonight."

A general sense of satisfaction fills the room. I finish my second plate of food and help deliver our dishes to the kitchen where Mary and Zona stack the dishwasher. The tables stand clear except for coffee cups. We prepare to work.

Denise says, "I don't want to rush you, but I have a conference call at one o'clock with the Superintendent, the Chief of Interpretation, Mary Ann, Anne Binnley, and the head of Resource Protection for the Southeast Region. Mary Ann and Zack have talked. She's willing to take our lead, but she can't leave the higher ups out of the loop for long without explanations.

"The Superintendent wanted me in the office this morning, but Mary Ann convinced him if I came to brunch, I could learn the details of the operation. While Mary Ann and Anne Binnley hold the fort at the park, what do I tell them? We walk a fine line here between telling them the Army included us and claiming ignorance of the details."

Zack says, "I would like to be on your call, if I may."

"Nothing would please me more. If they say OK, I'll conference you in."

"Bill, could I speak with you?" says Marty.

Bill nods, and they go to the front hall away from all of us.

Forty-Two
Cover Story

"Mary, do we have our notes from last night?" asks Barbara. "We're going to need pens and paper again, too." Mary goes into Bob's office and comes back with a few legal pads, pens, and a zip-lock bag of shredded paper. Marty and Bill re-join the group. Both are smiling.

Mary puts a yellow legal pad and pen at her seat, hands Barbara a pad and pen, and puts the rest on the table. Then she takes the bag to Bill. "Walt told me last night I should shred the notes we took. Here they are."

Bill says, "Thanks, Mary." He holds the bag aloft and looks at Zack, in effect saying, "I told you so."

Zack shakes his head and grins.

Pam and Myrna take pads and pens.

"We need a story that covers everything anyone outside this room knows or thinks they know about this exercise," says Myrna. "But without telling them anything they don't already have, right?"

"Exactly what we want," says Bill. "How?"

Ideas and questions fly back and forth across the room. Everyone contributes—all at once. The scribes' pens move across the pages with ferocity.

"Wait, wait, we don't have time for duplication, and you talk faster than I can write," says Barbara. "I see a pattern. If you can hold on a minute. Can we get the scribes together?"

John swaps seats with Myrna and sits between Mary and Pam. Barbara leans over to the others sharing her thoughts. The others seem to agree, and Barbara gives each of them a sheet with a heading. Barbara's reads *WHO*. Mary's reads *WHO RESPONSE*.

"Okay, we're all set." Barbara looks to the other three for agreement. "You can fire at will."

Comments fly again. Some folks remark to the group, and some talk one on one. The scribes write at a syncopated pace.

Bob and Daran pick up legal pads and jot notes. At one point, Pam points out we have failed to account for Bill's injuries.

At ten minutes to one, Denise says, "Time to go make my call."

"Come on. I'll take you downstairs where you can have some peace," says Bob. They leave, and Zack goes along in case he can join in.

Barbara says, "I think we've started repeating ourselves. Let's take a break. We'll compare notes and consolidate everything y'all have said."

"How about some more coffee, Zona? Mary, what happened to those brownies you promised us yesterday?" says Bob after he returns from downstairs.

"The last I saw of those brownies, they were on the way to the cave," says Mary. She and Bob have some banter going on most of the time. "You can suffer along with three kinds of cake. Such a hardship." She fixes Bob with her stern look.

Zona stands up, "I'll go get some highlighters. It looks like you could use some, Barbara." I don't know how Zona knows it, but Barbara loves highlighters. Barbara and Mary organize their notes. Pam goes to the kitchen to help with coffee. Myrna slices cake. Daran and Courtney help serve. Bob and I go into his office to set me up on his computer.

"I booted the computer. I'll bring up the browser, and you can get started," says Bob. "Are you looking for something specific?"

"I'm hoping to find some website that connects gypsum or its crystal relatives to crystal healing or herbal medicine or some other magical property. Not unlike the elixir from Mystic Onyx Cave." Bob leaves me to it.

My search goes well, and in less than ten minutes I have it. I find Zona.

"A million years ago, last night, when I was preparing to grill steaks with Bob, I saw several unbroken geodes around your koi pond. Would you be willing to sacrifice one to the cause?"

"Sure, Walt. You go right ahead."

"Walt, are you finished with the printer? I need to make some copies," says Mary.

* * *

I retrieve the rock hammer from our car and walk around to the pond behind the deck. I select a dark-gray geode about softball size, all in one piece. I use the edge of the driveway as an anvil and hit the geode with the chisel point. It breaks into three large pieces. A lucky break. An even luckier choice. On the inside, crystals of quartz, selenite, and barite almost fill the cavity. I take the fragment showing the most selenite, a mineral relative of gypsum.

Back inside, several small groups chat away. I make the rounds showing the rock to each group. Mary and Myrna have scissors cutting the copies Mary made into strips of various sizes. Barbara commandeers the dining table and lays out the paper strips in a huge spider-shape. Myrna watches Barbara and advises on the spider. Marty has called Daran and Courtney to join him and Bill. John, Keven, and Bob talk about the security officer. Zona makes the rounds lending support to all. I stand behind Bob and John.

* * *

Denise and Zack return, and Denise says, "The Superintendent seemed more than happy to have Zack included. Zack stalled like a career diplomat and promised the Southeast Region a full report. Zack told them the phone connection was not secure and promised if he could not find a secure line in the next twenty-four hours, he would fly to Atlanta to brief them and not breech security by conversing over insecure phones. They shut right up."

Bob and I read each other. We know all about insecure telephones.

Denise's phone chimes an incoming text message. Denise says, "It's from Mary Ann. She says, 'Thanks, Zack.'"

Denise, Zack, and I help ourselves to cake.

Marty and his group return to the dining room and den area. Daran smiles for the first time today.

* * *

"We think we're ready," says Barbara, standing and looking down at the paper spider.

"We have identified two principal lines of discussion. First, reacting to the gossip. Second, how to change the subject. Each of those lines contains two components. Mary and I took the first line. Myrna and Pam, the second. Because I come from a small town, I have always loved what Walt and I call the cave rock story." Barbara says, "Walt, tell Marty."

I repeat the story of how in the seventies, some local rock shops bought glass slag by the truckload and then sold it for twenty-five dollars a chunk. Marty laughs. Everyone except Zack claps in acknowledgement. The history major in Barbara loves organizing things like this.

She says, "The glass slag story seems to be the key to our misdirection. Myrna started off telling us we need to focus on what people outside this room know and account for everything they think or have heard. We don't want any mention of Wolfgang taking microorganisms out of the cave. If they can exploit something in the cave, the chance of vandalism or another threat like last night's escalates. We need to shift the focus out of the cave.

"I have organized our notes around the sources of our information." Holding up one finger, Barbara says, "First, we have identified three security personnel and two maintenance staff who have first-hand knowledge that something unusual happened in the cave last night. Those employees include the security officer John and Bob jumped—"

"We prefer, apprehended," says John, smiling.

"John did all the apprehending," says Bob.

"Yeah, after Bob charmed him by telling cave stories. He grew up around here and loves Mammoth Cave. I hope he will forgive us," says John.

"Duly noted, says Barbara. "The security officer whom John apprehended. What's a good reason for you to have *apprehended* the poor man? Also, we include the two PharmARAMA maintenance employees who delivered the refrigerated truck and some fresh lab coats and the two security officers who pulled a gun on us."

"Beyond those specific individuals, we should keep in mind the possibility the alarm system Keven and Denise disabled may leave some log on PharmARAMA computers or phones. And we have everyone from the hospital who knows something about Bill's injuries past and present."

Second finger. Barbara says, "Next, Catherine at the airport, anyone who saw Zack's group deal with the buyer, and the Homeland Security personnel we cannot be sure of. This group also includes locals who saw Zack's group moving around Cave City last night or this morning.

"Third." Finger number three appears. "Everyone who knows Bill got hurt last night."

"We neutralize those sources of information, and we're close to success with our mission. I turn the floor over to the retired schoolteacher and choir member to explain how we lie ourselves out of this. Seriously, Mary will explain how we manage things specifically for the Cave City audience."

"We have no choice but to stick to the facts to the degree possible," says Mary. "The gist of our story says Bill overheard Wolfgang talking about something significant from the cave being sold on the black market. Bill spent yesterday contacting a friend in the Army to help him find out how important it might be. Sorry Bill, but some of your past will leak out."

"A leak might not be all bad," says Bill. "If I'm going to take over Wolfgang's job—" A group gasp interrupts him. "It won't hurt my image for folks to think I know people in high places." Marty smiles. I look at Courtney, wondering how this affects their relationship. She looks happier than ever.

Mary eases into her chair.

"I don't plan for this to be permanent, says Bill. "I spent twelve years in the Army, and I don't see myself turning into a corporate management type. I enjoy guiding cave tours. I'll be on a two-year leave of absence from the Park Service—and the Army—sort of. But you're wondering about Courtney and me. PharmARAMA doesn't have a non-fraternization policy.

"That policy would have killed the deal." He glances at Courtney. "That for the moment I will be Courtney's immediate supervisor presents a potential problem. We have discussed it, and we'll get it worked out. According to Marty, Joan in Human Resources, understands the situation. Right now, we have bigger fish to fry."

"Our origins in Kentucky made sponsorship of Mammoth Cave National Park appealing," says Marty. "We have policies to protect against nepotism and sexual harassment. But PharmARAMA promotes company families. Several couples and many employees with family connections work for us. Excuse me, I need to get some employee handbooks delivered pronto." He makes more notes in his tablet.

"While we have Mary stopped, Marty, why don't you see what everyone thinks about your idea for Anderson and Floren," says Bill.

Marty looks up from the screen in his hand, "Prosecuting those two makes it all public. Additional publicity threatens national security and the safety of Mammoth Cave."

"And PharmARAMA's reputation, Marty, don't forget," says Bob.

"We do care about our reputation. You're right, Bob, but it's not our first priority here. PharmARAMA's research facilities occupy some remote spots around the globe. We'll separate those two. They will go into deep corporate exile. W.G. goes to a small, mostly unknown island in the Indian

Ocean that depends on Diego Garcia for support about five hundred miles away. He will work and live alone.

"Dr. Floren goes to one of the smaller islands in the Ulithi Atoll, which depends on Guam for its closest support some three hundred miles away.

"When Homeland Security no longer needs their help, they will depart directly to their new assignments. Zack believes he can convince Homeland Security to accept this plan which serves everyone best, especially the government folks." Marty looks to Zack.

"X-Ray talked with Homeland Security," says Zack. "And he convinced them Floren and Anderson going into exile meets everyone's needs. We won't—and Floren and Anderson certainly won't—mention any of this again. News reports of the recent, but illegal, interrogation methods obtain all sorts of cooperation from the likes of Anderson when they're facing the possibility of prosecution for terrorism. If any part of last night comes out, they void all agreements, and the government will prosecute them.

"Floren seems to be the one with the most backbone. I'm sure she planned a lot of this. She certainly made the initial contact with Hoa. We'll keep a close watch on her communications. She got involved with Anderson's scheme for the money. Anderson doesn't function well if he can't bully someone. They will go quietly, separately into obscurity."

"I hate to see him get away with it," says Keven. "But it sounds like the best solution for the cave. I am all for it." Everyone agrees.

"He won't be in custody, but he also won't be enjoying life much at all," says Marty.

At the pause in conversation, Mary stands and continues, "OK. Bill took the day off to coordinate Zack's participation. With that exaggeration, we account for Bill's missing work.

"Knowing Zack might not get here, Bill got Bob, Keven, John, and Denise to join him. PharmARAMA should recognize the security officer, maybe with a small bonus. That gets his good will. He may suspect nothing beyond his apprehension and the alarm. Good thought giving him the towel, John. He may feel less like your target.

"Wolfgang and Hilda's absence will make it clear the activity involved them. He can tell anyone he wants about his ordeal. Public opinion of PharmARAMA and of Wolfgang in particular will make it easy to accept cutting off the snake's head as it were.

"If the truck delivery guys were working off the clock, they will want to keep their part in this fairly quiet. If Wolfgang had them on the clock, PharmARAMA convinces them the refrigerated truck provided only window dressing for what Hilda and Wolfgang had conspired to do.

"Finally, the security officers who threatened the crew at the cave last night require more attention. From what you said, they are bullies plain and simple, especially the driver. Zack's apprehension of them last night probably cowed them for the moment, but it won't last. I doubt anyone will trust anything they say. Beyond that, we have the staff changes," she looks in Bill's direction, "I imagine PharmARAMA will make them aware their jobs depend on putting some distance between themselves and whatever happened last night."

"Major sensitivity training already in my planning," says Bill. "Additional re-education to follow regarding respect for the Park, Mammoth Cave, and Park Service employees. Afterwards we will have major discussions regarding drawing a weapon. If they ever carry weapons again."

"As for Catherine, and anyone else who saw or heard about any military presence," says Mary. "Zack and his company came because they felt unsure of Wolfgang's motives. Here again, we capitalize on the general ill-will Wolfgang created in the community." Marty groans. "Add to that the fact every community in the country believes they occupy top spots on the Russian's first-strike list explains why the Army would care what Anderson planned on doing. However, when Zack investigated, he discovered Wolfgang and Hilda were running a scam on the would-be buyer. Wolfgang used — what did you call it, Walt?"

"Selenite, a mineral chemically related to gypsum. Some of the geodes found around here contain selenite. My web research indicates some groups believe selenite can enhance one's telepathic powers. We say Anderson tried to sell selenite geodes along with four bottles of water from Crystal Lake to Hoa. Dear Leader, who boasts among his own people of his telepathic powers, constantly searches for enhancements to his natural-born abilities.

"The water becomes the focus because of its special qualities as a crystal elixir of particular potency. Anyway, the water explains why this scam took place in the cave. When we tell the story, we focus on the geodes, which occur in pastures and backyards all over Cave Country. Think our plan will work?" I hold up the geode from Zona's yard.

Keven raises an eyebrow and in a suspicious tone asks, "How do you know about the telepathic powers and crystal elixirs, Walt?"

"Dad! He Googled it," says Daran.

I nod toward Daran. "What he said. And I dreamed some of it."

"I knew it," says Keven.

"Now, Zona, if I could get some aluminum foil?" I say.

"You can indeed," says Zona. "Enough to wrap up your treasure?"

"Or a little more." She tears off about a foot-long piece of foil and puts it on the table. I set the geode in the middle of the foil. Barbara, seeing I am about to crunch the foil around the rock to resemble last week's lunch, intercedes and asks Myrna, the quilter, to wrap the geode neatly in the foil.

"Zona, do you have some mailing labels," asks Barbara. "I want to make a sticker with a PharmARAMA logo to dress this up."

"You don't need to," Marty pulls a couple of stickers from the pocket in his tablet and passes them over. Myrna places them carefully on the folds in the foil package making it look like official PharmARAMA contraband, and something Wolfgang would have had. She hands the final product to me. The pink and blue plaid scream out against the foil.

"Great, Myrna. Thanks," and I hand the package to Zack.

"A sample of the material Wolfgang was selling to the Dear Leader's henchman."

Zack grins, "Great! I hadn't considered what to do if someone asked to see the material. Can you give me another piece of the geode? I want to show it off and keep this piece wrapped up and sealed."

Mary looks at her notes, "Homeland detained the buyer, but they can only charge him because he came here to make an illegal purchase of material stolen from a national park. Since no security threat existed, the purchase and entering the country illegally will make up all the charges. With help from Bill and a few guides, Zack caught Hilda and Wolfgang, but in truth, Anderson was scamming Hoa, not committing treason and terrorism like Bill suspected when he raised the alarm.

"Catherine also deserves recognition from Homeland Security for helping catch the buyer. He may not have been buying anything dangerous, but he intended to do so.

"Courtney told us she dismissed all questions about Bill's injuries and hospital trip by explaining he is a veteran and does not like to talk about combat he has seen. Bill pretended to be in such awful shape, he required Courtney to speak for him. We follow their lead." Mary looks up from her notes, "Bill's replacing Wolfgang will buy him lots of goodwill in the short term, at least. The Bill versus Wolfgang story can morph into anything crazy, but the rumor mill will draw the right conclusion, and Wolfgang will be the bad guy. How do you like our story?" She looks to John and Pam, the ones with the first-hand rumor exposure.

John's all seriousness now. "Overall, it will work. I worry about an entrepreneur or two trying to exploit our cover story to expand their markets. How do we protect the cave, and the rest of the park, from poachers snatching geodes?"

Bob, theatre director that he is, looks up. "We engage in a little theater. We play up the geodes-come-from-any-backyard angle. Mammoth Cave doesn't represent a unique source for geodes. Or even a good one. Geodes crop up all over the fields. Everyone knows that. Why would they risk a federal charge stealing something from a National Park, when the rock shops already sell them by the bushel?

"About the elixir, no more than limestone spring water. The refrigerated truck's only purpose was to make the buyer think the water was special. It's not. It's merely water from the cave with the same laxative properties we know all about. The only clairvoyance it prompts is the foresight that drinking it means spending time in the bathroom. But the buyer didn't know that. Even if our misdirection doesn't work, Crystal Lake, because of its location, remains secure. Especially if the park receives support for additional ranger patrols," he says looking at Marty.

"No problem there. Right, Mr. Research Director?" Bill gives a thumbs-up.

"PharmARAMA under Anderson's direction became scary," says Bob. "The citizens of Cave Country don't like him. They see him for the real phony he is. Since we have local sentiment against Anderson, let's use it. Rumors of the involvement by Homeland Security won't hurt either. Marty can fund some additional ranger patrols, and while they're out there, they can address the problem with ginseng poachers."

Marty makes it clear PharmARAMA will pay the bill and consider itself lucky.

"A few weeks will pass, and the rock shop owners will either figure out they have no additional market for geodes, or they will decide the geodes from their own backyards will meet the requirement without risking going up against park rangers," says Bob.

"With your qualification, yes, it will work," says John. We turn to Pam.

"It seems plausible. It won't knock out all the speculation, but the big story of Anderson's firing will over-ride everything else. The locals will enjoy how the Army caught him and PharmARAMA removed him. Enough to prevent a hard search for holes in the story. Maybe."

"We have to decide how to spread this new rumor," says Myrna.

"I have that answer and how to include Catherine," says Marty. "We have a lavish and public dinner tonight at the hotel. Everyone here comes, and we invite Catherine too. You folks will tell your stories. The rest of us will listen in amazement. I think this grapevine you talk about will take it from there. We'll have a table full of folks, and it won't seem odd to speak loud enough for everyone to hear." Turning to Denise he says, "Don't you think we need to include Mary Ann and Anne Binnley?"

"I'll call them."

"Ray Valley must be good for something." Marty says. "Let's see if he can make dinner reservations. I count thirteen here, plus Catherine and her guest and then Anne and Mary Ann. Can someone give me Catherine's number? And what time do we want dinner? We should start early for the greatest exposure. Would six-thirty work for you? I better get something started on our security officer, too. The sooner he feels appreciated the less chance of an information leak we can't patch. Who in my company can I trust?"

We agree on six-thirty, and Mary goes to get Catherine's number.

"Marty, call Grace, in the office," says Courtney. "Wolfgang hated her. She retired from a big job up north and moved back home to help take care of her mother. She worked as a seasonal at the hotel back in her youth. She loves the cave. As a bonus, she seems to be a gracious person. Did I say Wolfgang hated her?"

"I don't want to overstep my job before I'm officially in it," says Bill. "But I wouldn't trust Valley. However, you can trust the concierge at the hotel with anything."

Marty enters more data. Mary puts a slip of paper next to him. "Thank you, Mary. If you will excuse me, I have to call many people and get things rolling. Thank you all." Zona leads Marty downstairs to make his calls.

"Zack, do you think it would be okay for Mary Ann to call the superintendent and tell him about the meal?" asks Denise. "Not much. But enough information that he can feel in the loop when he hears the tale from another source."

"Sounds like the way to handle it. Assure him I will report once I can access a secure line. Probably tomorrow," says Zack.

Denise leaves to call Mary Ann and Anne Binnley.

Mary says, "I think we've wrapped up the reactive part. Now we need to talk about the pro-active, or more accurately, distractive things we've talked about. Pam and Myrna have organized those thoughts."

Forty-Three
Nap Time

"While we're waiting for Marty, Zona, can I ask you about my head?" Bill says, motioning toward the restroom where she patched him up. Courtney looks up in alarm, but he pats her hand and points toward Zack, who tries to sneak a glance at his watch.

Bill and Zona return. Bill bumps Zack's chair when he passes by. He says, "Man, you are a disgrace to the uniform. You need a shave."

Zack feels his chin and says, "I could stand a shave. Marty set us up with rooms at the hotel, and even though you don't seem to need my help, we could maintain a lower profile from here. And one soldier sleeps here already."

"You need sleep more than a shave. We have things under control here," Bill says. Bill and Courtney slept for a few hours, but Zack stayed up all night. Who knows when he slept before?

"I have a straightforward solution," says Zona. "Use the bathroom downstairs. The sofa down there sleeps well. If we need you, we will wake you up."

"Guest quarters at the Cetera's outshines any hotel," I say.

Zack looks at Bill and seems to surrender to something. "Thank you. Let me get my bag from the truck. I wish all my assignments took me to Cave City, Kentucky."

"I'll meet you downstairs," says Zona.

Zack leaves to get his kit, and Zona heads to the basement.

Marty, having come up and passed Zack on his way down, looks toward the stairs and says, "Man, he needs to get some sleep."

"Taken care of," says Bob.

Zona returns upstairs, "I pointed him toward the bathroom. I put a pillow and a sheet on the sofa. He can use them if he wants."

"He'll use them," says Bill. "He's no fool. If a chance to sleep presents itself, he'll take it. Part of living on alert all the time means you sleep when you can."

"Marty, what did you find out?" asks Bob.

"We have dinner in process. Denise, I included Anne and Mary Ann in the count, but I need to add two more if they're going to bring guests. The concierge has everything under control. Valley didn't like his demotion or having to report to the concierge, but he's re-calibrated for the moment. Catherine and her husband will join us at seven.

"Courtney, thank you for sending me to Grace. Did you know Grace and the security officer are cousins? She claims he loves his job. And, she says he's scared PharmARAMA might fire him, but insists he followed standard operating procedure. She thinks a pat on the back will make him happy. He does what he's told and doesn't improvise. Bill, being the new director, you should present the award and make it clear we harbor no hard feelings."

"Should I call him now?" asks Bill.

"No, Grace handled it. She will call a staff meeting for tomorrow morning. We're inviting all the staff, but not requiring anyone off duty to attend. You can give him the award then. Sound right to you?"

Marty looks first at Bill and then at Daran and Courtney.

"A good start," says Daran.

"Mary Ann will come to dinner alone. I left Anne a message. When she calls me back, I'll tell her seven o'clock like Catherine," says Denise.

Bob says, "Walt, what do you think about some pictures of this group?"

"Great idea. Do you want me to get your camera?" I ask.

"Would you? It's still in the car. Here's the key."

"Anne called. She'll be there at seven. She'll be alone," says Denise.

* * *

I go out to the SUV. When I return with Bob's camera bag and tripod, multiple conversations overlap one another.

"The other ideas we collected center on focusing everyone's mind on something else," says Pam. "Keven, you said the FRC opposes PharmARAMA."

"FRC believes many things threaten the groundwater," says Keven. "And I'm with them on most of it. They fought this corporate sponsorship program from the start. It looks like they made the right call."

"Someone suggested we play up the groundwater issue. PharmARAMA comes in for a minor hit, but not much worse than the baseline dislike for it, anyway. Since this event did not affect the groundwater, they will find only good things," says Pam.

"I like the idea, but how do we get it in play? If there's nothing to refute, how do we stir up these concerns?" asks Marty.

"Same as always," says the group.

After an exchange of knowing glances, Myrna says, "Marty, you want to know what your PR and marketing people do well? Here it is. The PR department rambles on and on, saying nothing, and they stir up ill will with it. However, they can't hold a candle to what marketing puts out in writing." The PharmARAMA executive grimaces.

"They probably have a file cabinet full of denials about groundwater contamination," says Myrna. "When the cave community gets concerned, marketing tosses out another denial. The more the re-hashed stuff shows up, the more it convinces everyone on the conservation side something must have contaminated the groundwater. In this case, their fears might well work to our advantage."

"Boss," says Bill. "I don't want to throw money around before I start the job." He grins. "But if we want to make FRC suspicious, PharmARAMA could offer them a research grant. Not too big, but big enough to impress them. And make them nervous at the same time."

"I like it," says Keven.

Zona asks, "Do you think Zack could issue an official statement about the Army regretting the alert here last night. They could say the operation did not affect the groundwater. If you say it hasn't caused contamination, several groups will be certain the truth lies in the exact opposite direction."

"I'll ask him at dinner. Let's let him sleep for now," says Marty.

"I'm not sure the Army will make any statements about a group it barely acknowledges exists with soldiers who don't use their actual names," I say.

"I think you're right, Walt," says Bob. "Not likely to happen. On the topic of sleep, I don't know about you folks, but I could stand a nap. We are done here, right?" asks Bob.

"I'm all done," says Pam. "The actual work will be up to Marty and Zack. If asked, we repeat the assurances nothing affected the groundwater. I'm all for a nap myself, and we're going home. We'll be back between six and six-fifteen to go to dinner."

Barbara asks, "Marty, before you go, what's the dress code for dinner? Except for borrowing an iron, you see Walt and me at our fanciest."

Marty says, "You look great. We are a tourist hotel after all. We discourage bathing suits in the dining room, but we don't get much pickier. But since you mention it," he turns to Denise, "We might use this to reinforce the Park Service's position of authority at the cave." Marty glances at Bob, Keven, and John, and asks, "Would it be a great inconvenience to wear your uniforms tonight. If you think it might send the right message?" he looks back at Denise.

"I think having Bill come to work for you will make it clear enough, but it couldn't hurt if the guys don't mind. I will be in uniform anyway," says Denise.

Keven, John, and Bob voice their agreement.

Bob says, "It saves the trouble of looking for something else to wear. Now let's all line up in front of the fireplace, and I'll grab a few shots." I help Bob with the tripod.

"My executive VP wants me to tell you how much she appreciates what you've done and continue to do. I couldn't tell her much over the phone for security's sake. She asked about coming down to thank you in person, but we decided it would be counterproductive to the effort we're making to downplay last night. I'm sorry you have seen PharmARAMA at its worst. I'm not trying to excuse us. What could be worse than treason, assault and battery, kidnapping, and attempted murder? But I swear, you have not seen the true PharmARAMA. I hope to show you a much better side tonight."

"I approve of what PharmARAMA does. Mostly. I enjoy the work," says Daran.

"Me, too," says Courtney.

"I would not have taken the job unless I saw potential for a beneficial situation," says Bill.

"OK, enough of this mushy stuff, we have pictures to take," says Bob.

After Bob takes our picture, Keven says, "I remember someone mentioning a nap. Best idea I've heard all day. We'll see you at the hotel at six-thirty."

Bill and Courtney will be here then. We can go together and make the biggest splash. Mary agrees. Marty asks Denise for a ride back to the park, having sent Valley away in his car.

As everyone leaves, Juliet excuses herself to get to the door. In a minute, Foxtrot comes in, speaks, and goes into the guest room.

In less than five minutes, everyone scatters, and Barbara and I go to our room. We can hear Foxtrot snoring in the room down the short hall. It doesn't keep us awake.

* * *

When my phone alarms at five, Barbara and I head to the living room. Barbara finds the iron and ironing board Zona left out and presses a few wrinkles out of our clothes.

Bob hears us and pops his head out of the office. "I brought up some cave pictures on the computer, but we may not have time for them."

"You're right, but let's try a couple, anyway." At five-thirty, we tear ourselves away from the computer.

"I'll go wake the soldier in the guest room," says Zona. "Bob, if you will get Zack? Then we can dress for dinner ourselves."

"I'm on it," says Bob.

Once Barbara and I finish dressing, we move out to the deck and wait for the others to arrive. Mary joins us on the deck. When John and Pam join us, we move back indoors.

Zack emerges shaved and wearing the same fatigues. Not a wrinkle or smudge. He looks rested and eager. He and his two remaining team members will close out this operation and respond to anything else that pops up. Zack seems to enjoy this situation even with all his responsibility. Mary hands him a plastic bag of shredded paper. He smiles.

"This isn't my first misinformation operation, but this local variety works much better than anything imposed from the outside. More organic. More fun, too."

"Happy to oblige. Who's driving?" asks Bob.

"Marty is providing transportation," says Bill when he and Courtney come in.

"Is someone going to a prom?"

"Well, we all are, but why do you ask?" says Bob.

"Come outside and see," says Bill.

We walk out through the garage. Two stretch limos line the driveway pointed toward the road.

"Bill will ride with me in our vehicle in order to reinforce the powerful friends image. The rest of you will ride in the limos each escorted by one of my team members," says Zack. Juliet's and Foxtrot's uniforms appear ready for parade.

Juliet approaches Bob and Zona, "Mr. and Mrs. Cetera, on behalf of Foxtrot and me, thank you for your wonderful hospitality. This unusual mission definitely will go into our classified record book." She gives Bob a sharp salute, does an about-face, and returns to the lead limo. Exceptional courtesy must be near the top of the requirements for membership on Zack's team.

"The drivers and my team members will open your doors at the hotel, please wait for them. Foxtrot will stay with my vehicle to monitor the radio and weapons while Juliet escorts you into the hotel." says Zack.

"What about Keven and Myrna? And Daran?" I ask.

"I called Keven to let him know not to leave for the hotel. We'll pick them up instead. Daran, too. Denise and Mary Ann are already at the park," says Bill.

"I don't think you're going to get a limo up their driveway," says Bob.

"They'll meet us at the bottom of the hill," says Bill.

We all load up. On the way into the park, I fiddle with the TV, the minibar, the intercom, and the reading lights. Everyone else seems to relax and enjoy the luxury ride.

Forty-Four
Dinner at Mammoth Cave Hotel

When our limo approaches the hotel entrance, Ray Valley stands in the middle of a parking space in front of the door. He and a woman seem to be saving parking places for the limos and Zack's black SUV.

"She's the marketing manager," says Bob, for our benefit. "Those two are doing exactly what they're good for—traffic cones."

We wait for the doors to open. When we emerge from the limousine, I see Juliet opening the door for Courtney at the other limousine. When Bill joins Courtney, Valley walks toward Bill and then charges.

"You, bastard!" Valley shouts. "Anderson was a great man. You fool!" He brings his left arm up. A glint of light flashes in an arc.

Bill pushes Courtney behind him and turns to face the charge. He seems to have even more adrenalin in reserve.

Juliet comes out of nowhere, blocks the knife arm, and in a blur throws Valley to the pavement, both arms pinned behind his back.

"No, you don't," she says.

"Get off me. Let me go. I know people…" Valley's voice fades to a whimper after Juliet increases the pressure on his arms.

"Quit kicking now. That's not nice," she says. Valley whimpers again and collapses in defeat.

Foxtrot retrieves the knife with a camouflage bandanna. He takes it to the truck and returns with a couple of flex cuffs to secure Valley.

"Are you OK, Solo?" asks Juliet.

"Thank you, Juliet. Thanks *again*. I'm fine. Courtney, are you all right?"

"I'm good. Let's go inside."

"Juliet, you OK?" asks Zack.

"No problems. We'll stay with the prisoner, shall we, Zack?"

"Excellent. I'll see the rangers get here quickly and take him off your hands. Well done."

"Sir."

"Why don't we go in?" says Zack.

We all file into the hotel behind Bill and Courtney. The former head of marketing, much subdued, holds the door. No weapons appear. We stop at the maitre d' station. Marty and Grace appear and welcome us with all the formality they can muster. Denise and Mary Ann, both in uniform, stand behind them.

"Mary Ann, could you contact the rangers to pick up Valley out in the parking lot? They should charge him with assault and attempted murder," says Bill. "Zack's team took care of it. They have him secured at their vehicle right out front."

"What? How awful. Anyone hurt?"

"Valley's pride suffered another injury, and his shoulders may give him a twinge or two. But no. We're all good."

"I'll call immediately." She takes the walkie-talkie from her belt and steps outside.

"It's not over till it's over, is it?" says Denise. "What happened out there?"

"Apparently, Valley admired Anderson with real religious fervor," says Bob. "He charged Bill with a knife. I hope there aren't any more Anderson fans."

"I don't think there will be. Valley occupies the bottom of that barrel," says Grace. "I am sorry I did not understand he was this bad. He is. I apologize again. Do you think we can recover the celebratory spirit?"

"Please, lead on." says Marty.

The maitre d' leads us to the table.

The moment we get settled, servers fill glasses from pitchers of tea and water. The server helping Barbara and me points out bottles of wine on the table. He asks if he can pour us some. Barbara selects a Chablis since the local vineyards produce no white Zinfandel, and I order the same Norton vintage from lunch—yesterday?

The wait staff leaves but returns quickly with every appetizer on the menu.

We acknowledge our host with lifted glasses. Marty seems pleased, but he says, "Tell Grace. When I got to the hotel, Grace had everything well in hand. She put two and two together after she overheard what I told Valley. She ran everything from there. Valley got his new marching orders. You saw him saving parking spaces."

"Thank you, Grace. I'm looking forward to working with you," says Bill. Grace smiles.

"I, in turn, told Valley to report to Grace from now on," says Marty. "He left several messages at Corporate Human Resources. Apparently, he got no satisfaction there and started his slide over the edge. Joan put a new PR manager in his place. At least we're on record finally for recognizing his problems, if not exactly how severe they were. Are."

"I don't think anyone will hold you responsible, Marty. I don't," says Bill.

"Joan and I became one of PharmARAMA's first married couples. She didn't think cave sponsorship made good business sense from the beginning of this project, and she wanted me to oppose the goings-on in the cave. The fact Joan wanted no part of the cave project may have served to Anderson's advantage. If Joan had conducted the human resource oversight, she would have known Anderson was reassigning folks with a Kentucky connection or a strong interest in Mammoth Cave."

"Valley is awful beyond belief. Thank all of you for your patience this evening," says Grace. "I wish I could have known he was that crazy."

We pause the conversation and devour some appetizers.

* * *

The maitre d' comes in with Catherine, Catherine's husband, Jack, and Anne Binnley. Catherine and spouse sit in chairs saved for them between Zona and Mary whom they know from theater work. Anne sits next to Denise.

Once Catherine, Jack, and Anne place their drink orders, the servers pass around more appetizers.

"Zack, what can you tell me about last night and Anderson?" says Marty.

Zack takes Marty's cue and tells the story about Bill's calling his unit, and how they responded.

"As it turned out, we found no health threat and no threat to the groundwater. But, better safe than sorry."

When the wait staff arrives to take our dinner orders, Zack makes a significant point of falling silent. Since I enjoyed the fried chicken for lunch, I order pork chops for dinner. Barbara asks for the vegetable pasta dish. Once the servers take our orders and depart, Bill takes up his part of the story. Bob adds to the narrative making the security officer sound like a star employee.

Our meals come, and everyone concentrates on dinner for a little while. Servers pour more wine and whisk the empty bottles away. Marty speaks to a server who seems more attentive than necessary. The server goes to stand behind a food cart away from our table. Marty supports Zack's performance and does not speak in front of the staff, while making it easy for them to hear every word.

My moist pork chops yield easily to the fork. Like at lunch, they cooked the sides to perfection. Barbara says her pasta tastes good, too. There are baskets of bread beside each person. I eat more corn bread.

As the others tell their stories, Keven contributes where appropriate. Then he dives into it, improvising a story about their walk on the surface from the Frozen Niagara Entrance to New Entrance in the darkness of night. Keven borrows the owl story I told Daran. Keven tells the story well. For a moment, I forget they drove back in the SUV. They never made that walk.

Zack takes the floor again explaining how he learned through his network what transpired in Glasgow. He asks Catherine to tell her part in it. Catherine beams and gives us a detailed recounting of the request for ice and seeing Mary, then talking to Zona, and the arrival of Zack's team. Apparently, planes as large as Zack's seldom land at Glasgow. It created an actual sensation.

Barbara and I ask questions to allow Zack to expand on the lack of danger now the crisis has passed. Zack talks in a loud, and at the same time, confidential sounding voice when he talks about the geodes and the crystal elixir. John asks if we could see one, and Zack produces an official document pouch, removes Myrna's wrapped sample, and lays it down. Then he takes out the other piece of Zona's geode and passes it around the table.

We have done our best. We put the story out there. The nosey server forms the vanguard of the listening audience. The evening progresses, and the dining room fills up. Bob identifies many of the faces for me.

"The guy in the blue sports coat looks like the man from the Many Mart this morning," says John. "I wonder where he found that coat and tie."

"I suggest we adjourn to Bill's new office for coffee, dessert, and after-dinner drinks," says Marty.

Catherine says, "I would love dessert, but we need to get home to the babysitter."

"Catherine, thank you for joining us. You have been extremely helpful. Grace, please see they get to-go boxes with dessert." We all say goodnight to Catherine and Jack. Anne excuses herself and leaves with the Glasgow couple.

Juliet comes in, stops at the desk, and picks up two large boxes. She goes out again, this time with two servers following. One carries a tray of beverages, and the other carries more boxes. I assume she's taking dinner out for

Foxtrot and herself. The other dinners must be for the limo drivers.

*   *   *

Bill wanders around his large, future office.

"Solo, X-ray collected all of Anderson's papers for analysis," says Zack. "We will return what we can. I'm afraid you won't have much of his material to work with."

"Tell him not to hurry," says Bill. "I'll be glad to have the staff believe the Army confiscated Anderson's files. I want to talk to the research folks myself. I'll use the new staff assignments to start over. Joan and I discussed it. Grace oversees all public communication. PR and marketing merge into one unit, reporting to her. They will adapt to serious changes in their way of doing business. Daran and Courtney will report directly to me."

"Daran will use his combined knowledge of the technical, research side, and of the cave itself to roam around and make sure no one wildcats, and they protect the cave," says Marty. "We will filter all research reports through Courtney. With Bill's help, she will develop a team of scientists she trusts to explain and keep transparent, at least within the company, any research conducted in the cave."

Servers from the restaurant enter with coffee and a variety of desserts including Derby and chess pies, strawberry shortcake, and blueberry cobbler. We choose from the expensive brandy and liqueurs in Wolfgang's office.

As we relax, Courtney says, "Walt, what about you and that dream?"

I look around to make sure only people I trust remain. "Marty, Grace, please excuse me, but my dream seems to require some explaining. Bob, I will save the part about your commercial cave for a short story. About the parts of my dream which seem like foresight, I propose this theory.

"Mammoth Cave clearly exerts a pull on some folks. Keven seems to have felt it as a young kid. As Bob and Zona did, Keven and Myrna arranged their summers and then their retirements to be here. From things Marty said about his wife Joan, and Grace said about her cousin, they might feel it. John and Pam, something besides Bob's sparkling personality got you to move down here. Bill became a cave lover even before he and Courtney got together. I got hooked after my first summer of guiding. I propose the cave uses its pull when in distress, and it calls for help.

"Why the cave called out to me through the dream, I can explain too. You all live here. You agonize over the changes every day. Zona won't even go to the park anymore. Although I am connected to the cave, I haven't been here in a long time. The cave called all of us, but it got through to me. While I am attuned if you will, I don't live it day to day. Less background noise. And—this is no minor point—I may be crazier than the rest of you.

"In addition, I've been reading about the Potawatomi people and about their language. They may have descended from the folks of the Adena culture. Their language differentiates the animate from the inanimate. I'll give you an example. Their word for forest denotes animate. As does the word for large rocks. Why shouldn't Mammoth Cave be animate? So, I've developed a greater sensitivity to the distress of the *animate* cave. But I'm not suggesting I'm the only one."

Silence. I look at Barbara. She smiles.

Zona says, "Good job, Walt."

After the pause, Courtney says, "Works for me." Everyone in the room seems to relax and laugh. The men in the white coats will have to wait a bit longer.

Marty stands, raises a glass, and says, "Earlier today, I told you what will happen to Anderson and Floren. PharmARAMA will answer for all of this. Bill will bring us into harmony with the Park Service and a safer Mammoth Cave. To Bill."

"Here, here." Says Keven.

* * *

As we finish our desserts, Marty asks, "What can PharmARAMA do to show its appreciation to all of you?"

We shake our heads.

Zona speaks for us. "Marty, grand dinner and all that. I enjoyed it." The rest of us sound our agreement. "We are happy to have taken part in whatever did not affect the groundwater."

Everyone chuckles, but Zack's and Marty's laughter carries a degree of relief in it. Once more, we assure them we will keep these secrets.

"All of us are committed to the cave and to the cave area. You keep Wolfgang above ground and out of Kentucky, and we'll be happy," says John.

Marty addresses first Bob, John, and then Keven, "about your commitment, let me propose this idea. Would you help us with a set of programs to educate our staff about the cave? There used to be an orientation movie or slide show. I think I've seen some of your slides at campfire talks. No one working here should begin without basic knowledge of Mammoth Cave."

"They shouldn't. I assumed you gave them an orientation. Mary Ann and Denise manage our time and effort. If she needs my help, I'm glad to pitch in," says Keven.

"Me, too," says Bob.

"Count me in," says John.

"Great! Thank you. Local PharmARAMA operations are standing down for a few days until Zack gets the all-clear from his troops reviewing Anderson's stuff. We're going to use the time to get reoriented. At a staff breakfast, I will introduce Bill and explain where Grace, Courtney, and Daran will work. Sad, but the employees will pay for their meal by sitting through a reading of this."

Marty hands out sheets of goldenrod paper. "Unfortunate for the staff, but they will be a captive audience. Grace will introduce the topic and include references to protecting the groundwater." Marty holds up the sheet of paper. "Honestly, I can't tell you yet what this press release says. It gives me a headache You didn't exaggerate about the stuff PR and marketing put out, but if I didn't know the topic of this document, I'd have to ask.

"At eleven o'clock, we will meet in the picnic grounds. We've invited the FRC, all the staff from PharmARAMA, and park personnel who can be spared, and anyone else we can come up with from the cave community. Grace performed yet another miracle and got hold of suppliers on Sunday. They can make deliveries in the morning. She's paying overtime to kitchen staff who will come in to fix breakfast and lunch. We're serving bar-be-que and fried chicken. I would appreciate it if you folks would come, even though I can't recognize what you've done."

"Thank you, Marty," says Mary. "You have thanked us all you need to."

"OK, but I have one tangible way of showing PharmARAMA's appreciation. While our concierge stays with us, I am sure these won't be necessary, but—should he leave—you'll have these cards."

He passes out lifetime vouchers for service at the restaurant, including wine and beer.

Marty says, "My number is on the back."

We express our surprise and gratitude. And the lack of any necessity. However, no one hands back their card.

Barbara leans into me and says, "This is all nice, but I'm tired. If we're going to a picnic tomorrow and driving back to Atlanta, I need to go to bed."

I agree with her.

Keven says, "Very nice, Marty, we've run around for two long days, and my nap has worn off. Could we get a lift home?"

"Zack, you guys get some rest. Escorting us home runs into overkill. The limousines can carry us safely home. You've done more than enough," says Bob.

"Then this will be goodbye for me," says Zack. "We leave for Fort Campbell at 2200. It's been a pleasure working with all of you. When Bill told me he had involved civilians, I expected a disaster. You have conducted one hell of an operation. You all have my card. Call my number if you need anything from me. Or contact Solo—Bill. He will always be able to reach me. I hope to see you again under less trying circumstances."

On our way out, Barbara and I stop to tell Zack goodbye and shake his hand. Our limo delivers us to Bob and Zona's house. We say our goodnights, and once again climb into bed snoring as we drop.

Forty-Five
Picnic and Goodbyes

At last, the next morning gives me a chance to see Bob's cave pictures. They are very impressive. Mary arrives with fresh bagels from a bagel emporium in Glasgow. We munch bagels, sip hot beverages, visit, and look at cave pictures and portraits. Barbara and I break away to load the car.

At ten-thirty, we follow Zona, Mary, and Bob to the park. A man in white coveralls waves us to a prime parking spot right beside Bob's SUV. As we walk to the pavilion, Bob identifies the table on the left as folks from FRC.

Grace addresses the gathering from a small stage, where she introduces Marty. He takes the stage and welcomes representatives of the FRC. The FRC contingent looks uncomfortable. After a few remarks about cooperation and community feeling, Marty says "And, more importantly, how much we at PharmARAMA want to support Mammoth Cave National Park and to respect its resources." Applause.

Marty introduces Bill as the new operations manager and director of research, W.G. Anderson's former position. Bill introduces Courtney, Daran, and Grace, telling the staff what their duties will be. PharmARAMA personnel already knows this since the four of them have worked with the staff all morning. After the crowd settles, Bill introduces Joan's personal representative for the park sponsorship program. He does not speak but waves to the crowd. I look at Barbara for confirmation. She sketches the letter 'H' on the back of my hand. She's right. Hotel stands impressive, comfortable in a three-piece suit. Bill's driver to the hospital.

Marty explains how he re-assigned W. G. Anderson and Hilda Floren because they did not fit the Mammoth Cave culture and will not be back. The buzz in the crowd proves they understand Wolfgang left under duress and not in a routine corporate shuffle of management. I hope the story they tell matches the one we gave them last night.

Bill introduces Mary Ann. She reads a memorandum from the Park Service assuring everyone this activity did not compromise the groundwater. The general buzz of scepticism and the looks on the faces of those at the FRC table make me think this part of our plan might come together.

The recognition for the security officer follows, and he swells with pride. In his speech, Bill acknowledges all the staff that have served despite recent challenges. He promises things will improve. He asks everyone to help him by telling him what he needs to hear.

The picnic ushers in a new image of the sponsor. Choruses of "Ding Dong the Witch Is Dead" break out. The employees appear to be in good spirits. No fanatic jumps up to defend Anderson or attack Bill.

* * *

Barbara and I check the time. We work our way through the crowd to tell Bill and Courtney goodbye. They stand close together. Looking at Courtney for her consent, Bill lowers his voice, "Can you guys come back in September? If we have this mess cleaned up, we'll have a celebration. I understand several good marriages have occurred then." Courtney beams.

We whisper our congratulations and promise to make it back.

We ask them to tell Marty goodbye for us.

Keven and Myrna stand nearby. "Thanks, Keven. We had a great visit. Looks like we may be back in September," I say, looking toward Bill and Courtney.

"Great! Maybe you can visit without having to rescue anything. Or anyone," says Keven.

"Amen to that," says Myrna. "Y'all have a safe trip home."

"Bye, y'all," says Barbara.

We thank Bob and Zona for their hospitality and get promises they will come see us soon.

"Bob, tell them your news," says Zona.

"Mary Ann offered me a deal of sorts. Part time working out of the visitor services office and also guiding a few trips," says Bob.

"You're going to take it, right?"

"Yes. I am. Zona and I talked about it. This operation of Bill's taught me two things. I want to be part of the cave, and I want to guide tours. I can't predict how long that will last, but we'll start out that way."

"Splendid news. Good for all of us," I say.

"Congratulations, Bob," says Barbara and gives him a hug. We shake hands, I hug Zona, and ask them to tell Mary, John, and Pam goodbye for us. We navigate out past the visitor center parking lot, get on the main park road headed for Park City, and turn south on Interstate 65 for home.

Epilogue
Indian Ocean 500 Miles South of Diego Garcia - One Year Later

A bearded man wearing a straw hat and a faded swimsuit brief hunches over a microscope.

"Dr. Floren, will you pass me the next slide, please?"

No reply.

"Hilda, please. The next slide,"

No reply.

With a swift and vicious swing, he stabs a scalpel into cleavage exposed by a partially open lab coat. Air hisses as it escapes the ample chest.

"Oh, Hilda! My darling."

Later after the rage passes, he lovingly and tearfully uses his vinyl repair kit to patch another incision in the *lifelike* blow-up doll with real blonde human hair.

"There, there."

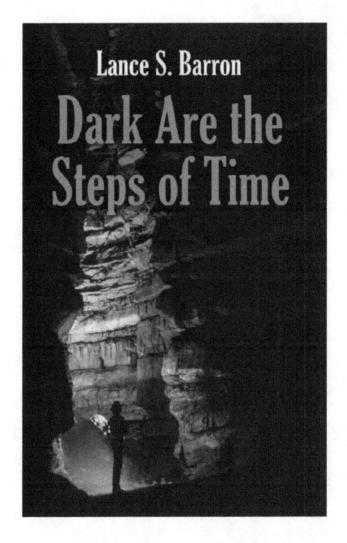

Available at: https://booklocker.com
More Information at: http://lancebarron.blogspot.com

CPSIA information can be obtained
at www.ICGtesting.com
Printed in the USA
JSHW042314250521
15193JS00001B/35